Camillus – Dictator of Rome.

The Fall of Veii (Part 1)

The cover design is by the very talented Ruth Musson, apart from that I have done this book as a complete Do It Yourself project. The artwork and story are the copyright of the author of this book. This book is the second in the series Dictator of Rome - Camillus

Other books in the Dictator of Rome series;

Prequel – The Ancilia Shield

Book 1 – Dawn of the Eagle

Book 2 – The Fall of Veii (part 1)

Book 3 – The Fall of Veii (part 2)

Book 4 – Vae Victis (Woe to the vanquished)

Book 5 – King of Rome

Published 2018 – Copyright F.M.Mulhern

Chapter 1

"Bolae has fallen" cried the herald.

Heads turned from the jostling crowd in the forum, their faces cracking into smiles as they instantly shuffled across to be closer to the man standing on the steps of the shops running along the eastern edge of the central Forum. The sudden surge of people rushing across to him caused a minor scuffle as one lady was knocked roughly to the floor by the passing crowd and her husband lashed out at the nearest bystanders. As blood spilt onto the heavy cobbled floor the herald continued to shout out the news.

"Publius Postumius, Tribune of Rome" he called, his employer would be happy with him today and he knew he would have many spies in the crowd so he had to put on a good show. He also knew how to milk a crowd, and today he would not only deliver his message but he would create enough mystery to get himself a belly full of lunch and wine in the local alehouse from this crowd, he thought, as he perused the urgent faces staring at him hanging on his every word. He waved his hands theatrically and continued.

"Has defeated the Aequian *dogs*" he hung on the word as he stared into the crowd around him. As expected they brayed their displeasure at the word and angry shouts soon turned to cheers as he added "at the City of Bolae, taking the town and sacking its contents for the glory of Jupiter, Mars and the people of Rome." As he finished he stared high into the air, he knew the crowd would like this supplication to their gods and he held the pose for a full thirty seconds until the crowd had begun to quieten, anticipating his next words.

"Our Tribune" he called to some cheers, but also a series of cat calls from the back of the crowd, which he ignored whilst trying to spot the perpetrators from the corner of his eyes.

"With the strength of Mars, war bringer, took three thousand good Roman men and crushed the enemy" more cheers from the crowd "and for you, people of Rome" he waved an arm over the heads of the crowd "he will bring back spoils; gold, silver and new slaves." He turned and dropped his head at this last word, a smile flickering on his face at the booing and jeering from the crowd. It was customary for heralds to hold their heads down when mentioning the taking of slaves from captured cities as it reminded all Romans that they too might succumb to such fate if Rome ever fell. Inside he laughed at his own skill, the crowd yelling abuse at the Aequian slaves, with some calling for slaves to be given to every freeborn Roman citizen and others wailing for the loss of freedom it brought to them. Romans are fickle, thought the herald as he stood and looked down the curve of his nose at the crowd. His deep brown hair, long and dirty from his ride back to Rome, lay in thick clumps on his head and his face was covered in a film of dust as he held his head high for a moment before the silence allowed him to speak once again.

"Our Tribune" he raised both arms to the skies as he spoke "will return with the glorious men in four days" his face turned to the crowd. "Word of his victory has been given to the Senate and will be posted within two hours" he added, knowing that this would certainly buy him lunch and drinks as he sneered at the crowd, now pushing forwards to be the first to find out the details of the fight, who had died, who had distinguished themselves in the battle and how many slaves would be for sale. As he moved from the steps and headed towards his favourite alehouse he had to fight off the crowd of people asking for more information, just as he expected. He held his purse tightly in case a pickpocket was in the crowd and jostled his way towards his lunch, with several bystanders already pulling at his sleeve begging him to let them buy him a drink if he told them more about the battle of Bolae. He knew at least one of Postumius's spies was at his heel and would make sure that his Master knew every word the herald said, so, as he trudged away to the corner by the Temple of Saturnus he praised the strength and ability of Publius Postumius, slayer of Aequians and bringer of glory to Rome, even if he didn't believe a word of what he said.

Watching him leave the forum Gatto turned on his heel and set off towards the Oppian hill at a leisurely lope scratching the thick scar on his chin, a relic of a battle against a shorter man and a long spear. He had grown his beard a full five inches over the winter as befitted the new Greek style that everyone was wearing, but it played with his scar, making it itchier than ever. As he started the slow climb past the temple of the vestals he watched two dogs chasing each other and splashing through a pile of slops thrown from a window in one of the rickety tenant buildings at the foot of the climb. The area had seen a sudden growth of new buildings as land was sold off to house the ever-expanding city. It was said that close to two hundred and fifty thousand people lived in Rome now, he thought, as he cursed the dogs which were so busy chasing each other they ran straight across his path nearly knocking him over.

Gatto had to give his report to a rider who he would meet at the temple of Tellus, half way up the hill and as he approached the corner before the temple he saw a man running away to his left glancing quickly at him as he did so. Without thinking, Gatto knew something was wrong and ran the remaining forty paces to the corner, stopping with his back to the cold stone and peering around the bend before stepping out in to the road. As he turned the corner the first scream came. Ahead of him, and spread across the front steps of the temple, was a mix of brown and red. The brown of a cavalry cloak, its dusty hue now mingling with the bright crimson and dark red of the messenger's blood. The man's face was twisted into an inane grin, as if he had laughed as his blood bled from his body. From the distance he stood away from the body, Gatto knew there was no point going any closer, so he turned and walked away with an imperceptible shake of his head, he would never catch the man he saw running, and Javenoli would not be happy.

*

*

*

*

Chapter 2

Marcus Furius Camillus was as healthy as he had ever been. His muscles were tight under his thick woollen tunic and his hair was thick and long, with his deep black beard grown into curls in the Greek style. His ability with the sword had grown as he had aged, and after successful summer campaigns he had gained a Junior Tribune rank earlier than any man for the past fifty years.

Following his return to Rome the previous summer, he had spent much of his time developing a machine which he hoped would launch a thick arrow, over three feet long, to a distance of over two hundred paces. He'd read about the machine in a Greek war scroll he had been given by Senator Gaius Javenoli and since then he had been fascinated by recreating it. He had spent weeks developing the machine with his friends Cornelius Scipio and Gaius Potitus, both of whom had excellent engineering minds like his own, but they didn't possess the foresight that Marcus had for its use in military campaigns. As he wrenched at the wooden wheel which connected the spring loading mechanism to the catch where the bolt was placed, he looked across at Scipio, his half smile causing Marcus to shout, "What? Why the stupid look?" at which both Scipio and Potitus fell about laughing.

"You could help" Marcus said, his teeth clenched as he twisted his body to use his full weight to gain as much leverage on the wheel as possible.

"By the time you've wound that thing up, my Grandmother could have snuck up on you from a half mile away, taken your trousers down and given you a damn good thrashing" snorted

Potitus, his eyes streaming as he received another slap on the shoulder from a guffawing Scipio.

Potitus was the son of one of this term's newly appointed Senators, a man that Marcus had fought with some years before when his brother had received the grass crown, Rome's highest military honour, for saving the besieged army of his friend Cornelius's father. The Scipios remained one of the foremost families in Rome and Cornelius, like his namesake father, had already seen success in his military career alongside Marcus.

"You'll see" smiled Marcus, his determination set in his eyes. "Once I get the mechanism" he grunted as he twisted "to load, I can start to see how the strain affects it and improve it". He laughed at the strained looks on his friends faces. Potitus was a better engineer than either Scipio or himself, but the man was happy to stay back and watch Marcus do all the hard work, he thought, finally standing back and looking at the machine with his hands on his hips, his breathing heavy from his exertions.

"There" he said "the tormenta" by which he meant the complex spring system developed to give the tension to the machine "is ready to load."

"Look out for Grandma" laughed Scipio as he walked to his right to the old olive tree where they had stacked three arrow bolts that Potitus had made. Each bolt was roughly three feet long with a thick iron spike attached to the end. Potitus had enjoyed developing the spike for the arrows in the forge at the back of Marcus's father's house and had developed the majority of the thinking for the machine that they now stood over.

"What are you going to call this machine then?" asked Scipio, smiling at Marcus, his brown hair cut short, more in the military style of the previous decade than the current Greek fashion. His green-brown eyes smiled at the invention, which they had failed, to this point, to actually fire. After a series of snapped strings and broken bows they had given up trying to develop the machine that Marcus had read about in his Greek studies into an efficient Roman war machine. But now, in the late summer heat of Marcus's father's house in Tusculum they had taken to the task with gusto. Marcus had worked the wood into a slightly longer bow than the previous one, adding three layers of thick wood together to create a bow which he couldn't bend with his hands but which the new mechanism did with the ratcheted gearing system Potitus had developed.

The machine stood three and a half feet tall on three collapsible legs – a change to their first design which they couldn't easily carry up the hill from the house. It had what looked like a large bow placed horizontally across a plate attached to the legs, with two large metal rods screwed into the same plate to be able to create tension around this central point. The first arrows they had made had been too heavy to fire and so Potitus had found some strong, but light wood in a boat building yard which he had fashioned into these latest three arrows. The two metal rods also served as a viewing gate through which the machine could be 'sighted', though they had not yet had the success of firing an arrow so didn't know how useful that would be.

"I'm not sure what to call it" mused Marcus, standing back and looking at the machine, "but I think that if it works it might sting a bit if it hits you" he laughed, looking to his friends with a wicked smile on his face.

"Like a Scorpion" said Potitus. "A sting in the tail."

"Exactly" laughed Marcus "A Scorpion. That's what we'll call it."

"Here" said Potitus with a flourish "You load your *Scorpion* Marcus" and handed the wooden arrow across, its heavy iron spike and thicker rear to counter-balance the weight held firmly in his hands. Marcus took the arrow and placed it on the top. "Stay" he whispered" referring to the previous five times when simply adding the weight of the arrow had triggered the wooden bow to snap or the string, tightly stretched across the loading mechanism, to snap with a loud twang. As the arrow sat neatly into the groove all three men looked to one another and raised their eyebrows, the smile starting to curl on their lips. Marcus smiled at the small eagle motif Potitus had carved into the arrow, a symbol Marcus had used in all of his military campaigns since the fateful day he had heard the prophecy which foretold the future of Rome.

"You hit the switch" Marcus said to Potitus. "You developed the thing, so you can have first shot."

Potitus stepped up behind the Scorpion with a twinkle in his eyes. "Mars and Fortuna, bring us luck" he said with a wink as he pulled the trigger switch and the machine clicked, throwing the arrow with such force that it crashed through the tree trunk fifty yards ahead of them, shattering the wood and knocking half the tree over at the same time.

Marcus, Cornelius and Gaius stared open mouthed at each other momentarily before they whooped with joy and raced to the tree to assess the damage it had done.

*

*

*

*

Chapter 3

"Sir, the Labici force is settling to the North, we estimate there are about a thousand men with two hundred horses."

The Centurion stood to attention as he delivered the message to his commander, his eyes staring vacantly into the top corner of the command tent.

Postumius sat in his chair and looked at the man in front of him, his tired-looking face showing the fact that he had ridden for three hours to bring him this news. His eyes searched for any dust or dirt on his uniform or a hair out of place, but annoyingly he could find none.

He turned to his left where one of his senior officers stood in the half shadow of the light which was coming through the open tent flaps.

"Sergius" he asked, calling the man forwards. "How many active men do we have?"

"Two thousand six hundred and forty-eight, sir" intoned the man without needing to consult any of his array of tablets and documents sat neatly on the table beside him. As the camp prefect Spurius Sergius had already gotten used to the constant questioning from his superior and had been fastidious in ensuring that every messenger was cleaned and fully de-briefed before presenting any information to Postumius. In this way, he could stay one step ahead of his commander and one step closer to keeping his dignity. Postumius had a way of keeping his favourites close to him and degrading anyone who posed any sort of threat to his command. Only three days earlier, he'd had a legionary whipped for dropping his shield whilst on sentry duty when the man was stung by a bee, the latest in a long line of punishments the commander had delivered, and another on the list that his soldiers hated him for.

"That will be all, Centurion" Postumius said standing from his chair and turning to smile at Sergius with a look of consternation as the Centurion saluted and left the tent as quickly as he could. "Do you think we might have a problem?" he asked Sergius as he picked at a hair that had landed on the ornate bronze breastplate that he insisted on wearing despite the heat of the day.

Sergius took a moment to compose his thoughts before answering. "We have detailed five hundred men to return the captured treasures to Rome. We have around three hundred slaves to transport, which will need another four or five hundred men to support them in case there is an attempt to escape or to free them, so that leaves us with an equal force to the Labici to support any attempt from them should they attack us. My guess, sir, is that they will be looking to do one of two things."

"Do tell" interrupted Postumius, his voice aloof as he meandered to the front of the tent, his back to Sergius.

"They could be looking to capture the treasures for themselves, sir. Which I think is less likely as we could easily outnumber them if we simply moved en-masse with the treasures to Rome. Or they could be moving to take the city once we leave it. They are the closest Etruscan city to Bolae and no doubt they see it as a good colony for them" he finished.

"Interesting analysis" Postumius replied in a quiet voice as he turned and moved across to the map sat on his campaign desk placed towards the back of the tent in the shadows where it was cooler. After a few moments, in which Sergius, from previous explosions from his commander, knew to remain silent, Postumius spoke again. "How many days until we have loaded the treasures and finished checking the city?"

"Two at most, commander"

"Then fetch me a messenger Sergius, I think we may need to call for some reinforcements from Rome. If you are right" his eyes flicked at his camp prefect who stood impassively next to him "then we will need to hold this ground as one unit until we have enough support to move out."

****

"Centurion Marcus Pomponius Rufus, sir" announced the sentry as Postumius started from a short nap and looked to see the sun had begun its slow decline over the skyline. He cursed himself for drinking too much wine as he took his meal and stood, settling his breastplate and tunic before he announced that Rufus could enter.

Rufus, his flame red hair shot through with grey as he entered middle age, stepped into the tent with a half-smile. He had known Postumius for many years and fought with him in many a battle. Maybe 'fought' was the wrong word he mused as he came to a stand-still in front of his commanding officer, who waved for Rufus to sit in the chair opposite him. Despite their years in the army together Rufus had never got to like the man who took his seat across from him, they had, at best, a respect for each other's rank, and at worst a working relationship born of necessity. Rufus removed his helmet and placed it on the floor next to him, running his hands through his hair as he did so.

"Well Rufus, what is it this time?" started Postumius, his expression showing a measure of exasperation which Rufus did his best to ignore but inwardly his blood began to boil.

"I ask again, sir" the Centurion said in a measured tone, his eyes fixed on Postumius "that, at the men's request, the older soldiers take Bolae as a captured city and colonise it. They have fought well here and done your bidding" he ground his teeth at this last comment as Postumius had been ineffective in the fight and without the Centurions leading the counter-attack once inside the city walls they would have been slaughtered. "And they ask your permission to start refortifying the walls and strengthening the town, sir" he finished, his jaw set firm.

After a moments silence, in which Postumius's vacant expression suggested he didn't seem to recognise that Rufus was in the room and had spoken to him at all, the commanding officer leant forward and pointed to a spot on the map on the table in front of him, his finger making a thudding sound as he placed it heavily onto the vellum, a flash of anger showing in his eyes.

"Here" he said "are twelve hundred Labici. And here" he pointed to another spot, "are the Capenates and the Falicians. They will no doubt want to re-populate this dust bowl as soon as we leave as well" he said dismissively. "If I leave a force of two hundred men here, Centurion, how long do you think you will last?"

Rufus shifted in his seat, his anger trying desperately to get out as he held himself in check.

"Sir" he started "two hundred men could hold this city for a week. New recruits from Rome could be here within four, maybe five, days and we could colonise this area, creating more land for old soldiers to move into and giving Rome a new colony from which we can control the roads here in the north and have reinforcements should Veii decide to march on Rome." Postumius looked at his Centurion and shook his head slowly. "We have had nearly twenty years of peace with Veii. Why would they attack us now?" Despite the rhetorical question, Rufus answered quickly.

"Sir, with respect, the Veientines have been stirring up the rest of the Etruscan cities for years, everyone knows that" he almost chided, quickly continuing as he saw the irritation start to rise in Postumius's face. "But, commander," he added the phrase as he knew Postumius liked to be named as commander of the army. "Whether they are stirring trouble or not, this position gives Rome good access to the mountains, a fortress in the north and an opportunity to reduce the burden of ex-soldiers on our City. Surely, sir, such a thing could only lead to better security for Rome?"

Postumius sat back in his chair. The same argument, over and over again, he thought as he looked at the man sat in front of him, noting the greying hair, creases in his brow and tired expression on his face. Postumius knew he could not grant the men's wishes, he had other plans for Bolae.

"It's not my decision, Centurion" he said, his voice sounding as bored as the last time they had held this conversation. "As I have said previously, such decisions are for the Senate, not for a mere field commander to make. In fact, Centurion" he added "if I hear the argument again I will personally kick the next man I hear speak of it into the latrine ditch" he said standing from the desk and waving an arm out at the front of the tent whilst staring down his nose at the frustrated look on Rufus's face.

"Rufus, Rufus" he cajoled as the Centurion looked up at him, his face a mask of frustration. "If I could make the decision you know I would, but I cannot."

"You could set a force to guard the town, Sir" replied Rufus flatly. "Two hundred good men, hand-picked" he added, looking at a spot away in front of him so as not to look his superior in the eyes.

"No. I have spoken" Postumius finished. "Tell the men that when we return to Rome the Senate will be presented with the idea of a colony and we will see what they decide."

Rufus sat motionless in the chair for a moment longer before speaking. "Permission to leave, Sir?" he said in a level tone which hid his frustration.

"Yes, yes" came the reply as Rufus saluted and turned on his heel, his helmet held under his arm as he marched stiffly from the tent to the sounds of Postumius sighing.

*

*

*

*

Chapter 4

"Bastard" spat Bassano, his teeth set into a grimace as he sat next to Rufus and several of the senior Centurions of Postumius' Legion. "What a load of crap. He could set up a colony here if he wanted to, he has the authority, and he knows it" he threw the dregs of his wine onto the floor. "Gods this wine is like latrine water" he said, his anger boiling.

"Calm down" said Rufus, his arm resting on his friend's shoulder as he looked him in the eyes. "He has Imperium here in the Legion so his decision is final. We have had our say and it will be recorded in the journals" he said as a few grumbles came from the men sat around him.

"This is good land Rufus, you know it" Bassano added with a shake of his head, his eyes staring into the fire around which they sat in the dimming light of the day. The officers all sat and looked at each other for a few minutes before a short man, his left eye covered in a thick bandage, spoke above the silence.

"A messenger went to Rome earlier for reinforcements" he said quietly, at which those who had not heard this news sat up with a look of interest. "I think he is looking for support to transport the treasure and slaves" he added with a questioning frown.

"Bastard better not lose that treasure" Bassano spat again. "I have enough money in those spoils to be set up for ten years" he grinned at the thought, as did a number of the men around him.

"Still doesn't sort the problem of where you'll be living though" added Rufus as Bassano glanced to him and shook his head with a wry smile.

"No, but with that I can buy a plot of land somewhere. Maybe just up the Tiber" he said with a smile. "Enough for the young ones to grow and maybe for Appius and his family to move to as well. I can't be living in Rome any more, too many people, too many beggars. I've had enough Rufus" he said with a dejected shake of the head. "Patres have taken everything, taxed it to the hilt and then closed every opportunity to become a magistrate and earn a good living in the City. The Plebeian leaders are not arguing our case strongly enough and we are little more than beggars to the rich" he sighed deeply. "Better to move to the provinces and see if I can get a magistrate's role out of a local town, they always want old soldiers, especially Centurions" he added to the agreement of some of the men.

The one-eyed man sat back with a grunt, rubbing at the patch over his eye before adding "I reckon I have enough from this campaign to see me through six winters" his grin spread across his face as he continued "how much do you reckon we will get for those slaves?"

As the Centurions set to discussing their spoils and how they would spend it, none of them noticed the man who had been lying next to the tent away to their left in the shadows. He crawled slowly backwards into the darkness of the gap between the tents and slid on his belly until he was out of sight. Postumius would be happy to hear that Bassano was bad-mouthing him he thought as he grinned wickedly and set off to his commander's tent.

****

"But father, the Scorpions are unbelievable" Marcus said, his voice strong but deferent as he spoke.

Marcus's father Lucius Furius Medullinus stood next to a small window in the exedra, the small garden room which was in the south-east corner of his villa in Tusculum. He looked at the warm sky outside as he turned to his son, his face serious as they discussed Marcus's latest 'invention'.

"Undoubtedly it is a good weapon" he started, waving away a fly that buzzed annoyingly around him, "but it is the cost Marcus. You have made twenty of these things, Scorpions?" he asked, his eyebrows raised. Marcus nodded a reply, his head lowered as he knew what was coming next. "The cost has used all of your reward from the last two campaigns, every scrap of bronze and silver has gone Marcus. If you are to bring up your children, pay for a good education and promote yourself for the position of Censor you will need money. Where do you see this coming from?" he asked, his exasperation showing that they had discussed this issue numerous times in recent weeks.

Marcus sat quietly taking slow breaths as he fumbled for words. Why did it always come down to money, surely his father could see the benefit of the Scorpions. Over the past month, he and Potitus had re-engineered the gearing system making it easier and quicker to load, developed lighter arrow bolts and fashioned an improved range finder which gave it a level of accuracy a legionary would never be able to achieve over a throwing distance of two hundred yards, three times that of any man.

"Father" he started, raising his chin and setting his eyes into a determined stare. "The Republic needs new weapons and new ways of fighting. With success, this could be a new income for the family. It could bring us a measure of glory as well" he almost pleaded, his voice rising slightly before he checked himself and took a deep breath. "Think what would happen if the Scorpions could send three bolts each, that's sixty bolts every minute into a phalanx. It would devastate a line of infantry and render the phalanx useless. The new version is light and can be carried by a man, or two men, on a horse, easy to pick up and retreat if threatened by cavalry."

His father stopped him with a shake of his head. "Marcus" he said "you would need two hundred, not twenty. The cost of each machine is prohibitive. How would any soldier be able to afford such a thing? Only the rich families would be able to provide them, and even then, each man would need a horse or even two" he added with another shake of the head. "We cannot afford it" he said with a measure of finality. "No more" he searched for the words "contraptions" he said with a wave of his hand.

"But father" started Marcus "the phalanx style is no longer efficient, I showed that with my Eagles. Didn't we win every battle with my new Maniples, my handfuls of soldiers fighting in smaller groups? Didn't our line take the phalanx at the river last year against the Capenates? With the Scorpions, we could have thinned those phalanxes to breaking point without any loss of Roman life. It is you and Lucius who are always saying that we lose too many soldiers each summer. The Scorpions are the future" he stated strongly, rising from the chair and stepping to the window, a cool breeze coming into the room from the garden outside.

Lucius, his deep-set eyes and thin nose a mirror of Marcus's own face, turned in exasperation and was about to begin his eulogy again when a knock came at the door and a slave entered, his eyes looking to the floor as he spoke.

"Master, forgive my presence. Master Fabius Ambustus has arrived and I have taken him to the study and ordered watered wine and food for him. He requested your presence and that of young Master Camillus."

Lucius looked at his son. "We will talk of this another time" he said as he placed an arm around Marcus's shoulder and gave him a light hug, his half smile and small shake of the head giving Marcus hope that their next conversation might go more in the direction he hoped.

****

"Fabius, an honour to see you my friend" Lucius Senior said as he clasped arms with the short, man, his wiry hair matted to his head as he had taken off his riding cap and run his hands through the tangled mess.

"Lucius. Marcus" nodded the man seriously before sitting down heavily in a thickly carved wooden chair and continuing to drink from the cup he had been given. "Forgive my unannounced visit" he said, wiping his mouth with a small cloth. "I have news of Bolae. Postumius seems to have won the day and sacked the town, but has sent for reinforcements." Marcus liked Ambustus, always straight to the point with no pleasantries and he smiled at the stern face of the man sat in front of him. "It seems he has Labici raiders on his tail and has requested a relief force to support the return to Rome. I have been given command of a thousand men, of which three hundred are Equites" he smiled. As leader of the horse, the Equites, Ambustus had been the first man to lead a charge on a phalanx, overwhelming the right wing of an attacking force, and his reputation in Rome had risen dramatically since that day. Marcus grinned as the memory of the fight flashed through his mind.

"The men" he continued, "are already a day's ride to Bolae but I have come to ask Camillus" at which Marcus turned his face with more interest to Ambustus "to join me. I think those Eagles of yours could be useful" he smiled, finishing the watered wine and standing to look at both men. Marcus flashed a grin, his heart skipping a beat as he contemplated the request. "I will be ready in thirty minutes my friend" he said, placing a hand on his father's shoulder and smiling at him. "I will take Narcius and Mella if that is acceptable Father? May I use a messenger to send to Rome for the rest of the men?" he asked as his father gave a resigned nod. The Narcius family had become clients of the Furii since the day that Publius Narcius had joined Marcus's Eagle troops at the battle of the three crossroads. Having been a poor legionary who struggled to wield the long spear in a phalanx he had taken to fighting with a sword and shield with such energy and expertise that his whole family had grown close to Marcus and allied themselves to him. As Marcus strode from the room Ambustus and Lucius sat and began discussing the latest news in Rome as they waited for him to return.

*

After half an hour of rushing around organising his equipment, Marcus had eaten a quick bowl of Satura soup and said goodbye to his wife Livia before leading the packing of the twenty Scorpions onto a cart and setting off with Ambustus and his small group of riders. After agreement with Ambustus, Gaius Potitus had been added to their group before they left, and the men rode off into the low hills with a wave back at the small huddle of family members who stood and waved at their departure. Marcus felt alive again; he was going back to war.

*

*

*

Chapter 5

"Damn them" Postumius said as he stared at the dead men lying strewn across the ground at the river. He spat, a long drip falling onto his leg, as he stared menacingly at the men around him. "Will someone get those damned archers?" he yelled at his officers, who cowered behind him unsure what to do against the fifty Labici archers stood across the narrow, but deep, waterway. The Labici had been raiding the outposts Postumius had set around his camp beside the walls of the fallen town of Bolae and, so far, had managed to kill a number of Roman soldiers without any loss to their own.

"Look at them" he called. "They are laughing at me" he said, his eyes searching the rows of men no more than a hundred paces away across the water, their brown leather breastplates and bronze helmets adorned with long black feathers showing which tribe they were from. "I want them dead" he said with anger as he whirled to one of his staff officers and pointed a finger. "You, Aulus Manlius, get me those feathers" he snarled, "I want them today".

"Sir" saluted Aulus, his face not betraying the resentment he felt for the constant jibes he received from his commanding officer. His brother had warned him that serving under Postumius might lead to some problems, but he hadn't realised how spiteful the man could be and this was another in a long line of unachievable objectives he had received from Postumius, all of them designed to make him look foolish and inept.

"Get on with it then, man" Postumius chided, his sneer bringing a smile to the face of his closest advisers.

Aulus nudged his horse forwards and called to Agrippa, his Centurion, "get me twenty men with horses and meet me by the ford." He stepped the beast slowly to the river-front, keeping as far from the bank as he could to avoid arrow-fall, as his mind ran through options for attacking the small war band.

A thump thirty yards ahead of him showed that the archers were testing the range, their black beards split with yellow-white teeth as they grinned and jeered at him. Below him lay a man he had had supper with the previous evening, a thick brown shaft through his throat as his lifeless eyes stared into the blue sky. A crow squawked as he neared the closest corpse, its wings lifting its heavy, well fed, body into the air as it shouted protests at being disturbed from its meal. Thump. Another arrow, this time closer. His horse edged backwards as he came to a stop as another arrow fell ten yards ahead of him.

"Don't stop man" came the laughing call from Postumius as he looked to his left at the commander, sat astride his large white charger. "Go on" called Postumius again "Get me my feather" he barked as he nudged his horse forwards, his eyes full of hatred.

Every fibre of his being wanted to shout back at Postumius and tell him exactly what he could do with his feather, but he knew he could not do that and that his Virtus, his bravery, was being affronted by Postumius. There was nothing he could do except obey his commanding officer's demand. The noise of horses behind him brought his mind back to the task in hand as he saw the approach of his riders. He looked across the river at the archers, three of whom now jumped from their horses and ran down the bank to get closer to the Romans, their long tunics flowing as they came to a stop and hefted their bows.

Agrippa appeared at Aulus's side, his face a mask of anger as he glanced at the archers and then back to Postumius, who was still walking his horse closer to the river. "I don't mind dying, sir" he said with a measured tone, "but for that prick?" he shook his head as he looked at Aulus and sighed "orders, sir?"

"The ford is further along, let's ride hard and come back as quickly as we can. Might as well get it over with" Aulus said as an arrow whistled into the water ahead of him. "Men, let's go" he called, waving his arm to the right and setting off at a canter, hefting the small round shield in his left hand as he gripped the reins with his right alongside his spear.

"Aaarrrgh" came a sudden scream from behind him which caused Aulus to pull his mount to a stop, the horse snorting as it stamped its feet and turned to a great cheer from across the river bank. Aulus looked back at his commander as he slipped from his horse, a long arrow protruding from his shoulder and a great scream coming from his lungs. Almost with a smile he called to his men "to the ford, we must get that feather" and rode off at a gallop to the cheers and calls from the Labici archers who were now racing to the river front and firing into the knot of Roman officers on the other bank.

*

*

*

Manlius stood, his white tunic bleached to perfection as he smiled at the assembled men of the plebeian council. He had been careful to dress down for the meeting, avoiding anything which he thought might show signs of self-importance to the men who had been asked to attend him in his house on the Capitoline Hill. Manlius smiled his warmest smile and nodded to the men.

"Calvus. Virginius. Cominus. Pomponius" he nodded as he welcomed each man, continuing around the table to several other prominent plebeian statesmen who all sat looking to him with measured smiles on their faces. "The candle has been lit and in the name of my ancestors I welcome you to my home" he announced, spreading his arms wide. "As you know I have asked you here to discuss the political *situation*" he smiled as a few of his guests smiled with him and nodded at his jest, noting that Calvus remained stoic, his bright eyes betraying no emotion.

"The annual campaigns are harder on all of our families" he started, seeing a few nods from around the table "and I have been discussing the issue with the Consuls. It strikes me that the cost of war, the taxes and such-like" he added as Calvus frowned at him "are becoming too much of a burden on many of our families and we should discuss potential options which may be to all of our benefits" he finished, picking up a honeyed oatcake and biting into the crispy biscuit.

"And which of the patricians do you have supporting you in your *discussions*?" came a reedy voice to his left as Manlius chewed the oatcake.

"Both Consuls have asked me for an opinion and the Senate will be discussing the issue in the next meeting at the Kalends" he added with a firm nod of his head.

"Hah. And no doubt they will be completing the sacrifices that only *they* can do. Or should I say that *you* can do?" came the reedy reply, alluding to the fact that only patricians could perform the religious ceremonies, of which there were many in Rome, that bound the state and Republic together. This was a particularly prickly subject but Manlius was prepared for it as it was a constant thorn in the way of any negotiations between the plebeians and patricians.

"I agree with your sentiment Pomponius" he replied, lifting the dish of oatcakes and handing it across the table to one of his guests as he spoke, his voice light and friendly. "Ten years ago, which of us would have thought that we would be sitting around a table even discussing such issues" he said, the crow's feet lines stretching at the corners of his eyes as he smiled a full smile. "But now here we are, brothers in the Republic. We have the same needs my friend, the same duty to the state and the same problems. Today is the start of the discussion to resolve the issues, not to keep bringing the old problems back. How can we step forward if we live in the past? I know the old saying 'one master and not two'" he added "the facts are simple, we are all getting poorer as the wars drain us of our children, our brothers and our money. But today I ask you, learned men of the plebeian council, for your views on resolution. How do we move forward together? We don't want another Secession" he said with a smile, his eyebrows raised and his hands out in front of him as a few 'huffs' came from the assembled men.

Pomponius narrowed his eyes and leant his head to one side. "So, Marcus Manlius, as the appointed" he smiled as he said this "patrician to discuss with us lower orders" he glanced around the table "what we feel should be done with regard to the taxes which we all pay for our safety in Rome, where would you like to start this discussion? Shall we start with patricians clearing all debts for their clients?" he sneered at the comment as a number of voices jumped in with agreement to this statement. Above the noise he added, pointing a finger at Manlius "you said it Manlius, one master and not two. Remove the debts of the people and we will be able to pay more into the coffers of Rome, not to the bank rolls of the rich. Your kind has all the money and you pay fewer taxes, yet we pay you as well as paying with our blood." Manlius growled inwardly as he sat erect in his chair to reply. "I know what you are going to say" sneered Pomponius before he could respond. "We *patricians* have the most to lose" he said, his voice sounding more nasal than before as he looked straight into the eyes of the bearded Manlius.

"No, no" Manlius replied as Virginius laughed loudly at Pomponius's comment. "The Consuls and Senate are looking at all options, my friends." He looked around the table as a number of the men shook their heads, their deep-set hatred of the patrician class too far gone to see any solution. "You are the new men of Rome" he said, his voice rising as the group were already shaking their heads again. "We are all in the Republic together, the Lex Canuleia..."

"The Lex Canuleia" shouted Cominus, his red cheeks pitted with thin veins "was a waste of good effort on the part of the plebeians. How many marriages have been sanctified? How many?" he called as he waved his hands theatrically around at the men sat shaking their heads. "You, Marcus Manlius, know nothing of the issue of which you speak. How can you? You are a patrician, you have the *'birthright'*" he spat these last words as he stared with anger at Manlius, his bravado starting to disappear under the barrage of the plebeian council. "Shall we talk legality, Manlius?" he added, his voice disappearing under a cacophony of calls from the men, who were quickly starting to become the rabble that Manlius saw out on the streets of Rome every day. Only Calvus remained calm as he sat quietly to the right of Pomponius and smiled a confident smile.

"Legally," continued Cominus, repeating himself as he asked the men to quieten and let him speak. "Legally the men around this table have one voice. But that one voice is nothing compared to a patrician's voice. How can we affect the laws of Rome and agree changes to tax as you request when we have no voice? Tell me that Manlius before I give you the benefit of my years and the fortune that my gods bring to me from my hard work." He had risen from his chair as he spoke, but now sat down, his eyes boring into Manlius, who sat impassively though his heart was beating like a drum in his chest.

Manlius lifted his hand, hoping it would be a placating gesture, as he took a breath and looked each man in the eye waiting for the mood to calm a little before he spoke. "My good friends" he said, seeing several men shake their heads and look away from him as he said the words. "We, the people of the Republic must find a way to work together, to do Rome's bidding and to be one people. I agree with everything you have said" he gestured "and we, yes *we,* must do something about it. But we can only do this together" he looked directly at Calvus as he spoke. "What say you Publius Licinius Calvus Esquilinus?" he asked, giving the man his full name as a mark of respect as much as a way of giving himself a few moments to collect his thoughts.

Calvus nodded at the respect shown to him and looked slowly around the table at the plebeians he had known since boyhood. Amongst them were men he had fought with against the Volsci, indeed he had seen many of their brothers killed in action. The meeting had started badly, as such meetings always did, the gulf between the patricians and plebeians was as wide as it had ever been despite the secessions and numerous vetos made by the plebeian tribunes. Calvus took a moment to compose his thoughts before speaking.

"Legally" he started with a smile to Cominus "the twelve tables have given a measure of" he searched for the word "*constitution* to what we all agree as our abiding principles for our home." He glanced at Manlius with almost a sense of pity as he continued. "But they are nothing more than a way of keeping order. The issue is, of course" at this he looked directly at Manlius "the Consuls have the direct power over the law and can decide in whichever way they agree what is best for the Republic. But as we know each Consul must be a patrician, and there lies our issue, Marcus Manlius" he smiled.

Silence descended on the room as each face looked expectantly at Manlius before Calvus continued.

"Rome is our home Marcus Manlius, as it is yours. To us and the *other* people of Rome it is imperative to be one nation under one law. But we cannot be that without the voice of the people being heard. How can it be?" Murmurs of agreement came from the assembled group of men. "The city has over two hundred thousand people crammed within its walls and more arrive every day as our armies win victory after victory. But Manlius" he looked to Cominus who was frowning as he spoke "release the debts of the people who have done well in this great city, free the land rights so that plebeians can buy good land and settle. But most of all, tell your Senate of patricians that they must give the people the power to make decisions, not just to be puppets that are asked their views and then ignored."

His last words brought a series of calls from around the table as the men agreed with Calvus's statement.

"Furthermore" continued Calvus as he looked at the plebeian faces, all grinning back at him as they came to silence at his words. "Now is the time to remove the law which states that Consuls and Military Tribunes must be patricians. Remove these limitations that hamper all freeborn men who have the desire to help the city to grow, and there will be greater benefits to Rome, Manlius. Take away the ideology that only those born into the older families of a Rome that has been and gone can make decisions about the here and now, change the world we live in Manlius, make this Rome the greatest City there has ever been by empowering the people who live in it to be a true Republic where each man has a voice." He finished with a stare into the corner of the room, his theatrical style pleasing himself as a burst of rapping on the table and some small cheers came from the assembled men, Pomponius gripping his shoulder and whispering "well said, brother" into his ear.

Manlius sat looking at the men around him. Something in his mind sparked as he listened to the words of Calvus, his heart beating fast as his thought processes caught up with the words he had heard. Somewhere deep inside himself he knew that these words were true and that Rome had outgrown the patricians, his mind worked feverishly to see how he could gain from this situation. He steeled himself as he stood and held his hand up to the guests around the table, his eyes holding a look of wonder as he spoke.

"Publius Licinius Calvus Esquilinus" he said with a small bow of his head. "I have heard your words, spoken with a passion and love of Rome and *our* people. A passion I recognise and hold dear to my heart. And, men of the plebeian council, I agree with your words. Indeed I" he paused as he spoke, a tear coming to his eye. "Yes, I Marcus Manlius will take your yoke and will carry your burden to the Senate. I will champion your words Calvus, if you will let me? But" he continued, as one or two of the men sneered and shook their heads at the drama of his speech. "*We* gentlemen, *we* must develop a case which cannot be vetoed by the

Senate, the very men who will oppose any eradication of their power. So, gentlemen, what do we do?" he asked.

*

*

*

*

Chapter 6

The leader of the scouting party that had been ambushed a day earlier watched from the ravine as the snake of men kicked up a dust cloud in the early morning heat. He wiped his brow as he considered his next move, glancing across the hillock to his right to see the hundred Labici warriors stop and search the ground for his tracks.

"Bastards" he thought. He had no idea if the column of men below in the valley were Roman or some other enemy, but he had to gamble, or he would definitely be caught. The Labici had tracked him for two days, killing his scouting party and nearly capturing him on two occasions. He gripped the wound on his forearm, the matted blood showed he had stopped bleeding but his fingers were still not able to grip strongly. He shook his head and clenched his teeth as he stared at the thin line of soldiers marching slowly to the north. It was now or never, he thought, as he kicked his tired horse into a trot and set off through the narrow causeway in which he was hiding, the steep drop to the road coming into view as a Labici rider called and pointed his spear at him.

The dust got in his eyes as he edged his mount onto the steep slope, the horse snorting and stamping its front legs as it searched for good ground. Behind him he heard the slap of an arrow, the damned Labici were good, he considered momentarily before a lurch to the right forced him to grip his reins tighter, the pain shooting through his arm as he did so. He peered into the distance to see one of the scouts ahead and below had seen him and was waving to the surrounding men, most of them on horses. His tired eyes could not make out the clothes or the colours as they watered in the dusty haze, his legs urging the horse onwards as it struggled to remain upright on the steep, rock strewn ground. Another crack sounded as an arrow skidded off a boulder to his right, the spark of light from the iron tip flashing into his vision. "Come on" he growled at the horse, dragging its head to the left and pointing it down the hill. He mumbled a prayer to Fortuna, a goddess he had become close to in previous weeks as he thought about how stupid such prayers were to him only a few years ago.

Ahead he heard a cry, the scouts were riding up the hill towards him. He glanced over his shoulder to see the Labici riders were coming to a stop, clearly not sure who the men below were. A sudden flurry of arrows thumped into the ground behind him as he made a last yell and squeezed his horse hard with his knees, its body almost jumping at his command as it staggered and trotted again.

The scout looked behind him and saw to his relief that the Labici were falling behind and coming to a stop. He sighed with such force that his grip slipped on his injured arm, sending him half over the front of the horse as it almost came to a standstill, unsure what its rider wanted. "No boy" he murmured, his grin allowing a fleck of white spit to form at the corner of his mouth, "Keep going, come on, good horse" he grinned as he looked ahead to see the red feathers of Roman cavalry dancing on the helmets of the men coming towards him, his face beaming as the first man came into view.

The Roman cavalry surrounded the rider, taking their time to make sure that he was not an enemy. Satisfied, one of the cavalry had swapped horses with him to allow him a better ride along the steep final descent, the scout walking the tired beast as the other men headed back to the marching column. As the rescued man drank deeply from the leather pouch he had been given, he looked up at the empty hillside, the Labici had gone, but were no doubt watching the men below and sending messengers to their main force. As he looked ahead he saw three men riding forwards of the column, their bronze armour glinting through the dust. As they approached and reined in he smiled, his grin splitting his face as he saluted and stared at one of the men in front of him.

"Marcus Furius Camillus" he said through his cracked lips "I never thought I would be so happy to see you again."

"Fasculus" came the surprised reply.

****

A couple of hours later Fasculus was cleaned up and sat on a rock as the column halted to take a short break from their relentless pace. The blue sky held a threat of rain as thick grey clouds were bunching on the horizon. Fasculus stretched his forearm, rubbing the thick bandage that had been wrapped tightly around it, and looked up at the sun as it blazed down on them from almost directly overhead. He shook his head and turned to his right "gods it's hot" he said, taking a drink of water and then splashing some over his neck , attempting to cool himself down.

"That rain will be here in an hour or so" came the reply from the man he had been introduced to earlier, Gaius Potitus. Potitus was Marcus Furius's close friend and as such Fasculus had made an effort to get to know him, picking up bits of information about what they were doing out on the road and where they were going. He was delighted to hear that they were going to

Bolae, his destination as well. After debriefing Ambustus, the leader of this group, with enough of his scouting reports to keep the man happy he had melted into the background of officers and kept his tone light, avoiding Mella and Camillus, as everyone seemed to call Marcus Furius these days, as much as he could. Mella in particular had reason to hate Fasculus and it was difficult to avoid the man's resentful looks and spiteful remarks.

Fasculus looked at the clouds away in front of them. "Thunderstorm?" he asked.

Potitus stopped eating and looked at the sky, taking a moment to glance at the few fir trees that were sparsely dotted around the low hills. "There's not much wind" he replied "so you may be right. It'd be best if we made Bolae before it hit" he commented without moving his eyes from the skyline.

"Aye" came Fasculus's response as he watched Marcus mount his horse and look over his shoulder at the column.

"Mount" came the shout as a clatter of noise started, men rising from the ground and shaking the dust from their clothes, horses snorting as they were pulled from the roadside where the grass was longest. Fasculus decided that he must get closer to Marcus and once mounted he slipped forwards in the line to walk just behind him, noting that Mella watched him like a hawk. He grinned at Mella with his best 'friendly' face before turning away as the man spat onto the ground and stared malevolently back at him. Javenoli had suggested he shouldn't dispose of anyone just yet, but Mella might be an exception that needed to be removed, he thought.

"Camillus" he said, nudging his horse forwards as he spoke. "Might I ride beside you, I have some things I believe need to be said" he asked, his glance at Mella telling him that one person, at least, didn't think there was much they could agree on.

****

The scout rocked on his mount, the red spot on his chest growing as he stared at it. His mind rushed with thoughts as he clutched at the iron tip that had appeared through his shoulder, a sudden flare of pain bursting through his body as another whack to his back announced a second arrow. He tried to turn the horse, but it screamed a nasal grunt and reared his weak hands unable to control the beast as it too took another arrow in the flank. His mind felt him fall, the pain was gone, how could that be? A darkness came to his eyes as he heard hoof beats galloping madly away from him.

"Is that the last of them?"

"Yes, three dead now" came the reply.

"Good, take the high point there, I will go to the bushes. Send the man to call them forward." He stepped to the side before turning again and asking "which one is he again?" as he patted the thick sword hanging from his belt "I want that reward" he grinned.

"He is the man with the Greek style beard and if they take the bait he will be leading the advance party. But we need to send a few warning signals to make sure they fall into the trap"

"Excellent. Make sure it happens. If there is no advance party, we will retreat until they approach the river. I must get this man alone" replied the taller of the two men, his head nodding slowly as he spoke.

*

Ambustus stopped the column. His nerves told him something was wrong, but he couldn't see what it was. The scout waved from up ahead, giving the signal to proceed and then turned away, trotting over the rise. Ambustus frowned, maybe he was getting too old for this, he considered as he waved the men forwards his eyes glancing at the rocky ravines on the right and low scrub bushes to the left. Had that scout taken off his helmet? Where were the other scouts? He felt an old, familiar, cold feeling creep up the back of his neck and he didn't like it.

"Camillus" he said quietly, an urgent look on his face which brought Marcus to his side.

"What is it?" asked Marcus, glad to get away from Fasculus who had spent a full thirty minutes attempting to distance himself from his actions when they had last met, blaming Postumius for 'orders' which had to be obeyed. The man had even gone as far as to apologise to Mella, at which Mella had snorted his derision and ridden to the back of the column.

"I'm not sure Camillus" replied Ambustus as he scoured the ground ahead of them. "Something in my gut tells me there might be a problem" he started to say before a call from behind caused both he and Marcus to turn. One of the men was pointing to the sky as a large eagle circled overhead.

"Your bird, Camillus" said Fasculus as he watched the eagle slowly circle and then disappear behind the rocky outcrops on the right. "I wonder what portent that brings?" he asked absently as his eyes turned to rove the ground ahead again, his nerves on edge. All he could see was the rise of the path, narrow and rocky, the perfect place for an ambush. His mind considered the options. A force of fifty raiders could probably hold the ground for an hour or two he thought as he glanced around at the land around him.

"Stop the column" said Marcus instantly, his instincts taking over. "Set out a force in front Ambustus, there is something wrong, you are right" he said quickly as Ambustus looked at him and then called a halt to the march with a stiff nod to Marcus.

"Take fifteen men Camillus" said Ambustus as he swivelled to his left and beckoned his first spear Centurion forwards to give him orders. "But be careful, the road is tricky and it's a good location for an ambush" he added as he tapped his sword, releasing it an inch from its scabbard nervously. The noise of the sword rasping on the scabbard made Marcus's eyes flick to Ambustus before he jumped from his horse.

"Narcius" he said as his Hastatus Prior, his own first spear, came forwards. "We are going to search ahead of the main column for a bit. Get fifteen of the men ready" he said, turning back to Ambustus. "Follow one hundred yards behind us, sir" he said as he slid his leather skull cap over his hair and thumped his helmet on top, tying the chin strap quickly before gripping his shield in his left hand. He hefted his sword, feeling the balanced weight as he took a deep breath and stepped forwards. "Follow me, Eagles" he called as the men trotted out behind him.

Ambustus watched as the last man in the line trotted along without a shield and with a long sword, its shining metal glinting in the sunlight as he placed it over his shoulder as he ran to catch up with the legionaries. Ambustus frowned as he watched Fasculus join the skirmish party, wondering what the man was up to.

Narcius called the step as the men crested the short hill, his breathing steady as he looked around at the countryside. His eyes searched the ground for any sign of disturbance or enemy. Nothing came to his view, not even the scouts. Something wasn't right.

"Sir" he said without looking to his right where Marcus was walking beside him. "This is a good spot for an ambush. Rocks to the right, deep gullies and that scrub bush to the left."

"I agree" came the reply as Marcus peered in both directions. "And it's too quiet" he added as he strained his ears above the clinking of the men's armour. He took a moment to glance over his shoulder, past the men in line behind him, at the forms of Ambustus and his officers who had crested the small rise behind them. "Narcius, get the men tight together..." Marcus started to say before a deep throated cry came from the roadside to his right and the blur of the shape of a man jumping from the small rocky outcrop appeared in his vision, the speed of the attack forcing him and the man to his right to twist manically to deflect the blow of a long-handled war axe. The legionary in front of Marcus caught the full force of the axe on his shield, but the blow was so forceful that it knocked him into Marcus and both men fell to the floor and scrambled to regain their feet. As the man smashed into the bodies of the legionaries another twenty men leapt from the rocks and started to hack at the Romans in front of them.

"Form up" called Narcius, gripping Marcus by the arm and hurling him upright as the warrior with the war axe fell at his feet, a gaping wound in his neck gushing a tide of crimson that soaked quickly into the dry earth. Marcus staggered and his feet slipped in the blood of the dead warrior as another man fell across his shield, at which Marcus pushed the falling body back into another attacker.

"Shields" called Narcius, Marcus thankful that the man's constant training and drilling of his legionaries was paying benefits as the men clunked their shields together as a flurry of hammer blows smashed into the wood. Marcus saw a movement above him and glanced upwards quickly to see a hail of arrows shooting across the road and into the officers along the road, Ambustus raising his shield to catch three arrows as his men called for defensive positions.

"Narcius" called Marcus "We need to retreat to the main column or we will be cut off" he said, his eyes flicking to a spear as it clattered over the top of his shield splicing a shard of wood into the air. The man who thrust his spear was grinning as Marcus moved his shield up and to the left and stabbed his shortened sword into the shoulder of the attacker, his dark leather breastplate no defence against the accuracy of Marcus's strike as it bit into the muscle on his upper arm. With a speed born of hours of training the man pulled back his spear, yelling in pain and cursing in Etruscan, a language Marcus knew well from his youth. Without a second thought, and despite the man's speed of movement, Marcus stepped forwards, closing the gap between the two men and sliced his sword across the man's neck, the flesh slicing easily on his sharp sword. The warrior opened his eyes wide, unable to understand how the Roman had managed to move so quickly and cursed as he fell to his knees, his shield falling from his grip as he clutched at the bleeding hole in his neck. Marcus stepped back to his right, closing the gap and parrying another attack with his shield, his focus on threats to come, not those he had dealt with.

"Behind you" came a scream as Marcus was pushed forwards, battering into the attacker in front of him and scrambling to retain his footing as Narcius, once again, gripped his arm and pulled him back into the line of soldiers. Whirling his head around he saw Fasculus smashing his sword with a two-handed grip at a long-haired brute of a man who had appeared from the shrubbery, followed by another handful of men. Each man wielded an axe or a long sword and small, circular, shields richly painted in reds and greens. 'Veientines' thought Marcus, his mind racing as Narcius called to the men to split into two fronts to face both directions.

Fasculus fell to one knee, his efforts to stop the repeated battering from his attacker starting to flounder as his breathing rasped in his lungs, his grunting sounding strained as he clashed swords once again with the heavy blade of the attacker from the bushes, his injured arm weakened under the constant attacks. Marcus stepped forwards, clashing his shield into the side of the tall attacker, his overly large sword rising to swing a double handed blow at him. The blow came in a cross-cut, down and around to Marcus's side. With a deft movement of his shield he managed to deflect the blow but the ferocity of the strike took Marcus off his feet for a moment as his shield buckled against the blow, his arm absorbing the impact and instantly feeling numb. Marcus stepped in front of Fasculus as another attacker jumped across with a low stab at the prone man. Fasculus, though, was no fool and was up on his feet, his long sword flashing into the arm of his attacker, slicing the sinews across the man's elbow as he screamed and dropped his sword to Fasculus's delighted yell as he plunged his sword into the man's chest, a small red line the only sign that he had struck his target as the man gasped and fell into the dirt as the strike through his heart killed him in an instant.

Marcus didn't have time to think, the brute in front of him pulled at his shield, his hand covered in grime as Marcus focused on the fingers gripping his shield. The man seemed to be staring at him, searching him as his eyes flickered from his face to his armour. He didn't have time to try and stab at the man's fingers as the man sliced his sword over the top of the shield, the deathly blade pointing directly at Marcus's eyes as he ducked to the side and felt the blade rasp along his helmet. With a mighty shove he launched himself forwards, catching the man off-balance as he leant in for the kill, but the man was good, he shifted his weight and fell away to the side, pulling his sword arm into a swing as he did so and screaming as his sword came crashing back towards Marcus, his full body weight behind the blow.

With a bone-crunching thud Marcus stepped under the attack and punched his short sword into the breastplate of his attacker, the speed of movement catching the bigger man off-guard, and slowing his sword arc which allowed Marcus to get his shield across his body as the blow came. The stab had been slightly off centre and baulked at the strong leather and thin bronze heart-saver the man wore, drawing only a small amount of blood as the man grinned back at Marcus and bared his teeth. Around him Marcus heard the unmistakable sounds of swords and shields clashing into each other as he stepped back into the line and peered at the black eyes of the brute that stared at him with a grin.

"*Combat*" screamed the man, spit falling into his brown beard as he repeated the yell, "*Combat*" and pointed his sword at Marcus, his face almost laughing as the point of his sword rose and fell along with his breathing.

Marcus froze as the sound of swords clashing and the grunts of his men started to dull until they eventually stopped, the sudden silence stretching as dust clouds settled around the standing men, all eyes turned to the Veienteine leader.

Combat! It was the right of each leader of an army to call for single combat in the field. It usually stopped all fighting and signalled that the two leaders would fight to the death, the winner taking all the spoils, the losers giving up armour, horses and in some cases the richer men giving themselves up to ransom. To decline single combat was seen as a mark of cowardice and Marcus stared at the man in front of him who simply grinned back at him, his breathing still coming in deep lungfuls as he stood with his enormous broadsword pointing at Marcus. Around him Marcus heard soldiers muttering, curses coming to his ears as the men stepped back from each other. Up on the rocky ground Marcus heard a thunder of hooves as the archers mounted their steeds and rode away. He glanced at the man, still stood staring at him with his sword pointed in his direction. His eyes flickered as he saw other men disappear into the bushes leaving only a small force of the ambushers standing to watch the 'combat' and something in Marcus's mind told him that this was a trap that they had been led into, with one purpose, to kill him.

With a step forward the combat would begin. "No" came the voice of Narcius, followed quickly by Fasculus, who stepped beside Marcus.

"Yes" replied Marcus. "It must be" and he stepped forwards, the grin on the man's face stretching as he nodded to Marcus without taking his eyes off him.

****

"They have a point" suggested Manlius.

"No, they don't" came the reply, cold and aloof as usual.

Manlius switched the cup to his left hand and tapped the table in front of him with his right. "This marble is the solid state" he said, reaching and tapping the ornate iron legs "but this is the support, the two work together and it functions as its purpose demands. Without the top they are just legs, with only the legs it's just a piece of marble" he postured with a smile.

"Ha" laughed the fat face of the man sat across from him, half a bowl of eaten grapes in front of him. "Manlius, where did you learn such prose? Have you been spending time with Calvus?"

Manlius looked at the face of the Senator and wondered whether he had his spies watching him, nodding his head as he laughed at the response. "Senator Javenoli" he said, his face a warm smile. "The plebeian council make some good points. We, as patricians must give as well as take. The senate asked me to review their thoughts before the Kalends and I have done so. You have read the report and its suggestions. I think the plebeians have good cause for anger and resentment. We should defer to their needs on many counts" he finished, sipping the wine he held in his hand as he narrowed his eyes at Javenoli.

"You have gone soft Marcus Manlius" said an elderly man, his thick stomach extended through the folds of his toga. "Maybe you are spending too much time with these men" he added, as Manlius sat forwards in his chair with a look of anger on his face.

"Senator Cicurinus" he replied, holding his breath and steadying his tone before he continued. "The new men work hard for their riches and they pay their taxes. All they want is a release of some powers to have a better say in the governance of the City. They are Romans too"

"They are *citizens*, my friend" replied the old man, his face cold and stern. "As new Romans, they do not understand the burden we hold to maintain the Republic. It was we who deposed the old kings, not them. We must defend Rome and our Republic. They are just the sheep that provide the wool" he added with a half-smile.

"I have to agree with Cicurinus" stated another man, his deeply lined face and bald head belying his younger years. "The problem with the plebeian council is that they do not understand the control the gods have given to the patrician families. Without the will of the gods supporting us we will have no Rome, and it is only through the patrician families that we have such links, directly through our blood lines" he smiled, a reference to the fact that many of the oldest families of Rome claimed direct family links from one Roman god or another. "And" continued the man, "how often do the plebeian tribunes simply stall every decision we make out of pure spite. They have no manners, no understanding of how things are done" he said, his head shaking at the thought.

Manlius sat back, his face resigned to another long and boring discussion on the role of the patricians in Rome.

Senator Atratinus, his bald head shining as the light filtered through the high window, turned to his peers. "Gentlemen, are we done? I have some business to attend to if we are" he asked in a bored tone, his eyes avoiding Manlius as he stretched his neck to look around the room.

"Is there anything else Manlius?" asked Javenoli.

"No, gentlemen. I thank you for your time and consideration" he replied, rising from his couch and placing the cup on the table as the men in the room shuffled from their seated positions and started to leave.

"Manlius, may I ask you something?" Javenoli said, his light touch on Manlius's arm making him turn to look at the shorter, rotund figure standing next to him.

"Certainly"

As Javenoli steered him towards the corner of the room and the Senators left a silence fell into the space, interspersed with the occasional laugh as the men leaving joked as they donned their outdoor cloaks despite the hot sun.

"My good friend" started Javenoli as Manlius's eyes narrowed once again. "Do you think that the plebeian council will accept any of the proposals you have heard today?"

"None Senator. Every request they have made has been ignored. Personally, I feel I have been used" blurted Manlius, his anger rising now that he was alone with Javenoli, who simply stared at him with his usual calculating look.

"What do you mean my friend, used by whom?

"The Senate" he said with frustration. "I have given good assurance, as I believed I could, to the plebeian council and now I must return to tell them that every point has been denied."

"Not every point" replied Javenoli.

"Yes, but the counter point to a relaxation of laws on land will be seen as an affront as the law has to be agreed by the Senate, marking it as null and void anyway" he added with a frustrated tone, his face turning to Javenoli who simply looked back at him blankly.

"The tax question is very difficult Manlius. We patricians don't earn the money as the traders do" he said. "Those who profit from Rome every day should surely help in its defence. We have paid for arms, walls, bridges, roads and even food in times of shortage over the years. Surely they see this?"

"They see today's problem Senator, not yesterday's solution. To be denied the opportunity to progress their families in civil roles and to support Rome is an affront to them. They are as Roman as you or me" he added dejectedly.

"Well, maybe there we disagree" added Javenoli as he stepped away from Manlius before continuing. "If they were to have junior roles in the Republic beyond their current limits what would they suggest?" he asked, his mind contemplating some thoughts.

"I am not sure Senator. They have two issues. Tax and Laws. If there is a role to support the decisions, then there may be a compromise."

"Compromise" said Javenoli with his finger to his lips, "Yes, a good word. Leave that thought with me Manlius. I will call on you tomorrow at your home. Do you still have that lovely fruity wine you served last month?" he asked, his eyes lighting up as he looked to Manlius.

****

Marcus took a deep breath as his senses told him that every eye was looking to him.

"Kill him Gastus" yelled a man from behind the bearded brute in front of him. "Yes, kill the dog" yelled a higher pitched voice. Marcus glanced at the second man, his young face screwed into a snarl of hatred, but the eyes were the same as his opponent, clearly the man's brother or some other family member. The man, Gastus, grinned again, one of his front teeth showing it had been chipped as he clenched his jaw into an angry scowl.

"Balance and footwork" he heard Mella shout, not daring to look in his direction as the two men began to circle each other. Gastus swung his sword in a circle, the action making Marcus flinch as he expected an attack, which brought a chorus of laughter from the men behind their leader. With a lazy swoop Gastus hit out at Marcus's shield, the heavy sword clattering into the wood as he stepped back, keeping his distance. As he had been trained to do Marcus watched the man's feet. Mella had taught him that good footwork was equally as important as a good sword arm, and he had proved this to him many times in their training sessions. Marcus smiled, the man had a loose binding on the left side, that might help him he hoped. He shuffled forwards in three quick steps, raising his shield and jabbing it forwards to test Gastus's balance. The man moved easily aside, leaning forward and slicing his sword into the gap between the two of them as a series of shouts came from both sides.

With a rasp Gastus took a dagger from a sheath strapped to his thigh, the long sword sweeping across his body as he raised the dagger high in the air in his left hand. Marcus had seen this move before, to try and attract the attention of the opponent's eyes with the sword and to dart in with the dagger. He allowed his eyes to wander as the sword swirled across his body, but he prepared his feet for a step forward just in time, as Gastus swept the dagger down as he made a feint with his sword. With a flick of his shoulder Marcus parried the dagger with the top of his shield and whipped the shorter sword up to catch the retreating dagger and hand of Gastus who smiled at the parry, nodding with some respect at the movement which grazed his skin but did no damage.

"Good Roman. I don't want this to look like I fought a woman" he said with his deep Etruscan voice, his eyes narrow as he stepped forward and Marcus saw him take the deep breath that every man took before he made his effort.

With a deep yell Gastus launched his sword high in the air and stepped forwards, the arc taking the weapon across to Marcus's left as Marcus stepped forward and to his right, a two-step movement which allowed him to keep his sword close to his shield and chop at Gastus's left thigh, missing by an inch as Gastus hit Marcus's shield with his heavy sword, the dull slap sounding loud in the calm clearing of the road. The momentum of Marcus's step allowed him to move right again and circle Gastus in a crouch, his eyes peering over the top of the shield as Gastus slid his dagger back in its sheath and took a two-handed grip.

Within a heartbeat Gastus raised his sword and battered into Marcus at a run, almost knocking him to the ground as his weight smashed into the wooden shield. Keeping his feet one behind the other Marcus pushed upwards against the weight of the man and felt the movement of Gastus's arm as the sword came around the left side of the shield, his body committed to the attack. Instantly Marcus dropped to one knee and smashed the bottom of the shield onto the foot of his opponent, using his bodyweight to twist the shield and block the sword strike, which clattered against the wood uselessly as Marcus stood and butted the larger man under the chin with the top of his helmet, a crunching sound coming as spots of blood and tooth fell in front of him to a dull groan from Gastus. With a final movement Marcus was able to shift his weight around to his right again and step clear of the man, who growled as he flicked his foot and hopped gingerly onto it, no doubt some of his toes broken by the thick wood of Marcus's shield. The Romans cheered as Gastus roared at the crowd, spittle and blood landing on the Romans in the front line who screamed "Camillus, Camillus" back at him.

Marcus breathed slowly and crouched again. Gastus stared at him wiping blood from a bleeding lip, a line of red held in his beard which made him look even more fearsome.

"What is this fighting style, Roman. Hiding behind a shield. Stand tall like a man and fight me" he called, waving his sword around as blood fell onto his torso from his wounded mouth.

Marcus remained motionless, crouching in the same position and smiled. "I fight as the eagle fights" he said slowly and with a curl of his lip. "I will snatch your life from you with my claws as I circle you" he said, as above him a screech came making several of the watchers' heads snap upwards and search the sky, a low mumble spreading amongst the soldiers. Marcus knew the screech was Mella, he had heard him do it before, but he smiled at the deception as a momentary fear came into the eyes of his opponent, his eyes glancing at the sky, before the man took another deep breath and ran towards him, raising his sword higher to strike. Marcus stood taller for a second, the movement causing a moment of confusion which spread on Gastus's face as his muscles twitched to re-direct the blow, before Marcus crouched and side-stepped, aiming a stinging blow at the man's thigh before stepping back as Gastus's momentum carried him past Marcus's left. Before Gastus had time to scream as the wound opened on his thigh Marcus had stepped back across his body and punched the sword into the man's ribcage, the crunch of bone resounding alongside Gastus's scream of pain as Marcus twisted his sword and stepped back in one quick movement. In two heartbeats, he had slipped away to the right and stood behind his shield.

"The eagle strikes" he said as he stepped forwards and Gastus, his strength seeping from his body yelled a curse and threw himself at Marcus again, the heavy sword swinging so high that Marcus had time to look into Gastus's eyes as he stepped close to the man and punched his sword through his neck, a jolt telling Marcus when he had severed the spine as a warm gush of liquid hit his sword hand. He whipped the sword back and returned to a crouch as the man collapsed, his legs jerking as a frothy foam appeared from his throat, his eyes screaming the curses that his voice could not.

"No!" came the yell from behind him as Marcus turned to see the younger man, the brother, launch himself at him, his sword glinting in the sunlight as it arced at his face. Whirling his shield, he batted the sword from the attacker's hand and stepped back as the man fell to his knees and crawled to the body of the dead leader, his sword landing with a clang on the dusty ground. *"Father"* cried the boy as Marcus looked at the body sprawled at his feet.

A sudden commotion behind Marcus made him turn to see a dozen or more Veienteine riders gallop away, other soldiers rushing into the bushes and scrambling up the rocks in an effort to escape as their leader collapsed.

"Combat has been won, as your leader demanded. Honour must be obeyed. Drop your weapons" called Ambustus as he stepped forwards in front of Marcus. The Romans cheered as they started to disarm the remaining ambushers who had been too stunned at the speed in which their leader had been beaten to make an escape.

"Brilliant" said the voice of Mella as he appeared next to Marcus and he jingled a handful of bronze and silver in front of his face. "Look what I won" he laughed aloud as Marcus stared at his beaming face. "What?" asked Mella, his bright eyes wide, slapping him on the shoulder before turning and striding away to join the rest of the men.

*

*

*

*

Chapter 7

Ambustus fumed. Silence hung in the air as the officers of the legion shuffled their feet and stared anywhere except at their commander.

"It is customary in such circumstances…" Ambustus started to say before Postumius rose from his chair cutting him off with a resounding slap on the wooden table in front of him which sent several maps and goblets jumping into the air.

"No" he said firmly, his eyes narrow and staring straight at Ambustus. Despite being the older man, Ambustus was junior to Postumius in the legion and could only offer suggestions, not give orders. Postumius stood, his shoulder wrapped in a thick bandage as he winced at the effort of moving, his free hand touching the shoulder as his eyes showed the pain he felt. Tucked into the bandage was a feather and Ambustus wondered what the black feather meant, its tendrils standing proud against the white cloth. Postumius stepped across to Ambustus and then turned to Marcus, the venom in his voice apparent to everyone as his whole body seemed to tense.

"*Camillus* you seem to live a charmed life" he sneered. "But a skirmish on the road with bandits doesn't warrant a phalera" he waved away the movement that suggested Ambustus was about to argue his point once again. "Bravery is for the real soldier, the man who stands in line with his spear, not for one-man combat, especially against what must have been a weakened opponent" he added, his insult stinging Marcus, who simply stood and stared at the far wall of the tent. "I deny your request Ambustus" he finished.

As he finished he turned to Ambustus, his face changing to a warm smile as he said "Fabius, please do come for dinner this evening, it will be an absolute pleasure to have you join me and my senior officers, you can tell them of the cavalry charge you led into the Aequian phalanx a few years ago. Now *that* was bravery." At this he glanced at Marcus with a look of loathing and grinned, his eyes betraying the friendly smile he portrayed to the assembled officers. "Don't take this personally Camillus" he chided "I am sure there will be other chances to prove yourself" he added as he turned and said, "you may leave" with a small wave of his free hand.

Ambustus nodded as the men began to file out of their commander's presence. "Fasculus" said Postumius over the noise of the men leaving "stay and make your scouting report" he ordered as Fasculus saluted and turned back into the tent with a glance at Marcus which seemed to portray his apologies for his commander's behaviour.

As Marcus's eyes adjusted to the brightness of the day outside the command tent he took a moment to wander across to the city walls, which were only a few hundred paces from the encamped Romans. Bolae was in an easily defensible location with ravines to one side, deep and narrow, hard to penetrate with a phalanx of men. On the other side there seemed to be a large cliff, dropping to the river which circled the city and created a natural barrier. Marcus stood for a moment wondering how Postumius had taken the city so easily. From what Mella had told him, Postumius's army had lost only two hundred men in the assault on Bolae and the gates had been opened by somebody from inside. It seemed typical that the story they had heard of a great assault and heroic victory was a long way from the truth of the triumph.

"It's a good location" came a voice which startled Marcus as he had been so wrapped up in his own thoughts. Turning he smiled and clasped arms with Bassano, who beamed back at him.

"It is good to see you again Marcus, or do I call you Camillus now?" he asked, his warm smile spreading across his face.

"Camillus is my chosen name" he responded warmly, his eyes scanning the Centurion he had not seen for a number of years and noting the better class of armour, a few new scars and how the man seemed to have grown thicker around the shoulders since he had last seen him. "You look well Bassano" he said, patting his shoulders appraisingly as he said the words and Bassano smiled in return.

"Hard work and long marches" said the man removing his helmet to reveal his short cut greying hair. "My time is nearly up in the legions" he said absently as his eyes moved to the walls of Bolae. "A few of us asked Postumius to let us settle here" he added as his eyes glanced to Marcus to look for any reaction. After a moment's silence he continued "he turned us down, flat. No reason, just said no. A bit like what happened in there just now"

Marcus looked at the walls, at the ground around them and at the Centurion, whose features were set in a grimace. "He must have his reasons" Marcus replied quietly, unsure what to say.

"Probably the same reason he didn't give you that phalera" Bassano said before turning to look directly at Marcus. "He has a nasty streak in him that man" he said, his eyes flicking around him as he spoke to check that no more of Postumius's spies were within earshot. "You know what he was like before?" he stated, a small nod from Marcus showing he understood the question. "Well he's twice as bad now" he continued as he turned, placing a hand on Marcus's elbow with a shake of his head.

"Denying you that phalera was" he shook his head again as he searched for the words "ridiculous" he said with a shrug. "Come on, let's get you some food and find you a place to sleep. You'll need all your energy to keep up with things in this camp" he said with a wry smile as he led Marcus away from the walls.

****

"The commander wishes to see you in his tent urgently" said the messenger, standing to attention as he delivered the message to Ambustus, Marcus and Potitus as they sat eating in a stuffy tent which had been hastily erected in the small clearing near Postumius's command centre.

"Better not keep him waiting" added Bassano, who was striding past rubbing a spot of grime off his helmet with a cloth. "And make sure your armour is clean" he added as he continued on his way, his voice disappearing as he marched off in the direction of Postumius's tent.

Within a few minutes all the senior officers were standing within the humid atmosphere of Postumius's command centre, his campaign desk and chair the only furniture in the room, everything else had been taken out and packed as the legion prepared to return to Rome.

"We have interrogated the captured soldiers who attacked you on the road Ambustus, though many more, I believe, escaped" Postumius said with raised eyebrows, the slur causing Ambustus to take a deep breath and turn his face toward him. The commander masterfully looked in the other direction as he continued to speak over the angry looks of the newly arrived officers.

"It seems" he said, with a look of confusion on his face "that someone has a bounty on your head Marcus Furius" he added, not bothering to use Marcus's new chosen name. Marcus looked at him with a questioning glance. "Yes, it seems that the Aequians have placed a hundred bronze ingots on your head, dead or alive" he smiled. At this Marcus looked to Ambustus, who shrugged back at him. "And" continued the commander "it makes these captives hired killers; Assassins" he said as he stood from his chair "and we all know what that means don't we?" he asked to the room at large, turning his head to Sergius who dutifully replied, "They will be sentenced to death, to be thrown from the Tarpeian Rock upon our return to Rome."

Ambustus looked to Postumius. "We will need to follow the correct procedure" he said, his indignant tone betraying the fact that he had been slurred moments earlier. As every Roman knew a series of legal reviews were needed to sentence prisoners to death followed by a ceremony to confer the deaths to the gods. Without such rigour, the deaths could not be ratified and agreed. Postumius looked to his officers and smiled. "Yes, I agree Ambustus. Aulus Manlius will lead the trial" he said as everyone's eyes moved to Aulus, his face showing no change of expression. "He is qualified to do it" added Postumius. "And" his eyes roved the tent "Bassano" he said, his searching finishing on the Centurion stood away to his left behind the more senior officers. "Yes, your son Appius can detail the guards, get him to set out four men to hold the prisoners when he is back from his scouting. It'll do him good to do some proper work" Postumius said as he returned to his desk and sat leaning forwards, his eyes watching Bassano closely for any signs of anger at his reproach. "Good" he said. "Then we must prepare to have the trial this afternoon and leave this forsaken place first thing in the morning." He looked at the assembled men, their faces all impassive as he spoke. With a leer at them all he called for them to leave.

As Marcus reached the tent flap and he moved to place his helmet on his head he heard a familiar voice call from within the tent. "Furius" came the voice "A moment of your time. I have a task for you" called Postumius as Marcus and Ambustus caught each other's eyes and Ambustus let out a low sigh with a slight shake of his head, patting Marcus on the shoulder as he turned to return to the tent.

*

*

*

*

Chapter 8

The light had faded as Marcus sat on his horse by the river, the quiet ripple of the water the only sound his ears could hear in the rapidly closing day. His eyes strained to make out the shapes in the semi-darkness which surrounded him and his troop of scouts as they sat motionless at the small ford that Fasculus's scouts had found a few days before. He turned to look behind him at the steep climb to the thick walls of the city, their heavy stones indistinct in the dim light and wondered why he had been chosen for this sentry duty. He shook his head, knowing in his own mind that this was just another way for Postumius to show him that he was in control. A splash turned his head back to the ford where Fasculus was walking his short-legged pony back through the slow-moving water, the horse attempting to drop its head to slake its thirst as he let the reins loose.

"Anything?" asked Marcus.

"Nothing" came the reply. Two other horses appeared from behind Fasculus and started to traverse the ford, the slopping of hooves in the water breaking the silence. Fasculus stretched his back and rubbed at a point low down, just above his sword belt as he pulled in next to Marcus.

"No tracks, no sign of anyone or anything being down here for days" he added. "Wish I hadn't mentioned it to him" he said, half expecting Marcus to chide him, but no reply came. The soldiers sat in silence, all eyes slowly turning to stare into the gloom of the surroundings, a few fir trees, the odd bush and a lot of empty ground with large boulders spread intermittently across the area all that they could see. After a few minutes Marcus turned to

Fasculus, "Well, we have another hour of light so let's get the pickets set up before we are relieved" he said as Fasculus saluted and called three men to him, issuing orders as they listened to his commands.

****

The assassin took a deep breath, his knees placed against the wood of the prisoner's pen. The knife sliced through the ropes, exactly where he had been told they would be weakest and the first wooden slat fell outwards against his leg. He caught it quietly, looking in both directions and seeing no movement. He smiled. The guards were busy with the fire and the prisoners had been beaten so badly that they remained slouched near the central pole, their hands and feet tied together so that they were almost curled into human balls lying on the floor in their own filth. He lifted his head, smelling the faeces as well as seeing the dark patches on the bodies and faces of the prisoners, their own blood he presumed. He snaked into the gap, crawling along behind the two prisoners, his body inching forwards as he had trained himself to do over the years. He smiled to himself as he heard the guards laughing, their banter telling him that they were paying no attention to the prisoners, just as he had expected. They wouldn't look in on them until just before changeover, by which time it would be too late. He crept to the first prisoner, clearly totally unconscious and slid the knife deep into the man's neck releasing a slow trickle of blood as the man's body moved slightly at the prick of his skin. The warm blood seeped into the ground as the man took a last gasp and his body went limp. Good, thought the assassin, now for the other one.

As he leant across and caught the head of the prisoner a burst of laughter came from the guards causing the assassin to grip the neck of the man a little tighter than he had planned. The prisoner's eyes opened, a momentary glint of hope in his eyes before the assassin sliced his neck and placed a hand over his mouth to stop him calling out. He watched as the man, more of a boy, wriggled for a few seconds as the assassin pressed harder onto his mouth before he too went limp. After a few heartbeats, he said a quiet prayer to the god Pluto, careful not to say his name in case the god noticed him and came looking for him too, and slipped the knife into the hands of the prisoner, wrapping the fingers around the blade and spreading a small trail of blood from the other dead prisoner to the knife, smiling as he heard the guards, again, laughing, oblivious to his deed. It was good to say a prayer for the dead, he thought to himself, as he slid back to the fence and replaced the wooden slat, and tied the rope he had left at the foot of the pen onto the fence posts to hide his entrance.

****

Marcus Manlius was angry and when he was angry he shouted a lot. Today he was shouting at his slaves, at his wife and at his children, his voice loud and deep as he chastised everyone who came near him. Maybe it was the wine, but whatever it was it was not good. He gripped the death mask of his father, shaking his head as he looked into the dead eyes of the face captured on his deathbed.

"Why?" he asked "Why is it that we are so lowly? Why couldn't our family be higher?" he asked in a low moan, the goblet of wine sloshing a red trail onto the floor before he pulled it up and took another long drink from it, gasping for breath as he drained the contents and looked at the other death masks sat in their tidy niches on the wall. He shook his head again and set off towards his study, shouting for more wine as he stumbled into a door post and yelled again, rubbing his arm as he moved past the doorway.

"I'll show them" he said, realising he was still clutching the mask of his father, the same blank expression looking back at him from the dead eyes. "You should have been more ambitious" he said, looking at the face and shaking his head "more ambitious" he continued as he slumped into the wooden chair knocking the cushion to the floor as he almost fell into the seat. "Ambition" he said, opening the wooden shutter and looking out of his small window over the roofs of the houses below his on the Capitoline Hill, their red and grey tiles just about visible in the low light. He smiled as thoughts began to race through his head. These plebeians were surely starting to gain power in Rome, their cause was justifiable and their claims to power should be heard. Javenoli. He almost spat the name. And men like Cicurinus, he thought as he put his hand to his face, feeling the two-day old stubble prickle his fingers. They had power now, but they needed to be taught a lesson. Manlius stood and turned to face the door as a slave came trotting around the corner, his hand holding the jug of wine.

"Take that filth away" yelled Manlius as the slave's face dropped and he cowered, his arm instinctively coming up to cover his face before Manlius yelled at him to get out of his way and trudged back towards the door to the garden.

"No more drink" mumbled Manlius, his thoughts a blur. "No more. They won't get away with it Father" he said, raising the mask to look at the blank eyes. "They won't" he said as he sat on the low wall running around the perimeter of his ornate garden. "I will see them humbled. They think they have it all, patrician blood, Roman values" he sneered as he spoke. "They won't have it for long" he smiled "I promise you Father" he said as he slumped to the floor, leaning against the wall as his eyes saw the first star coming into the sky. "I promise you" and with that his head nodded and he fell into a drunken sleep.

****

"Fasculus" called Marcus softly into the darkness, his log torch blazing as he leant it out across the water, silvery red light reflecting off the water, which oozed by relentlessly.

"Here" came the reply, as a splash made Marcus turn his head to the left and squeeze his eyes to focus on the man stepping slowly across the shallows lest he should slip and fall. A second series of splashes announced the return of one of the men Fasculus had left with and Marcus took a steady breath as he stood tall and stretched his back, realising he had been standing tensed for at least ten minutes whilst Fasculus and the replacement pickets had gone to the furthest point of their watch.

"All clear?" he asked as Fasculus came into the light of the flames.

"No problems, there's nothing out there, sir" replied the man as he stepped free of the shallows, the wet leather of his sandals squelching as he stood on the stones laid across the entrance to the ford.

"Right, let's get back to the camp" Marcus said, turning and walking away as the two men followed behind. Marcus placed the torch in the fire as he grabbed his equipment and slumped it over his shoulder looking up at the steep climb ahead of them as he did so. He shook his head at the thought of walking up that steep path in the dark and wondered if he should have set some burning stakes in the ground to light the path earlier, but it was too late now. A low breeze whispered along the path as he turned and called the several men of his watch into a slow march, wishing the new watch a good night as he stepped onto the narrow, steep incline.

As he neared the top of the path Marcus could hear Fasculus grumbling behind him, his constant moaning was almost as annoying as the fact that they had had to be the first group out on duty, a slur that Marcus was sure was aimed at him alone. He took a deep breath to settle his rapid breathing from the steep climb as he crested the final section, edging round the steep wall and seeing the glow of a hundred firelights away to his front. He smiled at the sight as he stopped and waited for the rest of his contingent to reach the top of the climb. He turned to Fasculus, who was sweating heavily, the glistening water dripping down his face in the light from the fires and was about to speak when a great cry went up from the camp and men started to run to and fro shouting for the guards.

"What?" said Marcus as Fasculus and he stared at each other for a moment before dropping their bags, drawing their swords and charging across the remaining hundred yards to the main camp, heading directly for Postumius's tent as they ran, their feet pounding the rocky ground. As they came to the command tent several other officers were already arriving and Postumius had just stepped from his tent, immaculate in his armour and pressed tunic, almost as if he had been standing waiting for the alarm to be raised.

"What is it?" he called to the man who had rushed up to the tent, saluted and stood waiting for permission to speak.

"The prisoners, sir" he said, his face looking away to the sky as he spoke. "They have been killed, sir" he added, his voice even and monotone.

Ambustus had arrived and was stood next to Postumius, his scruffy hair and half laced armour testament to the fact that he had not been sitting waiting in his armour as Postumius appeared to have done. He looked at Postumius, who had a calm air about him as the other senior officers arrived and looked at each other, their mouths open as they asked each other what the commotion was about.

"Come" pronounced Postumius as he set out towards the edge of the camp where the prisoners were kept, a small smile on his face as he stepped forwards and glanced over his shoulder as the men fell in behind him. As they approached the scene Marcus moved forwards to stand next to Ambustus, his glance telling him that he was concerned about the situation as much as Marcus was.

The gate to the prisoner's pen was standing open as they arrived and Postumius strode straight in without a glance at the guards, who saluted with worried looks on their faces. Marcus and several other officers filed into the small space, the smell of urine hitting his nose as he peered at the two dead bodies below him. Postumius used his sword, the same elaborate sword he had offered Marcus a few years before, to move the hands of the dead boy Marcus had last seen slumped across his father.

"Dead by their own hands" Postumius said without emotion. Ambustus stepped forwards just as Sergius stepped in front of him and bent down next to the body of the dead boy.

"Look sir" stated Sergius as he stood, the dagger in his hand as he pointed at the two bodies with his other hand. "This one killed that one with this knife. Both men took their own lives rather than face the Rock" he said, his meaning clear. Earlier that evening the prisoners had been thoroughly beaten and brought before the trial, at which Aulus Manlius had found them guilty of banditry and attempted assassination and so they had been sentenced to death by being thrown from the Tarpeian Rock in Rome. The two men had mumbled their innocence through their broken jaws, but Postumius had sanctioned the death penalty and the men were returned to their prison.

"How did they get this knife" called Postumius, his eyes scanning the assembled men, the officers closest to him but a hundred or more legionaries, armed with swords, stood outside the prisoner's pen staring silently at the scene inside. Postumius took the blade and showed it to the crowd. "Does anyone recognise this blade?" he called, taking it and walking slowly around the circle of men, all of whom shook their heads, the wet slap of Postumius's sandal as he walked in the blood of the dead prisoners broke through the deepening silence, many eyes drifting from the blade to the blood on the floor as he did so.

Then a small voice came from the back of the crowd by the gate "It is mine" it said as all eyes turned to Appius Bassano as the man stepped forwards, a look of utter dread on his face as the collective gasp of a hundred soldiers echoed into the darkness.

*

*

*

*

Chapter 9

"It's a damned plague" said Calvus more forcefully than he had intended as he stared at the magistrate, his white toga almost perfectly positioned across his lap as he reclined in the chair in front of him. "There are dead bodies in the street and you are doing nothing about it" he almost shouted, a drop of phlegm coming from his lips as he stood and stared indignantly at the face of the junior official who was listening to the plebeian council's latest demands for changes to the regulations in the City.

"My dear Calvus" the man said, his wispy, thin, beard showing his age as he handed a wax tablet to a slave, who bowed and approached Calvus with it, handing it over without looking up at the enraged man standing in front of him. "Your demands have no substance. A few drunks and layabouts who fell upon each other in the streets is all it is" he stated in a bored tone. "The Senate have reviewed the incidents you speak of and there is no evidence of a plague." As he finished he went to stand, as if his business with the representatives of the plebeian council were at a close, his air of superiority causing the plebeians from the council to raise their voices in angry protests.

"Gentlemen," the magistrate said, his eyes almost fearful as he stepped back slightly "your behaviour does you no favour" he said condescendingly as he looked at the men in front of him. "There is no plague" he added, his eyes wide and his effeminate face soft, his white hands held out in front of him. "If you have no further evidence to present?" he asked with a questioning look. "Then I bid you good day" he said as he turned and walked towards the door at the back of the room.

"Pompous patrician bast..." started Pontius Cominus before Calvus placed a hand on his arm and shook his head.

"Well Marcus Manlius" said Calvus, looking to the man who had used his influence to get the leaders of the council this meeting. "What do you say to that?" he asked, waving an arm in the direction of the closed door by which the magistrate had left. Manlius grimaced. Yet again another meeting he had arranged had gone badly. The conflict between the plebeians and patricians ran deeper than he had imagined. Spending time with these men and seeing at first hand their problems had certainly opened his eyes and his plans, born from his drink fuelled sleep, had been thwarted at every turn. Maybe now was a time for more drastic action.

"If the patricians have no interest in the plague then maybe it is because they see it as a suburban problem" he stated as he smiled at the other men. "Maybe if the dead were to die on the Oppian Hill or the Capitoline quarter they might take more interest" he smiled. Calvus cocked his head, his thoughts running as he looked at Manlius.

"Not on my doorstep?" Calvus said in a slow voice, a curl coming to his lips as he grasped what Manlius was considering.

"Precisely" replied Manlius as he turned and stepped towards the door. "We will need some men to transport the bodies" he said as he looked back over his shoulder.

"Oh, I am sure that can be arranged" came the reply.

****

Despite the early hour, the whole camp was in uproar. Soldiers were set out around the central command tent in full armour with swords drawn, their Centurions doing their best to get them to stand down, but to no avail. Hundreds of men were calling for order, others were calling for blood and some just stood watching. After the knife had been found to be owned by Appius Bassano, the five men detailed to guard the troops had been placed under arrest by Postumius, his personal bodyguards carrying out the orders. Aulus Manlius had approached his commanding officer and asked for leniency whilst he looked into the case, calling for a proper trial for the guards, at which Postumius had raged at Aulus, telling him that as he was the officer in command he, too, was culpable and would stand trial with the guards. At this he too had been arrested. Aulus was a popular officer and many of the men had pleaded with Postumius and the other officers for a review, but Postumius would hear nothing of it. Ambustus, Marcus and Rufus had managed to quell a total riot amongst the men, their bitterness at Postumius's treatment of them boiling over into a handful of scuffles which they managed to hide from their commanding officer as he retreated to his tent and had the prisoners chained to a post outside it, guarded by several burly bodyguards. Centurion Bassano, Appius's father, had been restrained in his tent by Rufus to stop him from tearing

Postumius limb from limb. But then at dawn the men of the Legion had surrounded the command tent and demanded an audience with their commander.

Marcus stood next to the prisoners and looked to Aulus and shook his head as the man stood, proud, facing the tent of his accuser. Inside the tent he could hear Ambustus shouting at Postumius, who was shouting back at him, their voices clearly audible across the ground to the men standing around the tent. A sudden silence came from the tent, making everyone stop and look at the tent entrance. After a moments silence Postumius appeared, to heckling from the men standing around, his dark look at Marcus showing spite and hatred as he placed his helmet on his head and paced to the centre of the space outside his tent. He waved a hand at his tent as a slave ran forwards with a small wooden mounting block, upon which Postumius stood.

He surveyed the faces around him, a look of loathing coming to his eyes as he took a few moments to look into the faces of the leaders of the troops.

"You men" he said, his voice strong as Ambustus appeared from the tent and moved next to Marcus, a quick glance showing that he had not achieved the peaceful settlement as he had intended. "You are men of Rome and the Latin League" he stated as he continued to look around the men standing silently listening to him. "You know the law, you understand the rules" he said. "This" he looked down at the floor "insurrection. This cessation of your duties" he added as he shook his head, his face showing wonder at the men around him. "Gives me great cause for concern". A loud murmur went up from the crowd as his head jerked to where a call for leniency went up, followed by an agreeing cheer. "How, soldiers, how can I give clemency to this act? The law is clear" he said, his arm waving to a slave who appeared at the tent flap and trotted across to where he stood with a small wooden chest. "This" he continued "is the law" he opened the chest and took out a rolled vellum scroll, the yellow hide covered in black writing. "You know the punishment. Should any prisoner condemned to death be found dead whilst under guard." He had picked up the scroll as if reading from it and turned to stare at the prisoners tied to the post near him. "Then they shall die in the same manner in which the prisoners died" he added as a cacophony of noise arose from the men, the bodyguards coming closer to Postumius as some of the men stepped forwards in protest. Without knowing it Marcus had stepped forwards too, not in protest but as a precaution in case any of the soldiers made a run at their commanding officer. Despite himself Marcus knew that what Postumius was saying had a grain of truth. The law of the legion was sanctified by the gods each year and each soldier had to swear an oath to it as the campaigning season started. He shook his head slowly at the thought.

"The gods wrote this law" shouted Postumius. "Am I to break it? Am I to challenge the gods?" he added, stepping down from the mounting block and walking around the circle of men, waving the vellum at them as he continued. Men dropped their heads as he passed them. "The law is sanctified by your sworn oath to the legion and to Rome. They know it" he said, pointing a hand at the men on the floor. "Will you break your oaths" he said as a gleam came to his eye as another thought crossed his mind. "Men of Rome" he finished. "Who will challenge the gods and the laws of Rome?" he asked, holding the velum up above his head as the hundreds of faces stared at him in absolute silence.

With a flourish, he turned and paced back to the mounting block he was using as a rostrum, stepping onto it and turning his face to the crowd. He stood, looking at the men around him. "I will hold a meeting of the senior officers and we will discuss punishments" he called. "Fabius Ambustus and Camp Prefect Sergius will argue for the state and Centurion Marcus Pomponius Rufus will represent you. I will decide" he said as he went to step from the rostrum before a voice called out.

A voice cried out "we want Camillus to represent us, he is beloved of the gods and will give a fair account of our wishes" at which both Marcus and Postumius looked into the crowd of men to see who had spoken, but the speaker was hidden too deeply in the crowd. "Yes, Camillus" came the call from one or two voices, then more and then even more until a great cry of "Camillus" was echoing around the camp.

Postumius looked at Marcus, his head shaking with a resigned frown as he stared maliciously at him. He raised his hands and waited for silence before nodding his head and saying "then Camillus too" and walking to his tent with a grimace on his face as he sent a fleeting look, his eyes dark and teeth grinding, at Marcus.

****

Manlius coughed at the smell. The bodies were putrid, their weeping eyes had fused with a thick gore which the crows clearly thought was a delicacy as they dived noisily onto the corpses and pecked hurriedly into the soft flesh.

In the semi-darkness of the pre-dawn morning he and the six men he had been given to help him had found several dead bodies down by the river and brought them up the steep climb of the Oppian Hill, dropping them outside the more prominent patrician family homes. As he let the last body fall he gagged at the open sores on what was left of the man's neck, the red raw flesh testament to the pain in which the man had died. He mumbled a quiet prayer to the dead, careful to use a few words he had heard the priests use, as the men looked to him. Only patricians could complete ceremonies in Rome and he knew that the men around him would expect him to do something to appease the spirits of the dead, so he had made up the invocation on the spot and smiled to the men around him who nodded in reply.

He stepped back and removed the thick gloves from his hands before wrapping them up and throwing them into an alleyway. He pulled the cloth from his face as he walked away, feeling the cold air hit his lips and taking a deep breath now that the cloth had been removed.

"Take the cart back" he whispered to one of his accomplices as a man nodded and set off pushing the heavy hand cart back down the hill, the clunky wheels bashing out a deep tone as he disappeared. Manlius looked around him at the clean street, the walls of the rich houses were tall and thick, but the stench of death was already pervading the area and more crows were appearing on the walls and roofs of the nearby buildings. He smiled as three men appeared and nodded to him, each one covered in a film of blood on their arms.

"All done" said one of them, his smile showing how much he enjoyed this work.

"Good" replied Manlius without looking at him. "Then let's get off to our own houses and see what comes of tonight's work, well done you men" he smiled, his grin infecting the men around him who looked at him with a measure of respect. One of the men stepped closer. "Sir" said the man, pulling his hood from his head to reveal his face, a light smile and dark eyes with a thin, dark, beard. He scratched at his chin, almost automatically and then looked at Manlius who had stopped and looked into his eyes, a look of curiosity on his face.

"Gatto?" he said "Is that you my old friend?"

"Yes sir" came the reply.

"That beard doesn't suit you" came the laughing response. "It must be eight, no ten years since you and I were in the Legion" smiled Manlius, stepping forwards again. "What are you doing these days? Not in service?" he asked looking at Gatto with a measure of caution as he knew the man to be a cold-blooded killer on the battlefield.

"Nah, I'm doing some jobs here in Rome" he replied with a shrug. "I'm" he looked around slowly to check that nobody was close enough to hear him speak "doing some jobs for Javenoli" he finished as Manlius's heart jumped in his chest.

In a voice which he hoped didn't betray any emotion he replied, "that old snake" and laughed quietly. "Shall we step to my house and have some breakfast Gatto? Catch up on old times?" he asked as his mind whirled through a jumble of possibilities

*

*

*

*

Chapter 10

The sun was beating down from a clear sky as Marcus stepped from his tent, his tunic scraped of mud and cleaned, and his armour polished vigorously. He knew that Postumius was likely to pick on any flaw in his attire or his words and he had spent some time preparing his equipment and mulling over what he might say, though in his heart he felt that there was nothing that could be done for the men. Centurion Bassano had been confined to his tent and a guard placed with him as he had raged at the situation, his anger spilling into tears before he had succumbed to the confinement. Rufus had spent a long time with him calming him and discussing options, of which they seemed to have few.

Marcus had sat and discussed the situation with Mella and Rufus as well, but they too had come up with no options, the law was the law. As he looked around him the camp seemed quiet, as if some spirit had come and taken away the men's energy, sapping them of the will to do their chores and keep to the camp activities. Soldiers went about their duties in almost total silence, men sat sharpening their swords, the grinding of the whetstone on the blades the only sound that came across the open ground of the camp, even the blacksmith was not busy, his tools sat forlornly against the wooden bench by his tent. As he wandered to the centre of the camp Marcus saw the despondent look on the faces of the men, many looking up and nodding to him as he passed. Marcus's heart was heavy as he felt he had no option other than to accept the judgement Postumius would no doubt give to all the men, death came simply in the legions, but to die in disgrace would bring shame to the men's families.

Aulus Manlius was another problem though thought Marcus as he continued towards the central command tent where the meeting was to be held. As a patrician, he could not be put to death for his failures in this situation, if they were, indeed, *his* failures. '*Nulla Spes*' he mumbled to himself, a no hope situation. For many patricians, Nulla Spes would mean the man would be in such a dire situation that the only escape would be suicide. He gripped the small wooden eagle on the cord around his neck and stood still for a moment as a thought came to him. He took a deep breath and exhaled slowly, seeing Ambustus enter Postumius's tent ahead of him, the man looking tired as he ducked to avoid the low tent entrance. There might be hope, he thought, but not for everyone. He would have to play the game with Postumius, but it might work. He stood for a moment composing his thoughts and trying to remember his lessons from his days back in Rome until his attention was drawn to Rufus, who waved from the side of the tent beckoning him forwards with a perplexed look on his face. Marcus looked to the sky and said a silent prayer to Fortuna and Juno, hoping that they would guide his thoughts and words in the next few hours before calling a legionary over and sending him on an errand back to his tent to fetch the items he thought he might need.

****

Postumius had seated Rufus and Marcus on one side of the campaign table and Ambustus and Sergius on the other, with himself at the thin edge of the table, his empty seat placed on a wooden platform looking down on the proceedings. Marcus gaped momentarily at the scene as he entered the tent, snapping his jaw shut almost as quickly as it had fallen open. Rufus rolled his eyes as Marcus neared his seat and then turned to face the empty commander's chair as Sergius nodded a welcome and placed a wax tablet on the table in front of him, no doubt containing his 'speech' for the proceedings thought Marcus.

Rufus leaned in close, a slight smell of garlic hitting Marcus's nose as he did so. "I can't see a way out of this for the guards, but I reckon Aulus Manlius has nothing to answer for, he set the guards but he can't be held responsible for their failure in a camp with nearly three thousand soldiers" he said, his eyebrows raised. Marcus nodded, he didn't want to speak yet, his thoughts still working through his mind. He had decided he would wait to hear what Sergius and Ambustus had to say before he spoke.

The tent flap opened and Postumius entered as he gave a final order to one of his messengers to prepare the baggage trains to leave at first light. Rufus and Marcus shared a glance at this news. All the soldiers stood as Postumius took his seat on the platform, shifting his backside on the thin cushion two or three times before nodding to allow the men to sit.

Sergius remained standing and nodded to Postumius, whose nod in response suggested that the two men had evidently met and discussed how the proceedings would work. As Sergius started to speak Marcus held up a hand, his eyes moving to Postumius as he turned his body in his direction. At his movement Sergius sat and looked angrily at Marcus before he too turned to Postumius.

"What is it?" demanded the commander, his voice a tone too forceful, after which he smiled a late, weak, smile.

"Won't we be lighting the candle to Justitia?" he asked, his voice edging on surprise as Ambustus cracked a smile before quickly wiping it from his face and turning to Postumius. "Camillus is correct, the proceedings must be overseen appropriately" he added, a nod to Marcus "The men would want it so".

"Sergius?" asked Postumius his face becoming impassive but with a nasty gleam in his eye.

"Er, we don't have the candle in the camp, sir" he started, his eyes glancing at Marcus as he spoke. Marcus edged his chair back and turned to Postumius.

"Commander" he said, "a sword and scales will do in times of war as you know" he stated, Postumius's questioning face suggested he knew no such thing. "And just in case, I asked for them to be ready, as these occurrences are so rare in the army" he said smiling at Sergius. "They are outside" he finished.

"You seem to have come prepared" stated Postumius, his hands gripping his knees as Marcus stood and went to the tent flap where the legionary was standing with his sword, a candle and the small bronze scales he had asked him to bring. As he turned he looked directly at Postumius. "If we do not follow the exact proceedings commander, you know that the men will find flaws in our decisions" he said walking across and placing the sword and scales on the table and taking a small candle, half used, from his clenched fist which the legionary had also brought him from Marcus's tent. "With the sword and scales, we can invoke Justitia to preside on our discussions and to guide your deliverance of the punishments, the balance of fate will be upheld by the gods will, sir" he stated, placing the candle in front of the men and stepping back to his chair before sitting.

Postumius looked at the items and with a slight shake of his head he leant forward and nodded. "You are, of course, correct Marcus Furius" he said. "Your time in the temples of

Rome was clearly time well spent" he added haughtily as he turned and called to one of the guards to fetch a flame with which he could light the candle and invoke the goddess. He turned his face to Marcus. "But as I am the commander here" he said, standing and unclipping his own sword "we will use my sword and your scales Furius" he added, continuing to avoid the use of Marcus's chosen name. He bent forwards and placed his own sword on the table and motioned for Marcus to remove his. Marcus bowed as he leant across and removed his sword, placing it on the floor by his seat. Ambustus sat watching and narrowed his eyes as he looked at Marcus, his questioning glance ignored as Marcus looked dispassionately at his hands, rubbing a finger as if it itched and then smiling to Rufus.

Once the candle was lit and Postumius had said a few words to include the goddess in the decision making of this camp meeting he sat back and nodded to Sergius, who stood and opened his wax tablet taking a deep breath.

"Gentlemen, this is a clear case" he said as he looked at the faces of the four men around the table. "Each soldier knows the law and took the soldier's oath. Each soldier is responsible for the duty in which they partake. Each soldier failed in his duty in this case and Appius Bassano's knife was found on the dead men. Therefore, each soldier must take his own life, as the prisoners took theirs. This is in accordance with the law." He looked up at the men before continuing, Postumius nodding with a deep frown on his face. "Aulus Manlius, as officer in charge, failed in his duty. The law is less clear for officers, yet he is clearly responsible for the death of the prisoners as much as the men themselves are. He cannot share in their deaths as he is of patrician blood" Sergius said as his eyes looked up from the tablet and he swallowed hard, making Marcus glance to Ambustus as Sergius suddenly appeared nervous about what he was going to say. "The state has decided that his failure should be punished by a fine of one hundred Ases and twenty bronze ingots." Marcus glanced to Rufus who nodded his approval at this suggestion, both men feeling that whilst heavy it was a good compromise. "And" continued Sergius, his eyes flicking to Postumius as he spoke "twenty lashes tied to the legions standard as a warning to other officers to do their duty as leaders of the Legions." At this Rufus, Marcus and Ambustus all stood and turned to the head of the table where Postumius's smile broadened on his face as the three men took a moment to take in the words. A patrician flogged? It had never been done before.

Ambustus grabbed the wax tablet from Sergius, who indignantly grabbed it back from him, his brows furrowed as he turned to Postumius before Rufus interjected.

"You cannot flog an officer of the Roman Legions" he stated, his mouth open wide as he gaped at Postumius. Marcus stared at Ambustus, who clearly had no idea that this punishment was being put forward by the state as the man sat back in his chair and stared at Postumius with a look of pure anger.

"Gentlemen." Postumius spoke once again with an air of superiority, his long nose raised high as he looked at the two defending officers. "If you would care to sit, maybe we can continue this meeting" he added, waving a hand at the candle and the sword and scales. "The goddess will be offended if you take such" his eyes wondered to the corner of the tent before coming back to focus directly at Marcus. "Aggressive stances" he said, the creases across his forehead growing into long ridges as he scowled at both men. Rufus huffed as he sat and Marcus simply stared at the candle, its light dancing on the table and reflecting off the bronze scales, before he too took his seat.

"So, if you two gentlemen would care to tell us what your defence is, maybe we could get this camp dismantled and leave for Rome" Postumius said in a bored voice, his eyes rolling to the ceiling, at which Sergius smiled and Ambustus clenched his jaw.

"Commander" said Marcus, his mind starting to form the argument as he spoke. "Justitia" he said as he bowed to the candle, noting Ambustus relax his jaw and sit forward as he did so. "Let us deal with the guards first" he said as he stood again and turned to Rufus, raising his eyebrows as he did so. "It is undisputed that the guards failed in their duty. It is also unclear how the knife came to be in the possession of the prisoners. They could not have taken it from Appius Bassano as he had not been close to the prisoners and his dagger was with his equipment in his tent, not on his person. Therefore, it is my suggestion that somebody else gave the knife to the prisoners after they had stolen it from Bassano's tent." He turned to Rufus before continuing. "Also, commander" he said turning back to Postumius, who he saw was inspecting his finger nails, his face a mix of boredom and irritation "the prisoners were tied at both hands and feet. It was impossible for any one of them to reach across and slit the throat of the other. They simply could not reach, I call for a check to be completed of the bonds and the distances between the prisoners." Postumius shifted in his seat, his head lowering as he looked like he was preparing to speak. Marcus quickly continued. "And commander" he said hastily, stepping to the wooden box Postumius had used with the scroll containing the laws that he had used with the men earlier. "The law states that an equal number of guards to prisoners should fall to the same fate as the prisoners in such circumstances. It is my view" at which Postumius and Sergius both sniffed in unison "that we await return to Rome before we pass sentence. The case is not as clear cut as we first thought and can be put to the Senate at the next meeting." Marcus finished with a slow nod to Rufus who smiled at him, his smile growing as the words began to sink into his mind. He knew that any court case in Rome would take months to settle, by which time the detail would have been lost and the punishments be less severe.

Postumius looked to Ambustus and Sergius. "Do you have any remarks, gentlemen, before I make my decision?" he asked.

Both men mumbled a negative reply as Postumius moved forwards on his seat. "A good argument Furius" he said, his hands clasping together in front of him as his elbows rested on the table. "I have checked the bonds as I feared the same as you" he said with a growing smile at the corners of his mouth, his eyes darting from left to right as he spoke. "And I concluded that the distance was achievable if the men turned to face each other, the bonds were not as tight as they should have been. Another failing of the guards" he said dismissively, his eyes narrowing to focus on Marcus as he spoke. Marcus put his best stoic face forward despite the fact that he knew Postumius was wrong. "It's a shame the bodies have been moved or we could have re-checked them" he said as he turned his head to look at Rufus. Marcus seethed inside, he had been outmanoeuvred by Postumius, who, as the senior officer, would out-rank his opinion of the positions of the bodies. "And I agree with your comments regarding the guards and the law" he said, sitting back and steepling his fingers as he leant back into the frame of the chair. "It does *suggest* that an equal number of guards face the same fate as the condemned prisoners, but that is also at the discretion of the Legion's Tribune" he added as he looked at Marcus over the top of his soft hands. "Therefore, in the interests of" he looked up at the ceiling of the tent before speaking again "*compromise,* I state that Appius Bassano and one guard will suffer the punishment. Two lives instead of five" he stated as his lip curled. Ambustus shook his head but kept quiet, in no position to argue with the camp commander who held imperio, total power, in this situation. Marcus took a deep breath, turning to Rufus who was staring with a look of horror at Postumius, before returning his eyes to the top of the table. "Commander, I beg a reprieve for Appius Bassano, the man was not at the prisoner's gaol and did not, in my view, take any part in whatever happened" he asked, his eyes growing large as he spoke.

Postumius's face remained impassive as he looked to Sergius. "Write the decision Sergius" he said "Appius Bassano and one other man, drawn by lots, will die by their own hands as punishment for their failure of duty. By the power vested in me as commander of Rome's Legion I state this, in front of Justitia, Mars war-bringer and the representatives of the state and soldiers" he said as Sergius smiled and began to scribble the command in the tablet he had placed on the table earlier. Marcus was about to speak when Rufus pulled gently on his arm and shook his head mouthing the word 'no' before he could speak. Marcus stared at his friend incredulously, his eyes flicking to Ambustus, who could not look him in the face, before he twisted in his chair and sat erect, his chest heaving as he bit back the anger he felt.

"And Aulus Manlius?" Rufus said. "The fine is acceptable but to flog a patrician?" he shook his head, a deep frown coming to his face as every head turned to look at Postumius.

"Gentlemen" started Postumius as he let out a long sigh. "Manlius must face punishment" he said, his eyes looking at the candle as it continued to flicker, the yellow flame jumping slightly as he spoke. Postumius leant forwards and picked up his sword. "The scales have been tipped" he said "see" as he pointed to the bronze scales sat next to the candle. "The balance of life has been changed, only one guard and Bassano will die and not five men as the goddess expected. The goddess will be pleased that justice has prevailed for the men of Rome" he said, his voice sounding superior as he continued to stare at the candle. "But punishment" he said, quickly rasping the sword out of its ornate scabbard and slamming it back forcefully as he looked up, his trance-like eyes staring at nothing in particular. "Punishment is needed to balance the scales. The gods would have it no other way, you must know that with all your training *Camillus*" he said, almost spitting the last word. He sat slowly back in his seat as the officers simply stared at him in silence.

"The man must face punishment" he said, his voice drifting as he lowered his head whilst he spoke.

"But, sir" said Marcus breaking the silence before Postumius raised a hand and scowled once again at Marcus, his face creasing into a grimace.

"Marcus Furius" he said with a shake of his head. "You saved my life once" he added as he cocked his head to one side and seemed to look straight through Marcus, his stare unnerving Marcus as Postumius sat silently as if considering him for the first time. With a sudden jerk Postumius sat straight and stared at his camp prefect. "Sergius" he said "add this to the records." He turned to Marcus, who suddenly felt as if he had been played into a corner, the words Nulla Spes coming back to his mind.

"Aulus Manlius will receive ten lashes not twenty. Another *compromise*" he said. "But" his voice rose as a mad glint came to his eye and he smiled at Marcus "Furius is correct. A patrician cannot be flogged by a soldier. A patrician can only be flogged by another patrician." Marcus gasped as Postumius glanced to him, his lips opening to a broad smile, his teeth glinting yellow in the candlelight, as Marcus felt a sudden dread come over him.

*

*

*

*

Chapter 11

Manlius stood next to the old stone lion, its mane worn by thousands of hands who had rubbed its long locks as it was said to give those who touched it bravery in difficult circumstances. It was also said that the bones of Faustulus were placed under the lion and it was a lucky place to meet relatives. Manlius didn't believe any of these old wives tales, and looked at the rough carving of the beast, its blank eyes and thick legs a testament to the talent of the sculptor. He frowned as he walked to the side of the statue, his focus taken up with his criticism for the sculpture when behind him a commotion in the forum caused him to turn.

The forum was busy, as it usually was at this time of the afternoon, the heat of the day creating a fog of dust in the open space as people milled to and fro. Around the outside of the forum there were sellers of baskets, fruit, vases and the usual troupes of players all attempting to barter for the coins or wares of the passer-by. Yet at the far end a cry had gone up and Manlius stepped forwards, his sandals kicking up a small cloud of dust as he set off in the direction of the noise. A mini swarm of gnats, their buzzing causing him to instinctively flinch, seemed to follow him as people started to move away from whatever the commotion was, one woman and her slave fleeing past him with a look of terror on their faces. Manlius smiled, swatting at the flies which seemed to be worse than ever today, as he came close to the source of the fuss.

Gatto, his newly shaved face, appeared at Manlius's side and nodded, a curl on his lips.

"Looks like another victim of the plague" he said so loudly that a handful of the closest watchers turned in his direction. "That's the fifth I've seen today and the Consuls are doing nothing about it. That man" he said theatrically, pointing to the wasted body of a man, which to anyone with any sense would know had been dead for days. "He was here yesterday and said he had a cough, look at him now." Gatto's voice resonated around the silent space as his eyes glanced at Manlius, who nodded his reply. "The plebeian council told the magistrates about this" he added, his face a picture of anger "but they did nothing. There are too many migrants coming to the City, they are bringing this plague" he added pointing again at the lifeless body slumped against the wall next to the new shops.

People started to leave, first a slow trickle and then all at once they left in droves, some running, some walking, but every one of them held their tunics over their mouths. Plague, it was almost as feared as fire in Rome. For the last few years they had been lucky to have no pestilence or plague, but now it seemed it might be back. Many more in the crowd gasped and covered their mouths as they scuttled back to their homes.

The sturdier men stood and looked at Gatto, his features creased into an angry glare. "What can we do brother?" came a voice from the remaining crowd. Gatto's eyes smiled but his face remained stoic.

"Here is a man who will know what to do" he said turning "Marcus Manlius, you were an officer in the legions, you *must* know what to do, sir?" he asked, his voice almost pleading. Manlius smiled, Gatto had played his part well and the men around them shuffled closer.

"Tell us Manlius" came a voice from one of the men, his eyes fearful.

"Have the gods forsaken us?" came another cry from back in the crowd of men.

Manlius grinned as he saw more men walking across the forum to see what was happening. "No, the gods have not forsaken us, they are merely showing us their displeasure. It's a *sign* brothers" he said, turning to the small crowd. "The Senate needs to do something about the disease and death in our streets. The gods are telling us that they are not happy with the magistrates. They are not happy that Rome is so crowded, that so many people beg on the streets and so much filth spoils our great city" he said to a chorus of agreement from the, now growing, crowd.

He waved to Gatto "Will you find some strong men to take this body and any others and burn them?" he asked "and I Marcus Manlius will go to the Senate myself and ask them for action. We need strong men, men of action not men of words" he chided, his chest expanding as he spoke. "I will be the people's voice as you seem to demand of me. You" he waved his arm out over the heads of the crowd "to the patricians. They must listen to us" he called. "But" he said, raising his arms and turning in a slow circle so that he could see each face in the crowd "you must follow me, men of Rome. You must stand proud and challenge the magistrates to do your bidding. They have money in the treasury, they can close the gates and clean up the city. Together we can make the gods proud of Rome again. And today there is a meeting at the Temple of Jupiter, we can go there now and challenge them" he added as a great cheer rang out.

Gatto winked at him as he grabbed two men, both of whom Manlius had seen with him earlier, and gripped the dead body as the crowd, now swollen to over fifty men started to walk to the Capitoline Hill where the temple stood. Gatto, with his insider knowledge from Javenoli had given Manlius this plan and as he walked, the crowd growing behind him, he saw Calvus, standing away to his left, smiling and joining the crowd as he had planned. In his mind Manlius spoke to his dead father 'see father, now your boy is a man now and he has a road to power that you never had' and his grin broadened as he felt men slapping him on the shoulder and cheering his name.

****

"People of Rome" called the Senator from the steps of the temple as the crowd shouted abuse at the white clad leaders of the Republic, many of whom had slipped out of the rear entrance as they saw the crowd approaching, but the remaining gathering of the leaders of the City stood at the top of the steps looking down on the crowd. "We must observe the rules, the laws" he shouted, his voice drowned by a chorus of booing and swearing.

"The law made by patricians" called a few voices.

"It's a plague sent by the gods" called others. "What will you do about it?" shouted a man to Manlius's left, his face soaked in a wet sheen from the humidity of the day and the stale smell of sweat rising from his body. Manlius turned his head away and took a deep breath.

"We must consult the gods, an augury" called the Senator, his thin frame and grey hair testament to his fitness despite his years. Manlius knew Fidenas well, the man had been tribune some years previously, but he was a staunch hater of improved plebeian rights and had spent many years building a fortune by buying good land around the Roman hills and then calling in debts when his clients, those plebeians he had rented land to, had struggled to pay their dues.

The crowd shouted abuse at the call for an augury, some voices calling for actions, not more words and others shouting for a bull to be slaughtered to appease the gods. Manlius smiled inwardly and turned at a movement to his right to see Calvus stepping forwards. What was the man doing? With a start he realised that Calvus was suddenly placing himself between the crowd and the Senators and he jerked into action, calling for quiet before Calvus could get a chance to speak, he needed to regain the initiative, or he would lose it to Calvus.

"Men of Rome, let me speak" he called, repeating the shout as the men around him turned to him and others stopped shouting abuse at Fidenas at this new turn of events. With a glance to Calvus he stepped forwards, his feet on the second step of the temple before he half-turned to the crowd, the Senator frowned at this action although Manlius had been careful not to turn his back fully on the Senators standing above him.

Manlius looked at the faces of the men below him, all turned to him as he smiled at them, the crowd now numbering at least a hundred. "Senators" he said, turning to the toga clad elite, who all frowned at him, some shaking their heads at the audacity of a 'nobody' a man with a poor lineage, addressing them in this way. "The people of Rome need action, not words.

Have you not seen the dead on your doorstep?" he asked, seeing a few of the Senators nod and turn to their friends with a cautious look. Gatto had furnished him with enough information to know that the Senate were discussing the pestilence and what they should do about it on this very day and so he had sacrificed a chicken to Juno and prayed that today his plan would be kick-started into action. So far it had gone as he had expected.

"We are one Republic and we have the same problems" said Manlius to a few angry snorts from the patricians and a few cheers from the plebeians. "And we live together in this great city. Death is at our doors, all of our doors gentlemen" he added, his arms raised from his sides. "The gods are not happy" he said, his head bowed as he spoke, many of the men below him nodding agreement, some clasping talisman's on chains around their necks as their heads bowed too. "We must have an augury to find out the cause of the plague. *But*" he held up his hands to a few dissenters in the crowd. "We need immediate action as well or the plague will spread and more people will die, your brothers, your sisters and your children" he added theatrically as he stared into the sky so as not to place the evil eye on anyone in the crowd, who now stood silently watching and listening to Manlius.

"Your plebeian council members are here today" he continued with a wave to Calvus, who scowled at him in reply "and I am sure they will support our leaders" he added with a turn to Fidenas "in all actions we agree today. I, Marcus Manlius will represent you at the augury if you wish it" he finished, stepping down into the crowd to a great cheer from the men, many of who gripped his arms and thanked him loudly.

A short silence fell on the crowd as everyone turned to Calvus, whose face was a picture of measured calm but Manlius could see that inside he was coiled like a spring, played into the scene well by Manlius's words.

*

*

*

*

Chapter 12

The legion lined up outside the walls of Bolae, the tall structure looking down on the lines of men standing in marching gear, sweat starting to trickle down their faces as the heat of the end of the day built to its most ferocious. Each group of men had dismantled their tents, packed their equipment and sent parties to fill in the latrine ditches as well as collect water for the march. Since Postumius had announced the decision, the army had gone about its business efficiently with only a few dissenting voices, many of whom had finally been shouted into silence by their Centurions.

Marcus had spent some time with Bassano discussing his son Appius's effects and what he wanted to do with them before Bassano had, himself, visited his son to say a final goodbye. Now the legion was lined up to watch the final acts of the sorrowful situation play out and Marcus was stood in the centre of the makeshift parade ground as Postumius stood on his mounting block rostrum and turned to the soldiers, all standing to attention and staring at him with looks of hatred.

"Bring the prisoners forward" called Postumius as the five men, Appius Bassano and four guards, were marched to the centre of the space, their brown tunics spotless as they had been cleaned up at their commander's requirement. Each of the guards held his head low, but Appius stood tall, his chin in the air as he marched forwards, his hands tied to the man in front of him by thin leather thongs. As the men came to a standstill Appius was cut free from the remaining men and moved two paces to the left where he was gently pushed to the ground, landing heavily on his knees. He stared at Postumius with a look of loathing, but he kept his head high.

"You men" called Postumius. "Failed in your duty. But I, as commander of this legion, have given you a reprieve" he said. "A chance for three of you to remain alive and live to fight for Rome another day." Postumius was pleased with these words. He had spent some time working through his speech, hoping to make it memorable to the crowd of soldiers so that they would see the clemency of his actions. He half smiled to himself before continuing.

"Sergius" he called as his camp prefect stepped forwards holding a leather bag.

"In this bag are four stones. One of them is black the others are white. The man who chooses the black stone will suffer the penalty" he stated formally.

"Cut their bonds" he commanded as the guard's hands were cut free, most of them rubbing their wrists and stretching fingers that had been unable to move for the past few hours. Sergius looked to his commander, who nodded.

"Step forwards" he called to the first man, who looked to his left at the other prisoners and shook his head with a deep sigh before stepping forward and, with a glance at Sergius, reached into the bag. For a second he rummaged around, his face creasing as he tried to discern which stone to choose, a look of terror coming to his eyes, at which Postumius grinned and stared more closely at his face. His legs were shaking as he pulled a stone from the bag, a sudden look of relief flashing across his face as he fell to his knees and looked to the sky with a moan holding a white stone clutched tightly in his hand.

"Get up man" Sergius called as he lashed out with a stick, whacking the man across the shoulders and pushing him backwards. "Re-join your unit" he said as the other three men simply stared at their fellow prisoner, now set free as he stumbled away without looking back at the remaining condemned men.

The remaining prisoners looked down at the floor, their faces drained of colour as Sergius called the next man forwards. He ran his fingers through his jet-black hair as his eyes stared wildly up to the skies, his lips working through some prayer or other to his chosen god. Postumius watched intently. This man had an unlucky look about him, he thought. His face was a mask of pain and he hadn't washed the grime from his legs, Postumius shook his head at the state of the man and made a mental note that all prisoners would be scrubbed clean before attending him in future. This time the soldier simply stepped up to the camp prefect, reached into the bag and dragged out the first stone his hand gripped, his eyes closed as he did so and his mouth mumbled indistinct words as he held the stone up high. White again. A small cheer, quickly stifled, came from the ranks behind him as Postumius looked at the location of the noise, seeing a Centurion lashing at a similar looking man to the prisoner with his vine stick, the recipient of the blows smiling despite the lashes he received. Postumius smiled at the small mercies he was granting.

The man turned and looked to the two remaining men and muttered a few words which Postumius could not hear, but both men nodded glumly as he walked away leaving them to their fate.

"You" called Sergius as the next man was pushed forwards, his head bowed low as he reached into the bag and closed his eyes, his mouth working but no sound coming out. Postumius glanced at the fourth prisoner, his chin against his chest as if resolved to his fate, as the man standing above him pulled a black stone from the bag and a small murmur went around the crowd of soldiers, the man with the stone instantly dropped the signal of his death to the floor as if it was red hot and shuffled backwards his eyes wide with fear as a small moan came to his lips.

"Hold him" came the stern reply as the soldier seemed to look about him for an escape route before he fell to his knees and put his head in his hands. The final prisoner had not moved.

He remained motionless as the man next to him let out a deep moan and slumped to the floor. Sergius stepped forwards.

"Release this man, he is free" he said as the fourth prisoner was ushered away, his head shaking and words streaming from his lips which Postumius couldn't hear.

Postumius waited for a moment, looking at the faces of the soldiers who had stood almost silently throughout the proceedings before speaking again.

"The fates have chosen" he said. "Proceed" at which a drum began to beat in the background, its low note heavy in the stifling humidity. Two men stepped forwards, hoods over their heads as they carried two long-bladed daggers into the space. Postumius looked around the soldiers standing in their ranks, his eyes searching for Bassano. Yes, there he was standing away to the right, his face a mask of sorrow. This would teach him, he thought to himself as his lips curled slightly. Nobody would get the better of Publius Postumius, especially not these plebeians with their thoughts of new settlements and new lands to farm.

The two condemned men were knelt facing the Legions standard and a few words were said to Mars to honour their deaths before each man was handed one of the knives, each blade glinting in the sunlight. A guard stood behind each man with his sword drawn in case the prisoner could not summon the courage to take his own life, ready to do the deed quickly if there were problems.

Appius Bassano looked to Postumius and smiled before ripping his tunic to bare his chest and placing the point of the knife under his ribcage pointing upwards. His eyes never left Postumius, a look of hatred filling his face as he plunged the blade deep into his chest and thrust the hilt left and right as he fell to the floor, a great red line rushing down his stomach as the man next to him moaned, his eyes staring at the dead body of Appius.

The guard behind the final prisoner stepped forwards and grabbed the man's neck before he shouted "no" and raised his own blade stabbing it into his chest with a ferocity that shocked many of the men around him, he punched the blade into his chest three or four times, howling at each thrust before his eyes went to the skies and he fell into the dust, his open mouth letting out a deep gasp as he fell to his death. Soldiers gripped their talismans and mumbled prayers at this sorry event, surely an affront to the gods.

The sound of the drum beat continued, but no sound came from the ranks of soldiers, other than their mumbled prayers.

Postumius looked up at Sergius, who was clutching the bag which contained the stones and staring at the bodies, his mouth open. He flicked a glance to Bassano who stood erect, his eyes staring into the space high above the walls of the city, his face betraying no emotion.

"Sergius" Postumius commanded, his voice loud and strong, "proceed" he added as the camp prefect turned to him before jumping to attention. The two guards waved to a legionary who ran across the ground with a hand cart and the two bodies were lifted slowly and placed within it before the cart was dragged away by both men, the arm of one of the dead falling over the side of the cart and dancing up and down as the cart bumped over the rocky ground. Sergius stepped forwards and called "Aulus Manlius. As officer in charge of the prisoners you have been found guilty of allowing their deaths through your inattention to details." He looked up at Aulus and his eyes flicked to Postumius, a curl coming to his lips at which Postumius frowned.

"You are sentenced to ten lashes" he called as two guards walked forwards with Aulus and the Legions standard was brought to the centre of the open ground in front of the troops, a heavy cart rumbling along beside it. A low murmur went around the men, some shaking their heads as the patrician, his jaw set firm and his step heavy, came to a standstill in front of the tall standard. Sergius looked to Postumius, who nodded. Three men began to fix the standard to the cart and tied two ropes on either side in which to fit Aulus's outstretched hands.

"Men of Rome" Postumius said looking around at the soldiers faces. "This officer is also guilty and will be punished as agreed by your representatives" he added with a glance at Marcus.

"Proceed" he finished, waving to a slave who rushed forwards with a large beaker of water. Postumius placed his hands out in front of him as Marcus watched the water poured onto them, the ritual cleansing of his hands for the decisions he made now complete. Marcus fumed. Postumius had been clever and had made it clear that he was punishing Marcus as much as he was punishing Aulus. Knowing the Manlius brothers as he did, Marcus was sure that this was not the last Postumius would be hearing from them and he shook his head quickly before stepping forwards and moving to the position from which he would have to administer the lashes, his face stony and cold as he did so.

Postumius had made it clear that Marcus had to administer the lash and that if he shirked in his duty then he too would receive ten lashes. Marcus had argued against the punishment, but his argument had been a waste of time, Postumius had already made up his mind and, as Tribune, his word was law in the camp.

Aulus Manlius was tied to the standard, his bare back, pale and white against the brown wood of the cart and the dusty ground. He was placed in a kneeling position and a box was placed beside him holding the whip. Marcus stepped forwards, at which a low grumble came from the soldiers, Postumius smiling at their discomfort. Marcus had determined to make it quick, ten quick lashes and then to return to his position, no emotion and no show of anger at the decision. He sucked in a slow breath as he stepped to the box and opened it, his eyes wide as he saw the whip within, momentarily stopping as he flicked his eyes to Postumius a measure of anger coming to his face before he closed his eyes, took another deep breath and stood, the three tails of the Flagrum, the slave's whip, hanging from the wooden handle in his hand. A gasp went around the soldiers as they saw the whip, its symbol clear to them all. The Flagrum was reserved for whipping slaves in Rome, its three leather 'tails' fitted with metal hooks which would rip the flesh but not break the bones so that the slave would not be rendered useless. To whip a patrician was bad enough; to use a slave's whip would be seen as an affront to the patrician's family. Postumius frowned at Marcus as he stood still and glared across at him. Postumius was almost laughing as he waved a hand at Marcus, telling him to proceed. The soldiers in their ranks went silent as Marcus stepped forwards, his muscles tensing as he tried to gauge the weight of the whip so he could use it quickly and efficiently. With a look to the sky he said, strong and clear so all could hear "Mars and Juno guide my hand as I administer the punishment", the age-old invocation used by Romans when dealing out the lash.

As the first slap of leather and metal hit Aulus's back it tore three red lines into his flesh, the pale skin turning to an angry red as Marcus drew his hand back and started his second swing, his mind cursing Postumius and his teeth clenched as he drew a deep breath.

*

*

*

*

Chapter 13

'Watch your back' Gatto had whispered to Manlius in the forum as he had passed him with a slight nudge on his shoulder, almost as if he hadn't known the man but with a direct look in his eyes, a look of alarm on his face as he scratched at the angry red scar on his chin. Manlius had whirled around to speak to him but Gatto had disappeared into the crowd quickly. His mind was suddenly alert as he felt his heart break into a new beat, his blood starting to course through his veins as he suddenly saw enemies in every face in the busy crowd. He took a deep breath, easing his hand to his small dagger under his long brown tunic, his wide leather belt holding the folds above it and allowing his legs freedom to walk comfortably in the heat. The day had started warm and the sky was clearing. The five dead bodies in the forum had been removed earlier, their remains smouldering on a pyre outside the city wall. What had Gatto meant? Had someone put a price on his head? A voice in his head told him that the Senate were not happy with him, but he sneered at them as he narrowed his eyes and looked for a path through the crowd which could see him back to his house on the Capitoline. The pestilence still remained, people were dying each day, but there were fewer now that they had taken the bodies and burned them, surely the Senate saw this as a good thing, he pondered, realising he hadn't moved for a few moments.

With a grunt, which startled a well-to-do lady who was stood near him, he set his head low and started across the forum, his eyes scanning the crowd for any untoward movement. His old soldier's instincts took over and he said to himself that the best place to attack him would be on the hill near to his house where the trees narrowed into a dark corridor and the walls of the houses were high. He clenched his jaw, his lips tight, as he walked and gripped the dagger tightly thinking of options.

It would be best if he could circle around the road to make sure he wasn't being followed, he thought, taking the road to his right and walking away towards the Clivus Orbis which led to the Esquiline Hill. In his head, he planned to start up the hill before doubling back on himself and heading across to the Capitoline. It was a long walk, but it would make it difficult for anyone who was following him.

****

The two men watched Manlius leave the forum, wondering why he was heading towards the road past the Vestals house rather than towards his house up on the Capitoline. They shrugged in unison and nodded to each other as each one set off in different directions, but both following their prey. The price on the man's head was enough to get them to work together rather than alone on this particular job. The first man was thin and wiry, his thin features criss-crossed with multiple scars, one which ran across his head from the front of his forehead to a point above his ear, its bare white line visible on the man's shaven head. He set off to the right, heading for the road to the Palatine, but keeping Manlius in his sights. The other man was much bigger than the first. His arm muscles bulged under a thick brown tunic, a thick green leather belt wrapped tight around his waist with a heavy pouch attached which bounced against his hip as he walked. His face was brown from standing in the sun and his hair was long and tied back in a knot behind his head. His right forearm was a map of thin, pale, scars and his wrists were bound with wristbands which held the face of a gorgon stamped into the leather.

After five minutes, the two men looked to each other and stopped following Manlius, meeting together at a well on the cross roads beyond the house of the Vestals.

"I say we head to his house and wait for him there. I don't fancy climbing around the hills for an hour just so we know where he is going. Better to wait for him to come home" said the burlier man, rubbing his wrist as he spoke.

"Right" replied the other. "You go ahead, and I'll follow in a minute, better to look like we are alone" he said with a nod, at which his partner nodded in reply and set off at a stroll. As he smiled he set off after Manlius, better to claim the reward for himself than to share it, he thought.

****

Manlius stepped up from behind the pillar in front of the Vestals and watched the first man move away. So, it was just two of them. With a turn of speed which showed his fitness he ran across the road and descended the steps to arrive at the corner by the temple of Castor and

Pollux, his angry mind telling him that it was ironic that this was a site often used for Senate meetings as he shook his head and narrowed his eyes. The thin man with the deep scar on his head was coming into view. The temple had a narrow alleyway along the side and he quickly glanced at it to check it was empty before crouching behind a tall grey pillar.

Two slaves wandered past, their foreign words drifting into the air, laughing as they walked, oblivious to Manlius crouched to their left. The scarred man was ten paces behind the slaves and didn't notice the figure behind the thick stone pillar as he walked along looking at the sky, where a few dark clouds were forming in the predominantly blue sky.

Manlius stepped out behind the man and gripped his tunic at the back of his shoulder, thrusting him to his left as he pushed his hand behind onto the side of his head and stepped across and thumped the man's head into the pillar in one swift movement, the deep ridges exploding into a red hue as his skull connected with them. Instantly Manlius dragged the body into the alleyway and knelt his knee across the man's chest looking back over his shoulder to check that nobody had seen the action and followed him into the dark, narrow, alley.

The man's eyes were glazed, his head raised in a thick welt, with two lines of almost black blood oozing from his broken skull.

"Who are you working for?" Manlius asked in a deep growl with his teeth clenched, gripping his hand on the man's windpipe as his eyes rolled in his head. No answer came so Manlius used his free hand to grip the man's face and move his head from side to side, a low groan coming from his chest as he did so. "Damn" spat Manlius realising he had been too violent, again checking over his shoulder and realising that his tunic was covered in blood, the red mixed into a dark stain along with the brown folds of the material. A spot of white showed in the indentation of the man's skull where the dark red blood was congealing already and Manlius shook his head. He would have to finish the man off, he would be no use to him now and he would have to tackle the brute of man with the wristbands if he was to find who had

put a price on his head. Slipping his dagger from its hiding place he sliced it across the man's

gullet, opening a gap from which a warm draught of air escaped before a gurgle of blood

rushed into the space and the man choked for a second before his life disappeared from his

body. Manlius jumped up and wrapped the folds of his tunic into his belt to hide the worst of

the stains before disappearing back out into the street, which remained quiet, as he headed

towards the Capitoline Hill.

****

Mella sat on the large grey boulder rubbing his feet and shaking his head. He glanced at

Marcus who was frowning into the distance at the long dust trail left by the marching army,

its men and pack animals loaded with the treasures and booty from Bolae.

"I hate the rear guard" he grumbled, shaking another small stone out of his sandal as he

spoke. Marcus ignored him, he had heard the same complaint for the past three hours.

"All the dust, all the dung and all the drop-outs" he moaned, wiping something brown from

his foot onto the rock he sat on before slipping his sandal back on and grunting as he tied it

tightly.

Marcus had called his small detachment to a halt as they had quickly caught up with the rear

of the marching column. As soon as the flogging of Aulus Manlius had been completed

Postumius had ordered the men to march, no doubt believing that keeping the men busy on

the road would stop them having time to grumble. Marcus had been ordered to bring up the

rear of the column, marching in a thick cloud of dust and open to any attack from whichever

enemies might be lurking behind the Romans.

It had been two days of slow movement, covering no more than twenty miles at most in that

time due to the heavy wagons and slow pack horses. As they had left Bolae a force of a few hundred Capenate horsemen had been seen riding into the City, many of the legionaries grumbling that they had lost any chance to claim the town now that the enemy had retaken it without a fight. Potitus and Marcus had discussed the issue at length, both agreeing that Bolae was a strong position which should have been manned, but neither having the strength of their conviction to bring this thought to Postumius as they knew his feelings on the subject. Marcus watched two birds circling high above them, unsure what type they were. Mella, seeing his eyes staring upwards, came across. "Eagles?" he asked.

"No. I don't think so, too small." Marcus replied. "They are probably crows. But" he peered around the location in which they sat "in this scrub-land there cannot be much food so they must be using the height to look further afield. Come on, we need to get the men moving again" he added as he moved away towards his horse.

The men were sitting and standing on the roadside with three guards, each looking outwards towards the open ground surrounding their location. A Roman scout, his horse walking slowly a hundred paces to their right, waved his spear horizontally in the air as he saw them begin to stand, the signal for all clear. Marcus nodded to Narcius, who smiled a toothy grin as he called the men into their ranks. The one hundred and fifty men of the rear guard set off at a slow walk towards the thick dust cloud that was the Roman army returning to Rome.

"Sir" asked Mella as he came up beside Marcus. "What do you think Manlius will have to say about his brother being whipped, especially with a flagrum" he asked, his face forward and his voice low. Marcus shook his head slowly and let out a deep breath at the thought.

"You know Manlius as well as I do. The man is prone to action and not thinking. I hope he doesn't do anything stupid, but I suspect he will" Marcus replied, his face glum. "And" he added, his thoughts coming quickly as he had not had time to discuss these details with anyone up until this point "he will probably take legal action against him which will cost him a small fortune." Again, he shook his head.

Mella glanced across at Marcus, his question forming in his head but he wasn't sure how to phrase it. "And how do you think he will react to the fact that you whipped him?" he asked, his voice low as he saw a grimace quickly come and go on Marcus's face. After a moments silence Marcus replied in a whisper "I don't know."

****

An hour later the men had arrived at a small ford, the clear fast-flowing water only ankle deep as the men splashed through. Marcus ordered the men to take a short break and to re-fill their water pouches and let the horses rest as he slid from his mount and tied it to a laurel tree, the grey trunk and thick green leaves providing a welcome break from the heat of the days march. Two scouts were sent out to check the flanks and three others continued for a hundred paces to keep an eye on the rear of the column.

Narcius wandered across to Marcus and saluted, his leather breastplate already undone as he wafted it to release the heat from his body. Marcus held out a piece of dried beef as the man approached and smiled at the face of his first spear.

"Nice spot" Narcius said looking around at the land in which they were sat. Away to their left were the low hills which led to Bolae, and to their right was the flat land of the valley through which this stream ran.

Marcus looked around at the trees and the thin grass with rocky outcrops before his vision came to the skyline. "Wouldn't be much good for farming, but it's a pretty place" he conceded with a nod as Narcius took the beef and thanked him. As Narcius took a bite of the beef a loud whistle came from away to the men's right, its warning immediately clear. Marcus, Mella and Narcius were on their feet and running to the highest point, a jumble of rocks thirty yards away from where they had been sitting. The men, swords and shields dragged into position, began to form up into three lines as they watched their leaders run to the vantage point.

Darting across from the low scrub was one of the scouts, his body leant across his animal as it thundered towards them, the hoof beats loud against the quiet gurgle of water. The scout reined in and saluted before dropping from his horse and stepping up to Marcus.

"A force of some fifty or sixty horsemen are following" he said, his breathing laboured as he reported. "Armed. Spears and round shields, sir" he added.

Marcus looked to Narcius with a half-smile. "Probably just those Capenates checking that we left the area" he said. "But we best get going and catch up with the rear of the column just in case. Let's get the men moving" he finished with a nod to the scout as he placed a hand on his shoulder.

****

The body lay across the thick stones of the low wall in the half shadow of a leafy Myrtle tree, a small crowd of locals standing muttering at the scene. The man had been dealt a heavy blow from behind, the back of his head a crushed mess of hair, brain and blood. Manlius shook his head as he stood looking down at the dead body of the second of his would-be assassins. He slowly scanned the road around him, the steep hill narrowing at this junction of the road was the perfect place for an ambush, with the low wall, the shadow of the trees and the steep rise. He shook his head at a question from one of his neighbours, his words indistinct as his mind raced through thoughts of who had killed the assassin.

"I'll send some of my slaves to clean up the mess and to take the body and burn it" he added to the man, who was busily asking questions of all the bystanders, his peaceful world on the Capitoline clearly disturbed by this murder. After another look at the body he stepped away towards his own home which was no more than fifty yards to his right where the road began its steep drop back down towards the short valley to the Quirinal Hill. As he approached his doorway the door opened and one of his slaves appeared, his face a mask of worry and his eyes almost pleading with him to hurry. Without thinking Manlius started to pick up his pace as his slave waved to him, his beckoning hand waving urgently and the words "hurry Master" calling to him.

"What is it, what is the matter?" he called as he approached the doorway, his heart now beating fast in case the assassin had already visited his house.

"A man, Master, inside" called the slave, peering behind Manlius as he ushered him into the house and closed the door behind him. In the hallway the tiled floor, its bright coloured mosaic, was hidden under a thin wash of blood. A number of house slaves were mopping up the mess, a series of circular red sweeping lines disappeared as Manlius's eyes adjusted to the darker interior.

"Here he is" said a voice which Manlius instantly recognised but took a moment to comprehend as his eyes swivelled into the dark corner where the door slave had propped up the dark-haired form.

"What?" asked Manlius incredulously as his eyes roved the scene in his house. He stared at the grimacing face of Gatto, his clothes covered in blood and his left arm hanging limply by his side. With his free hand Gatto held something up and through his clenched teeth said "Got you a present" as he handed them across to Manlius. Taking the two wristbands Manlius looked to the toothy gorgons and again at Gatto and smiled, a sudden relief coming over him. "Get this man some water. Where is my wife?" he called to another slave as he called for others to clear up the mess in the hallway.

*

*

*

*

Chapter 14

Postumius dismissed the officers with a wave of his hand, his angry face flushed purple as he had given the orders for the evening's camp, Sergius standing to attention by his side with various wax tablets holding the details of the working parties. As Marcus watched the man handing out the duties, he saw a sneer appear on his face as he handed a set of orders to Aulus Virginius, the man's face flushing as he quickly scanned the details he had received, snapping the wooden cover of the orders closed as he looked up.

"Sir" he heard him say, his voice strong and his head raised high as he stared with a look of loathing at his camp prefect. "May I respectfully request a change of duties for my men? This is the fifth day in a row that my men have been assigned latrines." He shuffled a little as he stood erect, his shoulders stiff as his eyes flicked to the shorter man stood next to him. Sergius glanced at him, a puzzled look coming to his face as he slowly turned towards Virginius. With a smile he spoke, his voice loud enough to carry across the tent and above the noise of the officers leaving the area.

"No, you cannot" he said. "The roles have been allocated. Your men will do as they are bid, they are good at digging ditches and their duties are assigned." He finished with a cold stare. The shorter man, whom Marcus recognised, placed an arm on Virginius's elbow and steered him away from the micro-confrontation that many of the officers had stopped to watch.

"What is that all about?" Marcus asked Potitus as they left the command tent, entering the coolness of the evening, the birdsong loud around them.

"It's a long story" Potitus started to say with a quick glance back over his shoulder. After a moment, he continued. "Virginius and Sergius go back a long way. They grew up on neighbouring farms and were always fighting and competing against each other. The lads say that Virginius bested Sergius at wrestling, horse riding and spear throwing when they were young and that he also got the pick of the ladies, if you know what I mean?" Marcus quickly glanced at Virginius, his tall frame, long dark hair and quick eyes marking him out amongst the shorter, stockier, officers around him.

"I can see why" he smiled with a wink to his friend.

"Well, since Sergius got the camp prefect job he's done his best to get his revenge on his former neighbour. He's had every shitty job since the day the army left Rome, so they say. He was left behind in the attack on Bolae, his lads got the baggage train. And so far, Sergius has seen to it that his men are humiliated whenever he gets a chance. They've been ditch digging, first scouts and latrines at each stop from what I hear."

Marcus shook his head, his thoughts going over the impact such treatment would have, not only on Virginius but also on his men. "Probably learned that from his master" he said with a frown as his thoughts jumped to Postumius and his own treatment from the Tribune.

"Barbatus keeps an eye on him though. Keeps him out of trouble" finished Potitus.

"Yes, I know Aulus Barbatus" Marcus grinned. "Fine soldier" he added. Barbatus had served with his brother Lucius in a number of campaigns and Marcus had met him on several occasions, his intelligent conversation and calm manner quickly winning him friends with many of his colleagues.

As they walked back towards their tent Marcus fumbled with the orders he had received. He had glanced at them quickly when he had received them and had nodded with a resigned frown at the orders, knowing before he opened the tablet that he would be guarding the rear and the baggage – he and Virginius seemed to be tarred with the same brush.

"Same orders?" Potitus asked.

"Same" he replied as a movement to his right caught his attention and he came to a stop looking away at a group of horses being led towards the command tent. With a quizzical look both men turned and walked back towards the horses, their frowns expressing their lack of understanding as the horses were those of Postumius himself. As the two men approached the central square of the marching camp Ambustus strode from the command tent, his face a picture of anger, his dark brows furrowed and jaw set into a firm grimace. Seeing Marcus, he stepped across quickly. "Keep your head down and say nothing" he whispered as he moved away to the horses, his hands flexing into tight balls as he walked.

Potitus and Marcus glanced to each other and stepped back, moving away towards the numerous guards who were now appearing from the tent and lining up to create a funnel from the entrance to the horses. Ambustus stomped away grumbling to himself as Marcus watched him shouting at a legionary who just happened to be standing watching the proceedings at the commander's tent, the man winced under the barrage of abuse and turned to run towards the horse enclosure with an impressive turn of speed as Ambustus gave him a string of orders. Potitus raised his eyebrows at Marcus at this strange turn of events. Marcus shrugged in reply, his frown clearly showing that he, too, didn't understand what was happening.

Postumius's white horse stood stock still, its breathing quiet as the legionary handling it stroked its thick neck whilst three other mounts kicked the ground and snorted, their handlers struggling to keep them still. Marcus nudged Potitus and the two men edged further away, the warning from Ambustus still ringing in his ears.

"Yes, yes" came the voice of Postumius before his frame appeared in the entrance to the tent, his shining armour resplendent in the late sun of the day. His back was turned to Marcus as he had stopped in the entrance. "You have the orders Sergius" he said in an exasperated voice. "Tell the men whatever you feel is needed, but I have urgent business in Rome. Just make sure you get that baggage back to the city" he said with a shake of his head.

"At this hour, commander?" called the voice of Sergius from inside the tent, his voice sounding almost as infuriated as Postumius's.

The commander simply shook his head and stepped from the tent, his right hand slipping the ornate sword from its scabbard with a clink to check it was well oiled as he walked across to the horses. He looked up and scanned the camp, a satisfied smile coming to his face as he saw a number of horses appear from the baggage wagons before he turned back to see Sergius coming from the tent with a handful of wax tablets.

"Sir" he said, "you haven't signed the orders."

Postumius laughed. "You are in charge man, you do it" he said as he stepped up to his horse and gripped the reins proffered by the legionary, who quickly knelt to the floor to become a mounting block. Two heavily built men stepped from the line of soldiers and mounted next to him as Postumius turned and looked away in the distance with a grim look on his face.

"Where is he?" he said quietly, almost to himself before turning back to Sergius.

"I want that baggage back in Rome in two days Sergius. Two days, do you understand?"

"Yes sir"

"No mistakes" he added with a measure of venom in his voice as he looked back up and instantly smiled "ah, here he is" he finished.

Marcus glanced to the left and watched as Ambustus and his Equites appeared, the men dishevelled but attempting to dress and pack gear as they came, clearly driven from their tents by the angry Ambustus whose face retained its dark countenance as he rode across and saluted to Postumius.

"Ready. Sir" he growled at Postumius who simply smiled back at him.

"Lead the way Ambustus" came the order as the Tribune and his entourage headed for the camp gate, men streaming from all sides to watch their commanding officer leave the camp, their questions coming in great shouts as Postumius rode on and ignored every one of them.

****

Sergius had immediately called the officers back to the command tent. A great deal of noise and confusion had descended upon them as they all stood waiting for an update from Sergius, who couldn't gain control of the men surrounding him, his voice flat and low in the hubbub. Virginius had sidled across to Marcus and shook his head at the melee of men standing in the tent awaiting the final officers' arrival before Sergius could start the briefing.

"The man's a fool" he said with a glance to Marcus.

Marcus smiled agreement but said nothing as he exchanged greetings with Barbatus, who formally introduced Virginius.

"I'm delighted to meet you Camillus" said Virginius. "It seems you and I share the same enemy" he said with a flick of his head towards Sergius. "Well that trained dog and his master anyway" he smiled.

Marcus nodded slowly and smiled a wry smile. "Indeed Virginius" he replied, "but all dogs have their day until a bigger dog comes and barks louder" he added with a wide grin as a small, but ironic, cheer went up. Marcus looked across to see the last Centurion had entered the tent, hastily saluting and apologising as he panted from his near quarter mile run to the tent, long streaks of sweat running down his temples.

A silence fell over the assembled men as Sergius stood behind the campaign desk, a series of tablets spread across its length in front of him. Marcus knew the military ran on efficiency, but this man seemed to make a meal of every order, with triple tablets created for everything from the sick list to the supply lists.

Sergius took a moment to survey the officers, his weak smile hiding the fear he evidently felt inside.

"The Tribune has been called to Rome on urgent business" he started, his eyes flicking nervously to a few of the men in the tent. "His instructions are clear, as presented earlier this evening" he continued as a low murmur went around the tent. "We will" he raised his voice as the murmur grew "camp here this evening and start at first light back to Rome. With the will of the gods we will be back in Rome within two days march. All current orders stand for the full march" he added as Virginius shook his head and let out a deep groan, at which Barbatus shook his head and stared at his friend.

"Why has the Tribune left so urgently?" came the voice of Bassano, his head held high as the men nearest to him visibly shifted, leaving the Centurion looking like a small island in a sea of anxious faces.

Sergius's chin dropped slightly as he peered at Bassano, his face dark and eyebrows drawn closely together. Bassano stared back at him malevolently as the camp prefect took a moment to collect his thoughts before answering.

"He has had an urgent message to which he must attend" he replied levelly, his tone suggesting that he would broker no other questions as he lifted a tablet from the table and was about to speak again before Bassano replied loudly.

"A Tribune should never abandon a camp mid-campaign" he said to a number of nods from the men around him. "Even Cincinnatus waited until the war was won to return to his farm" he added with alacrity as Sergius gritted his teeth and slapped the tablet on the table to gain silence from the gathered men.

"The business of Publius Postumius is of no concern of yours, Centurion" spat the camp prefect, his anger spilling over into his facial expression as his eyes bored into Bassano, who simply stared back at him un-moved.

A number of men gripped Bassano's arm and tried to pull him aside but the man's blood was up and he turned his face back to Sergius, his eyes flashing dangerously. "What is of concern to me, *Prefect*" he replied "is what the soldiers will think of their commander riding out of the camp without explaining to his officers why he is leaving. Do you understand how the army works and how men think?" he asked aggressively, as a few grunts of agreement came from the men closest to him in the tightly packed space. "He's taken the majority of the cavalry support with him and taken all the gold and silver from the baggage wagons" added Bassano to a sudden gasp from the enclosed group of men.

As Sergius' eyes betrayed that he did not know this fact, Bassano laughed at the sudden worried looks from the men around him, almost all of them turning to look at Sergius, whose jaw dropped at the news.

"So" continued Bassano, his voice rising to a new level of anger as he pointed at the various wax tablets on table "what do your precious reports tell you about that" he finished with a snarl as he crossed his arms and stared straight at the camp prefect, who seemed to wilt under his intense glare.

"I, I" started Sergius, his eyes darting from Bassano to the wax tablets and back again before a multitude of calls came from the assembled officers, many angry at the news that Postumius had taken much of the rich spoils from Bolae when he left the camp. Marcus looked to Potitus, both men sharing the alarm that the other officers faced. A push came from the men in front of Marcus and the table, full of wax tablets, was rocked as the men at the front had no choice but to stumble into the furniture and knock some of the wax tablets containing lists and orders to the floor, a well-placed foot smashing some of the wooden hinged tablets as they landed on the packed earth.

"Stop, stop" called Sergius, losing control of his men almost within a heartbeat as Bassano stood smiling at the sudden change in circumstances. The noise grew as Bassano was pushed from behind and turned to raise his vine cane at another officer, a patrician named Tullus, who shouted angrily at him. Marcus saw the sudden movement of several of Bassano's supporters as they spread themselves into the tent to support their friend, the mood suddenly becoming very dark.

Marcus took a deep breath, something inside him realising that someone had to gain control of this mess before it became too uncontrollable to manage. He pushed forwards and took a stance in front of Sergius, whose eyes showed that he had lost control of the officers, fear staring back at Marcus, who simply turned and called in his best parade ground voice.

"Officers of Rome. Officers of Rome" he called, the nearest men turning to him as he shouted, others gripping the collars of their fellow leaders and still snarling hatred at each other.

"You" called Marcus "Centurion Bassano" he said, his voice level, but loud. "Here" he commanded, pointing to his side and glaring at the man he had known and respected for many years, hoping that the respect would be returned now. "Centurion?" he asked in a quieter voice as the noise began to die down and all faces turned to him. Bassano's face went from anger to acceptance as he nodded and stepped across to Marcus, his jaw set firm as he moved but his eyes searching Marcus's as he did so.

"Officers of Rome" Marcus said again as silence descended within the tent and men shuffled, with a few pushes, to stand and look at him as he placed a calm hand on Bassano's shoulder. He waited until all the men had turned to him before he turned to Sergius and pointed to the small box behind him.

"Sir, may I ask that you light the candle so that we officers of Rome can discuss" he turned back to the group of soldiers "in a calm and orderly manner" he added more loudly "what you require of us, as your *oath sworn* men" he said with a look at Bassano. Marcus knew that the invocation to the gods and mention of the oath would stop the officers arguing for a moment as his words sank into their minds, but he stepped forwards and turned to the men closest to him as he heard Sergius open the box and search for the candle to Mars which was usually lit for all meetings of the camp officers.

"Fellow officers" he said, his eyes wide as he looked around at the faces of the men in the tent. "Are we base-born men who must fight with our fists, or are we officers of the greatest city the world has known?" he asked. "The Centurion asks a question, as is his right" he nodded to Bassano who simply stood and stared back into the crowd of men. "That question cannot be answered here as the Tribune has been called away" he held up his hands at a few men who raised their voices demanding to know why Postumius had left and why he had taken all the rich loot from the baggage carts. "Gentlemen" he said firmly, his grim face causing silence to fall once again into the tent. "The prefect is best placed to record the facts and to explain matters. If he cannot answer them then we recourse to the *process*. If we have any questions you may have them written down for review when we return to Rome. Every man here knows how the system works" he said flatly. "The lists here show what items are held within the spoils, and each tablet is written in triplicate" he added with a nod at the table indicating that whatever Postumius had taken was clearly shown in the lists maintained by Sergius. As he turned to look at the men one of the group looked shiftily at the broken tablet on the floor, his foot twitching as if he wished to push it away from him in case it incriminated him. Ignoring the red flush on the man's face Marcus continued.

"Discipline, gentlemen" he said as he looked into the faces in front of him, marking each eye movement as the men glanced to their friends. "It is our discipline as Romans that sets us apart from those we conquer. The men out there expect it from us, their leaders. Without discipline we become the barbarians we despise, gentlemen, and I, for one, will not lose my discipline, or my dignity. Rome expects us to lead its men to glory and to return its sons to their mothers. Rome is more important that one man or any number of spoils we take from our enemies and we have laws, gentlemen, laws which support all of us to achieve these things. Discipline, gentlemen, discipline for us, for our men" he raised his arm and pointed towards the tent entrance. "They need their officers to be unified now more than ever. The camp prefect has his orders and we must obey them. My friend Centurion Bassano has raised concerns, but we must remain disciplined as we seek answers, and we must follow the correct procedures. The men need discipline and we need it too."

He turned to Sergius, who was fumbling with a heavy wax tablet, the cord bindings frayed after many uses. He glanced at the candle and nodded to Sergius. "Sir. The candle is lit, what orders do you have for us?" he asked as Sergius seemed to stare through Marcus as his thoughts came rushing back into his mind.

Sergius coughed as Marcus placed a hand on Bassano's shoulder, his eyes catching those of his old friend who nodded slowly in reply as he placed a hand on Marcus's forearm. Both men then returned to the throng of officers. As one every eye turned to Sergius, who took a deep breath and let it out slowly to regain his composure before he looked up and spoke. "Marcus Furius Camillus is right. We must retain our discipline as officers of Rome. We have orders to camp here for the night and return to our home within two days." He looked to his right and bent to pick up a small box, taking out a four-leaf wax tablet, the new wood almost white in colour as he placed it in front of the candle. "I ask Mars war bringer to give us strength in our camp and to lead us safely to our homes." After a moment's silence he looked up at the officers. "I will remain here and collate questions should any officer have them" he said with a resigned frown as he touched the new tablet on the table in front of him with his index finger. As the men shuffled their feet he raised his voice, "dismissed" he almost shouted as the men moved towards the exit, some grumbling whilst others discussed the briefing with glances towards Marcus and Bassano.

*

*

*

*

Chapter 15

The day had dawned with a hazy hue of grey mist which had quickly cleared to reveal blue skies, a chill in the air quickly dissipating as the sun rose along the skyline. Scouts had been sent in all directions and the troops called from their slumber early. As the wagons were loaded with the wooden palisades and the gates from the camp the first sections of the legion had set off on their march, the silence in the marching ranks showing their mood as much as the early hour of the day.

"They're not happy" Mella said as he chewed on a thin biscuit, spitting a particularly hard bit off the end of his tongue as he stood next to Marcus watching the dust rise ahead of them. Marcus took a deep breath and sighed. The night had been one envoy of men asking questions after another. There seemed to be near panic amongst the men that Postumius had left the camp, with many irrational explanations becoming the gossip of the hour as the night wore on. Marcus and Potitus had been called to see Sergius on three separate occasions and each time the camp prefect seemed ineffective in his ability to quash any rumours. Marcus had suggested tripling the guard to keep the men busy, but Sergius dismissed this idea claiming it would slow down the march the next day. In the end, he'd simply allowed the gossip to hang in the air and the mood of the men to become more sombre.

"I don't like it either, Mella" Marcus replied as he stared at the back of the last man leaving the space where the camp gate had stood only an hour previously. "But until we get to Rome there is nothing we can do, so I suggest we get the wagons loaded and get moving" he said with no conviction in his voice.

Mella looked at the biscuit and scratched at a thick lump with a finger nail "the sooner we get back home the better."

The two men turned to see Narcius and a legionary named Falcius appear through the thin layer of trees which covered the ford by the river. With a raised hand, suggesting that all tasks had been completed, Narcius called to the men of Marcus's Eagles and the newly detailed two hundred men picked up their marching gear and hefted it across their shoulders. Marcus and Mella took a moment to mount their horses and walked them to the edge of the road, waving to Narcius to get the rear column into motion. With a call from the first spear the wagons were kicked into movement and the men fell into a steady trudge along the slow rise of the dusty road. Narcius trotted across to Marcus and saluted, looking up at his officer with a brown-faced grin.

"There are still about a hundred horsemen just beyond the river, sir" he said, his eyes alert as he spoke.

Marcus turned his head towards the tree line, the green and brown leaves still in the morning sun. He scanned the horizon to the left and right and his brow furrowed. "I wonder what they want? They can't attack us and it seems odd to trail us this far from Bolae" he said as he continued to look to their rear.

"The scouts will keep an eye on them" Mella added. "Maybe you should set a few extra just in case?" he asked, a genuine look of concern on his face.

Marcus glanced at Mella and pulled his lips tight. "You may be right" he said as he waved at a fly that buzzed in his ear. "Narcius, double the scouts and keep me informed every hour on the situation with our followers" he said with a smile as he nudged his horse forwards into a walk followed by Mella who twisted on his horse to look back over his shoulder as they moved away from the river.

****

"More bodies?" questioned the white clad Senator, his bored face sweating under the constant heat. He sighed deeply as the junior magistrate picked up the list from the table, scanning the contents quickly.

"Maybe Marcus Manlius and the plebeians were correct, sir" he replied, his deep brown eyes looking at his elder statesman with a sympathetic look. "It seems that the areas closer to the river are infected much more than the upper hills" he said as he tapped the list with a stylus, the thin bone instrument well-worn from many years of usage. "The Tiber has receded recently due to lack of rain and from what the report suggests" he picked up another wax tablet and opened the cover "there are more rats in the grain stores than usual at this time of year." As he finished a pained expression came to his face as he looked up at the senior magistrate.

"Commoners though?" the Senator questioned with a measure of distaste in his voice.

Lars Herminius Aquilinus was the grandson of a former Consul and had been working as a junior magistrate for almost a year. He had quickly learned that having no opinion, at least not openly, was the way to grow your status within the Senatorial group and its many hangers-on. He had spent some months working his way into the Senators inner circle and had finally been given the job of personal secretary to Cicurinus, a title which he knew would afford him a good start to his political career. He also knew that it would gain him the power to elicit a few extra bribes and a better income. He knew, though, that he must be careful to appear to be an eager fool or else the Senator would have him removed quicker than a pox-ridden whore.

"It would appear, Senator, that there are no cases reported in anything other than the lowest classes of citizen" he looked at the list "or indeed *non-citizens*" he added with a shake of his head.

Cicurinus huffed at these words, bringing a wry smile to Lars face as he looked up from the list with a questioning movement of his head. "Is there anything you would like done with regard to this?" he asked the older man, who wiped his sweaty brow. Cicurinus frowned and sighed again, his eyes looking tired.

"Seems minor. Continue the reports and send a message to Antoninius at the docks to give me a more detailed report on the grain and the rats situation, that could be a concern" he said as he stood from his chair, a grimace coming to his face as Lars stepped up beside him and helped him to stand.

"Thank you, Lars" said the Senator as he patted his left thigh "this old wound is getting worse. It won't be long until I'm using a stick, just like my father used to" he almost laughed as he spoke, Lars smiling warmly as he picked up the tablet.

"If you'd make the impression here, sir, I will get the orders sent straight away."

****

The sun beat down furiously on the men as they heaved at the wagon, the thick wooden wheel smashed in three places. The parched ground beside the road was strewn with equipment and brown cloth sacks of loot from Bolae, the men having removed objects to lighten the load.

"It's no good" said a thick-set legionary, his muscles tense as he strained to lift the back of the cart from a deep hole at the edge of the dusty road. "It's too heavy, we need more men" he added, kicking the wheel lightly as he shook his head. The wheel had dropped into a deep rut in the worn road and instantly snapped, causing the wagon to keel to one side, exacerbated by the sudden shift of the heavy load on top of the wagon which had also shifted across over the broken wheel. The men had lifted many of the sacks from the wagon, but they had quickly become exhausted due to the heat and weight of the heavy sacks.

"Titus" called another legionary as a smaller man stood from his seated position on the ground behind the cart, his youthful face alert and smiling as he responded to his name. "Run up to the front and tell them to stop, this thing's not going anywhere" he added as he turned to look at the broken wagon and then up at the last of the wagons in front of him as it moved steadily away from them. "Let's take a rest lads until the others get here" he said to the agreement of his three fellow legionaries, their sweat covered bodies testament to the efforts they had endured in trying to lift the wagon.

Titus, his young legs tight from months of marching, jogged along the track and caught up with the wagon in front of the one he was stationed with. As he passed he called out to the driver to slow down as the wagon behind had a problem, a wave from the man sat atop the bouncing seat showing he had understood the call. Within five minutes he had passed several of the rear wagons and each had received the same message. Ahead he saw the feathers of one of the officers, his helmet still sat on his head despite the general order for men to march without helmets due to the heat of the sun. Titus pulled up next to the officer who turned to him with a questioning gaze.

"Soldier?"

"Sir, I have to report that the last wagon has lost a wheel and is" he struggled for the word "stuck" he added eventually with a slight shrug as the officer grinned at him.

"Thank you legionary," he said "take a moment to get a drink and return to your unit" he added as he turned and called orders to a man sat on a horse ahead of him.

The call to halt was issued and Titus set off back to his unit in a slow jog. As he neared the last wagon before his broken one he noticed that a gap of some two hundred yards had opened between them, the men of his unit sat under the wagon to avoid the baking heat of the sun. As he got close to the wagon the men jumped up from their seated positions and Titus heard the drum of hoof beats as three horses passed him, reining in by the cart as they arrived. "I've sent eight men" said one of the riders, his young face slightly red from being in the sun, as he slipped from the horse and handed the reins to one of the other riders.

"Let's have a look" he said, walking around to the side of the wagon and peering at the wheel, kneeling low to see the shards of wood that had split. "Looks like the spindle has cracked" he said quietly as he ran his hand along the wheel, his eyes flicking around the underneath of the wagon. Standing he turned to the bare-chested burly soldier who had been attempting to lift the wagon earlier.

"Spurius, I doubt we will get this fixed today" he said looking around him at the sacks on the side of the road and the remaining items within the wagon. "Best to get those loaded on the other wagons I think."

"Sir" came the reply as Titus arrived at the scene, his breathing heavy from the run. A movement behind the officer caught his eye as a horse appeared on the road, the heat haze making it difficult to see clearly. Without thinking he raised an arm and pointed to the rider. "Horse" he said, his voice loud but not shouting as heads turned to him and then whipped around to stare back down the road. The low scrub bushes and thick piles of rocks on either side of the dusty road suddenly looked menacing as the men around the wagon were now acutely aware that they were some distance from the rear wagon of the column and the relative safety of the marching men.

"Is it a scout?" asked the young officer who had been looking at the wheel, his eyes peering into the haze.

"I'm not sure sir" said the burly legionary, quickly grabbing his kit and strapping a leather scabbard to his belt. Two other legionaries were picking their spears from the ground and coming to stand in the road with anxious faces as the rider picked up speed and galloped at them, his hand waving though the Romans were unsure if it was a placating gesture or a call to charge. Potitus, his fear growing in his stomach, grabbed his reins and pulled his sword from his scabbard as he mounted, his eyes straining at the approaching rider who had increased his pace.

"Only one of him" said a voice to his left as Potitus pulled his skittish horse into a standing position and relaxed slightly, his hand gripping his sword tightly. "You men get your weapons, we'll see who it is and what he wants."

Potitus nodded to the two riders with him and they trotted off towards the approaching man. As they closed the distance the man became recognisable as a Roman scout, the light colours of his tunic marking him out as a member of their force. The urgent look on his face caused Potitus to look beyond him in case he was being chased, but he could see no sign of an enemy beyond the lone horseman.

As the scout dragged his horse to a stop, a thick dust cloud erupting from the floor as the white-laced sweat of the beast dripped from its neck, he half saluted as he gasped for breath, his eyes almost frantic as he searched the three riders in front of him.

"A force of" he panted "a hundred horses coming this way, fast!" he exclaimed as he snatched a glance back over his shoulder. Potitus peered back behind the rider as he started to turn his horse, its nostrils flaring as it read its riders sudden urgency. "Quick" he called "back to the wagons." Not needing a second order the men turned and kicked their mounts into a mad gallop, Potitus calling to Spurius and his men to run.

****

"Are you sure this is correct Aquilinus?"

"Indeed" replied Lars as he looked around the grain store, walking away behind the owner so that the man wouldn't be able to look him in the eye. Antoninius glanced at the order from Cicurinus and frowned, his thick eyebrows meeting in the middle as he cast his mind back over the last conversation he had held with the Senator. Something wasn't right with this order, but he knew that Cicurinus wasn't a man to be kept waiting and that the patricians changed their minds as quick as the weather. He shook his head slowly and wiped away a bead of sweat that was running down his cheek.

"Right then" he said with a deep breath. "What do you need for your report?" he asked cautiously, looking at the back of the junior magistrate who had brought the order for him to personally review the grain merchant's ledgers and stores. After a moment Lars turned, his face smiling at Antoninius.

"What would you suggest?" he asked as he held out a hand for the order to be handed back to him, his eyes flicking between Antoninius's and the tablet held in his hand. Antoninius had seen these upstart patricians come and go and knew a rat when he saw one. He pursed his lips as he narrowed his eyes, his mind working through offers and suggestions. He knew this man's family name had been high a generation or two ago, and that he was ambitious, but he wasn't sure where to place his gambit.

"The last magistrate got three sacks a month plus first go at the new slave boys" he sneered, unsure if this man's tastes were that way inclined.

Lars remained with his hand out, his face impassive as he simply stood and looked directly into the eyes of the grain merchant. The merchant shifted uneasily, had he made a mistake or did the fellow want more? He gulped as his eyes flicked upwards, a movement that Lars knew meant the man was thinking through options. He had spent years learning the movements of the eyes and what they pertained to and in an instant, he knew he had his man. He let his head move slightly to the side as he raised his hand to request the return of the order, a move which caused Antoninius to sweat again, a long drip running down his temple and onto his cheek.

"Three and the slave girls?" he asked, his eyes narrowing again as he peered at Lars.

Lars dropped his arm slowly, seeing the corners of Antoninius's mouth twitch as he suppressed a smile as quickly as it started to come to his face. Turning towards the doorway he shrugged and waved a hand "Four, you can have the slaves" he said as he looked back at the face of the merchant, his eyes narrow but his teeth showing through his grinning mouth.

"Deal, and this?" he asked with a wave of the order from the Senator.

"I will complete my report to say that you are beyond reproach, but the increased problem with mice and rats has lost, what, twenty sacks of grain?" he asked with his expression neutral but a curl at his lips showing that the merchant would see this as a chance to profit immediately from their arrangement. The man's grin split his face as he handed the tablet back to the junior magistrate and replied, "I will have the evidence of the infestation in my office for you to take back to the Senator after we have had lunch" he said slapping Lars on the shoulder, at which the younger man winced but smiled.

As the men walked back across to the open doorway Gatto slid from his hiding place, the smell of rotten fish almost making him gag as he slipped over the wall to the back of his cousin's garum factory, a new venture which had seemed expensive but was providing a lucrative income for the family. Gatto carefully avoided the barrels of fish entrails which would be sold to the fishermen later that day, a good secondary income from the business. As he dipped under a long line of air dried fish he considered his options, Javenoli or Manlius, who would pay him best for this information? Having a junior magistrate in your pocket could be good for both men and he looked to the skies and thanked Fortuna for putting him near the entrance to the grain store when he saw the young Aquilinus enter.

****

As Potitus reached the broken wagon he twisted to look behind at the road, no sign of riders was yet visible, so he slowed slightly and glanced around at the retreating Romans as they ran for the back of the column, calling a warning to the men there as they did. A thought flashed through Potitus' mind as he dug his heels into his horse's sides and shouted for the animal to pick up its pace.

Sliding from the horse he called to Narcius, who was lining up two rows of men across the road, their spears and shields creating an effective barrier, "Narcius, bring me ten of the Scorpions" at which the primus pilus had grinned wickedly and sent a number of the men rushing away into the wagons beyond them.

Marcus appeared with Mella as Potitus ran back to the line of soldiers and stared into the distance at the lonely wagon, its contents spilled out onto the road where the soldiers had left them.

"What is it?" asked Marcus as he dropped to the ground and ran alongside his friend.

"Raiding party I reckon" came the reply as Potitus was kicking stones off the road and looking up and down, his head bobbing like a chicken as he strutted along kicking the ground. "That bunch that have trailed us for a few days, looking for easy pickings I guess."

"What are you doing" Marcus asked, his voice quiet as he glanced at the men, also looking strangely at their officer, who seemed intent on kicking stones out of the road behind them.

"Clearing the ground Camillus" he looked up with a wicked grin "for the Scorpions" he added as Marcus took seconds to comprehend his words. He glanced back along the road at which a handful of riders had appeared and reined in beyond the last wagon and clenched his teeth, a sudden rush of excitement coming to him.

"You think they will attack the wagon?"

"I would" replied Potitus, still kicking stones. "Look at it, a wagon of spoils left unattended, the men two hundred yards away and no-one left to defend the loot. What would you do if you were a raider Camillus?" he asked as the first legionary appeared, his breath rasping as he ran with the wooden body of the machine clutched tightly to his chest.

Marcus looked up at the riders, who were discussing whether they would make the wagons before the soldiers could run back to it. With a whoop, the lead bandit dashed forwards, his horse's ears drawn back and its nostrils flaring as he charged forwards.

"Will we have time?" asked Marcus as another two Scorpions arrived, Narcius quickly setting them up and calling forward the men he had trained in their use.

"I hope so" Potitus said as he stood and clutched one of the bundles of bolts which had just arrived; five bolts wrapped in a blanket and tied with a thick cord in two places. Pulling his dagger from his belt he sliced the cords and glanced back along the road. The riders were now almost at the wagons, the faces of the men clearly visible as they peered at the Romans, a mad look of lust on their faces.

Marcus looked at the strained face of one of the men as he twisted the locking mechanism on the Scorpion, hearing another grunt as he did the same to his machine. He grinned, this would be interesting.

"Quickly" he found himself saying before he chided himself for the order, it was down to these men now, and they knew they needed speed. He placed himself behind the first bolt thrower, the mechanism being wound and the sighting line being drawn. With a clunk, the first bolt snapped into the firing mechanism and Potitus fussed over the angle for a second, the legionary furrowing his brow as Potitus twitched the angle and looked to Marcus. "We need a brass plate here with lines for the angles" he said, almost to himself as he tapped the housing of the mechanism before he stepped across to the second Scorpion and went through the same motions.

At the wagon, the first raiders stooped from their horses, their mad eyes glinting as they grabbed at the sacks and attempted to haul them up onto their horses, one man slipping and falling from his horse as the weight of the sack was too much for his precarious position as he leant over too far from his tall mount, a burst of laughter coming from his companions as he stood and yanked at his snorting horses reins.

As he fumbled with the sack he glanced over his shoulder at a loud thumping sound, which to his ears sounded like somebody throwing a large sack of flour to the floor. In his peripheral vision, he saw a black blur, reminding him of a bee or a fly which was flying too close to his eyes, but he twisted to grip his horse, such minor concerns didn't worry him today. He knew that this sack of loot held enough for him to sell at the market and make him a good profit. As he grinned and considered what a good idea it was to join this raiding party he heard another thump from close behind him and turned to see Arxitus taken from his horse by a thick arrow which split his body as it drove straight through his chest and dragged the man, screaming momentarily, onto the floor, the scream dying before his dead body bounced in the dust. As his eyes widened he felt a great shove from behind as his horse whirled and screamed, its legs kicking madly as both he and his horse leapt in the air, joined together by a thick shaft of wood which sent a searing pain through his body.

The legionaries cheered as the second bolt thumped into the man trying to regain his mount, the wooden shaft bursting through the man's stomach and into the belly of the animal, a mad scream of the man-horse coming at the same time as the animal jumped and dashed in a frenzied circle before crashing to the ground, man and horse legs thrashing for seconds before they both came to a limp halt.

Thump. Thump.

Two more bolts were let fly as the raiders screamed and turned their horses, the look of fear etched into their eyes as they watched the thick arrows of death thrown towards them. A crowd of legionaries had rushed to the scene to see the bolts flying and Marcus, surprised, turned to call, half-heartedly "back to your positions men, they could be approaching from other sides" though he knew that the only real danger was facing their rear.

Potitus was calling the crews to load and fire, his mind ticking through the timings and mechanics of the action as the men worked efficiently to load and fire the machines. One bolt missed its target, skittering along the road, the iron tip scraping into the dirt as the wood bounced along to the groans of the firing crew, who were already re-loading. The majority of the raiders had turned tail and fled, those at the back of the attack had seen the devastation of the bolts and turned to flee instantly, but those near the front were almost in two minds whether to try and grab some of the sacks or to turn and race away.

"There" called a voice as Marcus saw a man jump on his horse from behind the wagon, a sack under his arm as his horse circled as he tried to mount it.

"This coin to the Scorpion that gets him" called Potitus, picking a thick bronze coin from his purse and holding it aloft to a cheer from the men. Marcus looked at the faces of the soldiers, all grinning madly at the scene and saw Mella grabbing arms and shouting odds to the soldiers, many eagerly waving coins, trinkets or ingots at the man as Marcus shook his head at his actions.

Thump.

The man bit his lip as he leapt onto the horse, the sack pulling his arm and swinging into the rump of the animal with a metal clanging sound at which he smiled, his thoughts suddenly going to what was in the sack and its potential value. The taste of blood in his mouth made him curse loudly as he watched the rest of the raiders scurrying from the hail of iron bolts, his heart pounding with a sense of fear he had never felt before.

Thump.

The first bolt smashed into the wagon, blasting the wood into shards as his horse reared at the sudden explosion by its side.

Thump.

The second whistled over his head, his eyes watching it as he kicked furiously into his horse's sides, his free hand dragging the reins as he struggled to lift the sack as the animal stomped back onto four legs and kicked into a gallop, it's mad eyes staring accusingly at its rider.

Thump.

He felt the horse gain its feet and kick into its stride, a sense of relief coming to him as he gripped the sack more tightly and set his jaw in a grin, he was free, there was no way they could throw an arrow this far, he thought.

Then with a sudden crash his horse went from under him, the bolt slicing into its hind quarters as the beast twisted and screamed in pain. The rider's leg was pushed forward as the bolt passed straight through the horse and into his calf, ripping the lower part of his foot away as he felt himself fall, pain scorching through his body. He heard a great cheer from the Romans and then his head hit the road and everything went black.

*

*

*

*

Chapter 16

Publius Postumius felt angry. He looked at the three Senators, their faces expressionless as they sat in their gilded chairs watching him.

"The priests have agreed, and my case is clear" he added, his words firm as he stared from man to man. The room, with its high ceiling, was stiflingly hot as the wooden shutters to the windows had been closed for this legal meeting. Postumius sat back in his chair and placed his arms on his thighs as he sat tall and took the stoic pose his Greek tutor had taught him all those years ago.

"The soldiers refused to obey their orders, they broke their oaths and as such they lose all claim to the rewards of the campaign" he said calmly "as I stated in my report" he finished. A mumble came from the Senators around the room, many dragged from their baths for this extraordinary meeting of the council.

The room was filled with as many of the Senators as had been able to attend, with three appointed as the senior judges to preside over the case Postumius had brought. As the three men looked to each other Postumius glanced at the man he hated most in all of Rome, Gaius Javenoli, his fat face watching him like a hawk as the three Senators looked again at the words from the priests. Postumius knew that all legal matters had to be ratified by the priests of Rome, and he also knew that the Pontifex Maximus could over-ride any decision that the priests made and that at present the man was outside the city visiting his sick mother in her villa on the coast in Campania. Timing had been everything and he had rushed to the city as soon as his spies had confirmed that the Pontifex Maximus was out of the city and unable to influence the proceedings.

He smiled to himself as the three men continued to discuss the situation in hushed tones, their animated faces and gestures showing that the money he had used to bribe both the priests and one of the judging Senators had been well spent. With any luck, this loot from Bolae and the retainer he had secured from the Capenates for some of the land deeds around Bolae would clear the enormous debts he had built up over the last two years since Javenoli had stopped his patronage. He glanced again to Javenoli as the man leant and whispered to the younger man next to him. Postumius wondered what the old fool was saying, but his mind was brought back to the three Senators as they seemed to have come to a decision, a nod from each head and deep sigh from the paid Senator suddenly causing his heart to jump in his chest as he shifted on his seat and frowned, trying not to look concerned.

The older Senator stood, his face blank as he turned to the audience of old grey-haired men who sat around the room awaiting the chance to review or influence the decision. Adjusting his toga across his arm the man looked directly at Postumius, taking a small drink of watered wine before speaking.

"Your report details that Roman soldiers drew their swords against their commander" he started, a stern look coming to his face as a murmur went around the room. "It states that the men of your Legion surrounded your campaign tent and demanded your prisoners be released, aided by" he glanced at the report "Aulus Manlius." Shaking his head, the old Senator continued. "Furthermore, despite your requests for the men to return to their units they refused and remained" he looked at the report again *"against their own Centurions' wishes"* he read as he looked up at Postumius with wide eyes. Postumius nodded, his face downcast as if he had been greatly offended by such an act from the soldiers. "Such a thing has never happened before Tribune" he said, his face glum as his eyes looked up and around the room of Senators, all ex-soldiers themselves.

"Yet" continued the Senator "you held your nerve against this angry mob and agreed to a trial of the prisoners, presided over by the senior camp officers and Marcus Furius Camillus, who was appointed by the men" he added with a confused look on his face, a number of voices rising in the seats around at the room.

"You've all read the final outcome" he said to the room at large as he turned to look directly at Postumius, his Tribune's armour polished to its brilliant best.

"The priests have completed the auguries and agree that the situation is dire, Tribune."

Postumius' eyes flicked to his paid Senator who sat coolly listening to his colleague, his attention fixed on the man standing beside him. Postumius fumed, a sudden thought that he had been duped crossing his mind as he licked his lips as the standing Senator continued. "Dire" he announced to the room with a genuine look of concern on his face. "We cannot allow the soldiers of Rome to ignore their commanders, it would cause chaos" he added as he licked his lips again and took a nervous drink from his silver goblet. As he drank he glanced around the room with wide eyes and a shake of his head. "Gentlemen, we live in troubled times. Clearly our Tribune has acted within his rights and followed the codes and laws of the army. The troops had to die as they were culpable for the death of the prisoners." He looked at Postumius as if he was going to add something else, but a flick of his eyes to Postumius's paid Senator suggested that he had been over-ruled in his desire to speak out with regard to Aulus Manlius's whipping. Postumius smiled to himself as he saw the Senators eyes glance back at the report, his fingers fidgeting on the wooden frame as he regained his thoughts. "Yes, the law is clear" he stated as he looked around the room. "Before we proceed, is there any challenge to this part of the process?"

After a moments silence in which Postumius held his face high and sat with bated breath waiting for any challenge, the Senator leant forward and pressed a seal into the wax on the tablet in front of him. "Then this part is clear, the records will show that the deaths were in accordance with the law. Furthermore" he glanced to the Senator sat on his left and then to Postumius, a small sigh suggesting he suspected foul play but could not confirm it. "Furthermore" he repeated "it will be recorded that Publius Postumius, Tribune of the Legions of Rome showed leniency to the soldiers under his command by allowing lots to be drawn for the equivalent deaths to the loss of prisoners." He took a deep breath and passed the tablet to his left, where the Senator looked at the writing and nodded, handing it back to the speaker, who passed it across to the other Senator, who also read and returned the tablet with a nod. As this happened a small number of whispered conversations started in the room, at which the speaker stood taller and raised his chin as he awaited silence.

"The second matter is slightly more complex" the Senator said with a frown, his brown eyes alert as he peered at the men around the room. "It is stated that the soldiers of Rome took matters into their own hands and *against their own Centurions' wishes* they demanded that the men guilty of the crime were not punished. This is highly irregular, gentlemen, and calls for more discussion." At this Postumius stood, the usual movement that allowed the speaker to give him the floor. The Senator turned his head towards the Tribune in surprise as he was about to speak again and held up a finger to Postumius. "If I may finish Tribune?" he said, with a small curl at his lips as Postumius nodded but remained standing. "The position of the council" at which he waved a hand slowly across to indicate the three senators sat on the podium "is that the men did indeed give up their right to any spoils of the campaign, as they clearly" at this a great noise erupted in the room, Postumius smiling as he returned to his seat.

"Gentlemen, gentlemen" the Senator called, his voice hoarse as he raised it above the noise. He slapped the table with his hand, the loud noise stopping some of the calls, but not all of them. "Gentlemen" he shouted again, his eyes roving the room as numerous Senators stood waving clenched fists at Postumius as their clients were clearly going to lose out due to this ruling. "You know the process, you will have time to put forward your comments" he added with a stern look as he shook his head in exasperation. "Where was I?" he mumbled as he ran a finger along the edge of the second tablet he had produced from the pile on the table.

"The soldiers gave up their rights to the spoils of war because they, by law, took arms against their commanding officers and despite many attempts to return them to their posts they refused. At this point the law states that they were, in effect, no longer soldiers of Rome and lost all rights to any spoils from the campaign." The Senator raised his finger to show he had not finished as he turned the wooden tablet to read from another underneath it. "Tribune

Postumius" he said loudly as a few voices had started to speak despite his motion for silence "has provided a list of the officers, Centurions and men who responded to his call for a return to duties" he finished as a number of men stood, some waving arms and others simply staring at the Senator with indignant looks on their faces.

****

Manlius sat. His arms ached from the sword practice he had completed no more than ten minutes previously, his body still covered in a glistening sheen of sweat. He looked up at the messenger, who cowered for a moment under the look of rage that came to the patrician's face as he read the message he had been handed. He looked to the message and then to the messenger and back to the message in his hands.

"I" he mumbled, his jaw dropping as his eyes widened "is this true? Whipped?" he said his voice rising. He stood, which made the messenger take a small step back with a look of fear in his eyes. "Tell me." Manlius spoke forcefully as the small man, his clothes still dusty from the ride, took another step backwards and then took a deep breath. Aulus Manlius had written the note to his brother from his sick bed where he was recuperating from his ordeal at the hands of Postumius. He'd then passed the note to the messenger and told him to ride directly to his brother's house and give him the message but to temper the delivery so that his brother did not do anything stupid.

The messenger took another deep breath as Manlius scrutinised him, returning to his seat as he scanned the message again. "Sir" he began "your brother asks that you await his return before you act on this message and he has requested that until his arrival you keep the details to yourself."

Manlius looked at the messenger and controlled his urge to lash out at the man. He knew that he must respect his brother's wishes, but he also knew that Publius Postumius would be getting a visit from him sometime soon. Nobody whipped a member of his family and got away with it. His teeth ground as he mulled through a series of options in his mind, the messenger standing uncomfortably in the ensuing silence.

"Fine" he stated suddenly as he stood and strode away towards the inner rooms of his house. "You can go. Tell my brother I look forward to speaking to him" he shouted back over his shoulder as he left.

****

"It makes no sense for the men of the Legion to simply put down their arms in mid-campaign, especially when they have already secured a great victory and are only a day or two from their homes" the thin Senator said, his bald head glistening in the heat of the confined room. "I agree with the suggestion that Gaius Javenoli has made, that we await the return of the officers and question all the senior men" he added with a movement of his toga-covered arm towards the figure sat a few places along from his position, who nodded at the gesture.

"Such an act" replied the other standing figure as he swept a look towards the seated Tribune "would put in question the authority of the rank of Tribune and make it clear to any trumped-up career soldier that he may question the imperium of his commanding officer." There was a loud murmur of agreement from a section of the attending Senators. "This would lead to the degeneration of the rank, gentlemen, and I am sure we do not want that" he stated as he turned to a chorus of agreement from his left.

"Never" replied the thin Senator with a shake of his head.

"It is true" came the defiant response as a series of coughs rang out around the room, one Senator visibly in distress as he caught his breath and continued to hack out a barking cough as many of the men around him looked to him with concern. As he waved a dismissive arm to inform them that he was fine he started to cough again.

"Yes, it is true" continued the white clad standing figure. "Without the imperium of the Tribune as untouchable we will lose control of the men of Rome. Without the strength of leadership, the armies will collapse and we will find ourselves open to attacks from all our enemies." As he finished speaking he looked to Postumius with a smile. Postumius glanced around the faces in the room quickly, knowing instantly that the argument was won as he saw the majority of heads nodding, many with deep frowns on their faces. These men knew what it was to stand in front of thousands of soldiers and they knew that imperium, the total power of the most senior officer, was one of the reasons that men fought for Rome. They also knew that without the fear invoked by this total power the army could crumble.

The coughing man rose from his seat, still gasping for breath and waved wildly at the crowd around him as he stepped towards the door using his forearm to cover his mouth, a slave running forward and catching his other arm as he stumbled. Postumius twitched as the man coughed and another Senator away at the back of the room repeated the noise, the deep throaty cough echoing in the high-ceilinged room.

The Senior Senator sat on the podium stood and raised both arms as a hush came across the room, most eyes watching the man being led from the chamber as he continued to cough with unmistakable red spots of blood appearing on his forearm as he left.

"Gentlemen" he said as all eyes returned to him. "As lead Senator in this review I, Papirius Mugillanus will sum up the arguments and decision." He looked to his fellow Senators who nodded in agreement as silence fell around the room. Postumius took a slow breath, training his eyes on the older man, an ex- Military Tribune with Consular powers who had been elected when Gaius Curtius had been found guilty of not following the correct procedures for the reading of auguries some years before.

"The case has been well argued by both sides. The argument against centres on suggestions that we need to request information from the other officers to be clear on the motivations from the soldiers. However, we have signed statements from the camp prefect and two officers which confirm the statement made by the Tribune." He pursed his lips as he placed a hand on a tablet on the table with a glance to Postumius. "There is no question that the Tribune acted within his powers and that he acted with leniency in calling a council with representatives from the soldiers themselves" he added with a firm nod of his head. "The question of apportion of goods from Bolae has been discussed and the augury completed." At this he took a moment to look up at the shuttered windows and his shoulders seemed to tense before he spoke again. Another deep cough came from the back of the room, turning a few heads towards the noise.

"The augury finds in the favour of the Tribune. The priests have concurred that the spoils should go half to the treasury and half to those men identified in the Tribunes report." At this a number of calls and jeers came from the assembled men, at which Mugillanus stopped speaking and looked angrily into the assembled men, his face flushing as he called "gentlemen, the time for disagreement has ended" and turned back to his notes.

"Therefore, with the will of the gods in agreement, we, the men of this council, accept the statement of Publius Postumius and will add to the report that he has acted in good service for Rome and its people." At this he looked up at Postumius and half-smiled before pressing the seal into the wax once more and turning and handing the tablet to the men sat beside him. Postumius stood and nodded to the three Senators as he turned to face the sitting men to his right. Before he could speak a great shuffling started and the majority of the men rose, a babble of noise rising into the room as they started to file towards the exit, many of the men fanning themselves due to the heat as they stood.

Postumius looked aghast at the men flooding from the room. He had prepared a long speech which praised his friends as well as denouncing the plebeian Centurions and those he saw as political enemies, but the noise and the sudden exit of many of the Senators put away any ideas of his being able to say his piece. As he bit his lip in frustration he turned to see the furious face of Gaius Javenoli staring spitefully at him. With a tip of his head and a broad smile Postumius turned and walked towards the exit, avoiding another man who was bent double, red spots of blood appearing around his lips as his chest heaved into a long and noisy coughing fit.

*

*

*

*

Chapter 17

Lucius Decius had spent years climbing to the top of the plebeian ranks, his position as Plebeian Tribune being the culmination of those years of hard work. He eyed the figure standing in front of him with trepidation, his pox-scarred face and the smell of urine coming from the man instantly marking him out as one of the capite censi, Rome's lowest class of worker.

"It's almost killed all of the slaves in the factory" the man repeated indignantly, almost as if Decius hadn't heard him. "What are you going to do about it?" he asked, his voice angry but a measure of fear showing in his eyes. Decius glanced to Calvus, who was standing on his right. Calvus had brought the man to his morning meeting amidst a series of others who had the same complaint. Each man had lost friends, slaves or members of their families to some kind of illness, a pestilence which they said started with a deep cough and led to a fever and death within two days. Calvus stood impassively at Decius's side and scowled. For days, he had badgered the Tribune with regard to the illness, which had grown out of all proportions within the last week, at last the Tribune seemed to be listening.

Decius clapped a hand on the shoulder of the man, a light dust rising from the thick woollen tunic as he did so. "Leave it with me" he said. "We will see if there is anyone who can send you some slaves while you purchase others for your tannery" he added as the man shook his head and sighed. Before the man could ask for compensation, as he had done three times in the past three minutes, Decius turned to Calvus and said, loudly "Calvus we need to take these concerns to the Senate immediately."

Calvus smiled and motioned for the tannery owner to leave as a slave ushered him out, his mumbling complaints about compensation still ringing around the room. "The patricians won't like this" he said to Decius as he watched the man leave.

"Hmm" came the non-committal response, one that Calvus was used to.

"Well, Marcus Manlius was right when he said, 'not on my doorstep.' He understands the workings of the patrician mind better than we do. You pay him a visit Lucius and I will arrange a meeting of the plebeian council and the Senatorial council. Manlius may have his faults but he does seem to be swayed towards our cause" he added with a smile.

"I agree Calvus" replied Decius. "This pestilence wouldn't happen if Rome wasn't filled with more scum every day. Each time I look from my door I see more beggars bringing more filth into our streets and more death on the road from bandits." He shook his head. "If the council had listened to me and agreed to send men to Bolae as Rufus had said in his message we would be free of these patrician laws regarding our home. We would have control of our own destinies" he added with a glance around the room to check nobody was listening.

Calvus looked at his fellow plebeian, seeing the tight balls his fists made as the old anger welled up inside him. "We've discussed this over and over Lucius. We are making ground my friend. The patrician's stranglehold on Rome weakens every day, the people will prevail, but I say it again" he said as he came closer to the younger Tribune "Rome will be the greatest city in the known world and we will be part of it. Setting up a new colony will bring greater problems for all of us. We stay, we grow and we make Rome stronger by being the voice of the people." He stopped to look directly into his friends eyes. "The Delphian portent was good my friend, remember" he smiled as his friend nodded his head.

"Yes, I know, I know" replied Decius. "When the people fall and the greatest of Rome re-takes the city the people will rise" he said mechanically as he shook his head "whatever that means."

Calvus grinned. "I think it means more than you know my friend" he said, placing an arm around Decius. "Let me tell you a story I heard from an old soldier, a story about an eagle and a prophecy" he said as Decius cocked his head, a quizzical frown coming to his face.

*

*

*

*

Chapter 18

"Veii again" Marcus said as he shook his head with an exasperated sigh. "It seems that whatever plots there are all start with Veii. First the price on my head and now these raiders harrying our rear" he said as Potitus and he left the camp prefects briefing. Under questioning the one remaining survivor of the attack on the baggage wagons had told how the raiders were from the city of Veii and were a mix of Veienteine and Volsci warriors hoping to catch stragglers on the road back to Rome and capture some easy loot from the Roman force. To his credit Sergius had set new pickets and sent scouts further afield, each scouting party consisting of four men, 'safety in numbers' he had said. Sergius had also been impressed with the Scorpions and had asked for a demonstration, which Potitus had been only too happy to agree to as Marcus frowned at him.

"It seems that way" Potitus agreed as Rufus caught up with the two men.

"Camillus" he asked as he walked alongside "I know it has been said many times" he started as he looked away into the distance "but we must do something about Veii. Your brother has the standing to raise it in the Senate and to take our complaints to them. Giving harbour to bandits, allowing and even condoning attacks on our roads" he shook his head angrily. "Sir, surely you would agree that we must send a deputation to them?" he asked as he came to a standstill at the intersection of two lines of tents within the camp. Marcus looked at Rufus, his straggly hair losing its colour.

Marcus took a moment to answer as he considered the words. "I think you are right Centurion" he said with a grasp of the man's forearm. "Veii has caused us great concern over the past years. They say they uphold the treaty, but all this evidence points to them undermining us at every opportunity. I will speak to Lucius when I return to Rome tomorrow. In fact, I will write to him tonight Marcus" he said, using Rufus's first name, at which the man smiled.

"Then, Camillus, come and join the men and my officers tonight at our campaign feast. It would be good to have you complete a reading of the last chicken" he said with a wide grin. "I hear you have learned the art of the Etrusca Disciplina?" he asked as his face lit up into a bright smile.

"Ha" laughed Marcus as he turned to Potitus. "I wonder who has been gossiping about that" he said as Potitus shook his head innocently. "Yes, I will do. I will join you just before the moon rises above the hills" he said as the two groups went separate ways.

****

The campaign feast was a small, but rowdy, affair in which each officer gathered his men and they toasted their lost friends from the campaign, adding libations to their chosen gods and drinking until they fell asleep. In many cases the augurs gained some quick coins by completing readings of the entrails of the chickens or small goats, if there were any remaining after the long campaigning seasons. In this case the campaign had been short and food was in plentiful supply so the unfortunate animals were prepared for the rituals by the men in each unit.

Divination, or the reading of the future from various god-given symbols had been a feature of Roman life for centuries, with the formulaic processes being learned by the sons of patricians as they went into the priesthood. The Etrusca Disciplina was the code of conduct, or rules of process, which each priest must follow to understand and glean the information the gods gave to mortal men. Marcus had, indeed, studied one of the three elements, Libri Haruspicini, the theory and rules of divination from animal entrails, extensively, not just during his times as a Camillus in Rome, but also through long conversations and discussions with his Uncle, the Pontifex Maximus. He had learned the texts, drawn the symbols and even divined a few portents from animals over the past few years. Potitus had been impressed with his skill and how precise he had been with the small details of the process of divination. The Etruscans, and to a similar extent the Romans, believed that the will of the gods was paramount. The Romans also believed that if the gods had already decreed the future of mankind, written in the Sibylline books, then they must have a plan for every single man within that future. It also made sense for the gods to communicate their plans to men in complex rituals and signs and it was the job of the haruspex to look for the signs and attempt to interpret them through divination. In this way men could gain glory and honour their chosen gods.

The light had faded and the air turned chill as Marcus wrapped his woollen cloak around his shoulders, laughing as the soldiers of Rufus's century sang a bawdy song of Volscan women and Roman stallions, each line of the song growing more vulgar as the song progressed. Potitus had indulged in too much wine and was attempting to sing the chorus along with the men, but his late shouts simply caused more hilarity from amongst the men as they whooped at his drunken, mistimed, words.

Rufus tapped Marcus's foot and flicked his head in the direction of the camp gate. "I'll be glad to see those gates packed up for the last time this season" he said with a weary smile, his face lined with shadows from the glowing fire at their feet.

Marcus shrugged, his glance to the gates making him think of Livia and his bed at home for the first time in a few days. They had not been immediate lovers and he had taken some time to get to know the headstrong girl, but now they had a bond between them that he hoped would never break. A yearning came to him as he thought of her and he looked into the fire long and hard as he smiled.

"Time for the ceremony" Rufus suddenly said, breaking Marcus's thoughts as he noticed the singing had finished with a final late call from Potitus, at which a group of the men had thrown the wine from their wooden cups at him with more hoots of laughter. Potitus looked affronted for a few seconds before falling to his knees and bursting into laughter as three of them jumped on him and started to rub his hair with sand. Marcus shook his head at the stupidity of the scene. Potitus, a patrician of noble blood being man-handled by a number of the rough soldiers. Rufus laughed. "They won't hurt him, come on" he said as he took a sword from a pile leaning against a rock and rapped the hilt on one of the shields wrapped in a thin leather sheet which stood next to them, the leather designed to stop the wood from becoming damp and useless.

"Men" he called, stepping forward and kicking a soldier who was being a little too vigorous in his attempt to pour sand into Potitus's underwear. Potitus' eyes rolled in his head as Marcus waved to Mella and pointed to the figure of his friend as he simply laid back on the ground with his mouth open, and his glassy eyes staring into the sky. With a wave, he pointed at Potitus and flicked his thumb towards his tent and Mella nodded, a grin splitting his face as he nudged the man next to him to help him carry the prone body.

"Marcus Furius Camillus has offered to prepare and complete a reading for us here today as we close this campaign." A few cheers and much head nodding greeted this statement as Rufus walked to the nearest tent and returned with a chicken in a small wicker cage, the animal clucking noisily as it was lifted into the air and struggled to retain its feet on the thin wooden cage floor. Marcus had been to Rufus's cook and been given the chicken earlier in the day and had asked the cook to pluck the feathers from the breast of the bird as the ritual required. He lifted the cage and looked at the panicked face of the chicken, the bird almost accusing him as he looked into its eyes. Shaking the thought from his head he picked up the small bundle of instruments he had prepared earlier, the ceremonial knife with its fine bone handle shining in the firelight. He put on his white robe, the cloak warming him in the slight chill of the evening. The men around the fire had suddenly fallen silent, even the bawdier, more drunken of the men seemed suddenly sombre and sober.

The stone was laid down and Marcus lifted three small containers from his bag, laying them out on the floor next to the stone as he knelt in front of it and pulled the hood of his white cloak over his head. As he placed the items by the stone he spoke quietly "Nundina, purify this place and make it sacred as I look to interpret the will of the gods. Allow me the sight and understanding as the gods will it so that we, mere men, can achieve your glories." He heard the shuffling of the men as those behind him moved to the sides and front to gain a better view. Unstopping the first container he poured a small amount of the oil onto the stone, wiping it with a piece of white cotton and saying an invocation to the gods as he did so. The second container contained oil with fine cuts of herbs and grasses from around the camp that Marcus had picked himself earlier in his preparations with Mella following closely behind to ensure that everything was bundled exactly as he requested.

He raised the knife and placed it on the stone as he opened the cage for the chicken, picking it up by the legs and quickly, efficiently, laying its head on the stone as Rufus, just as Marcus had shown him in advance, put his hand over the chickens head and held it down. Instantly Marcus sliced the neck, the chicken's kicking legs continuing as the blood mingled with the oils. Within a second Marcus had whipped the knife across the bare chest of the bird, slicing through the breast bone and into the lower stomach expertly to remove the intestines intact. The removal of the feathers prior to the ceremony made this act quick and easy and Marcus was satisfied that the process was going to plan. He lifted the long trail of thin guts and placed them on the stone next to the bird and then quickly cut the heart and liver from the carcass, placing them onto a small silver dish he had to his side, they would be the offerings to the gods at the end of the ceremony when he had sliced them to interpret any messages they may hold.

Rufus took the empty carcass and placed it on the grass, pouring the remainder of the oil with the grasses over the bird as Marcus had instructed. As he heard a few comments from the men around the fire, Marcus placed the knife on the floor and picked up the entrails, his eyes searching for spots in the important areas he knew from his learning of the disciplina. His eyes grew wide as he turned the thicker intestines and ran a finger along a series of lumps, a frown coming to his face.

"What is it Camillus?" said a man from the crowd of soldiers as a general murmur of sound came from the gathered men.

Ignoring the question, Marcus laid the intestines along the stone and counted, using his thumb width as a measure. At seven he stopped and picked up the knife to slice through the thin guts. Using the sharp point, he picked at the thin opening and squinted into the gut lining, the blood and half-digested material thick along the inner surface. He nodded to himself as a few more sounds came from the soldiers. Placing the innards back on the stone he picked up the liver and held it to the firelight and spoke for the first time.

"The intestines are unclear" he said, adding "though I am only learning this trade they suggest three problems may lie ahead of us before the season is finished." A murmur went up from the men as they all stared at Marcus as he moved the liver in his fingers. "The three problems are not clear, but they are unmistakable. The liver will give more clues" he added as he placed the small liver on the stone and sliced it in three places, taking the first slice and pouring a drop of oil onto it from the first container.

"Another war" he said with a frown "or maybe just another skirmish, I cannot tell" he said as a few groans came from the crowd around him. "But victory" he added as he viewed the second slice of liver, placing it aside quickly as he contemplated the last. After a moment, in which the silence of the countryside grew above the occasional spit of the fire, Marcus placed the three slices of liver back on the silver dish and picked up the heart. There it was again, he thought, three ridges, three lines across the heart as he had seen in the liver and three lumps on the intestines. The dark patch on the liver had shown war, directly over the 'Mars point' of the liver.

The heart was very small and quite difficult to cut, but his sharp knife made easy work of the tough outer skin. He looked up and said, "the blood is clean in the heart, a good sign" at which a few sighs of relief came from the men, some of whom he could see were clutching lucky talismans or other objects to revert the evil eye that all soldiers tried to avoid. He strained his eyes in the semi-darkness as he scanned the chambers for spots or signs, but could see none. He placed the heart with the remains of the liver and leant the dish forwards over the fire, dropping the two parts of the bird into the flames and whispering an oath to the gods as he did so.

"My reading" he said, sitting back on his knees and looking at the expectant faces of the men "is this." He stood and then sat back on the campaign chair he had sat on earlier. Turning to Rufus he added "I must warn you that I am no expert at this" at which Rufus half laughed and some of the soldiers called out to him 'tell us Camillus' their tones nervous.

"I see three concerns, one of which involves a skirmish and one is a sickness. I don't understand what they are, and the will of the gods is hard to interpret without years of training. The third I understand fully. It means that whatever happens with the first two we will be victorious in the end. Rome will endure but it may be many years until we can conquer the enemy who is close at hand. Seven or more years" he added as he closed his eyes trying to understand the meanings he had read about in the rituals and codes he had learned.

"I wish I could add more, but that is all I see" he finished as Rufus and all of the men around the fire looked at him in silence.

*

*

*

*

Chapter 19

Postumius laid another libation at the foot of the statue in the Lararium, the small carving of the house gods looking down on him with a blank stare. His forehead lay against the cold stone of the floor as his whispered entreaties to the gods streamed from his mouth.

"Apollo, give him strength, heal his body and mend him" he intoned as he rocked backwards and forwards, light tears dripping onto the grey tiles. "Aesculapius, give your help" he added as he lifted his head and poured more of his best wine into the bowl in front of the statue, his eyes blurring as he bent back to place his head on the floor. "I offer the goat and the calf" he added, alluding to the sacrifice he had paid for that morning "in return for his safety. I ask this of you my gods and my ancestors" he said, his voice trembling.

Behind him he heard another grating cough and his head twitched as his heart lurched in his chest. He had returned to his house from the meeting with the Senators to find that his son had continued to deteriorate; the pestilence that seemed to have appeared suddenly in Rome had spread rapidly to the patrician streets. He had called for the best physicians and they had clawed all over the boy, his thirteen years of strength dripping out of his body as he coughed, sweated and bled the fever that had taken control of his body. It had been two days since the hearing and in those two days the city had become swamped with people coughing blood and dying in the streets. The return of the army had become secondary to the pestilence as the people of Rome hid in their houses for fear of contracting the disease, with many patricians leaving the city for their country houses in an attempt to avoid coming into contact with the sick and dying.

Postumius stopped his supplicant prayers as his son hacked again, the noise lasting longer than before. He rose from his position and shuffled to the doorway of his son's chamber, his hand gripping the doorway with white knuckles. Inside his son lay pale and ghostly on a cot, a thin woollen cover spread over his body as he jerked at each cough, his eyes bulging and red. The physician sat at his side and wiped his brow with a damp cloth, taking another blood spotted cloth from the boy's hand and placing it into a pouch which he would burn later. The physician had stated that he must sweat out the fever and eat no food until the coughing had stopped. Postumius, like most men, mistrusted these Greek physicians. What did they really know of the sickness that was eating away at his only son? He stared helplessly at the boy, his eyes pleading with his father as he drew a deep breath and lay back on the cushions under his chest and head.

"Father" his weak voice said. Postumius entered the room quickly, his nervous steps pattering on the hard floor, and knelt next to his son, taking the thin hand that was raised towards him. He grimaced at how weak the boys grip was, his thoughts turning angrily to the sacrifices and whether there was something more he could do to buy the favour of the gods or bargain for their help.

"Will I live?" the boy asked, his frail face pallid in the low light of the room "do the gods answer your prayers?"

Postumius looked deep into the eyes of his son. Two of his children had died in infancy, yet this boy had grown quickly and vigorously, his healthy appetite and boisterous fitness bringing great joy to his parents after the losses they had endured.

"Yes Megellus" he replied, "they listen." The boy's eyes seemed to know he was lying to him and Postumius couldn't hold his stare for more than a few seconds before he turned to the physician. "Have you seen any improvement?" he asked angrily.

"There is a glimmer in his eyes that was not there before" the man said in his thick Greek tones. "He is a strong boy and I believe that within a day this fever will pass. When that happens, he must eat" the man's voice spoke in staccato tones as his eyes flicked from father to son. "He will need meat and he will need fresh air" he said with authority.

Postumius stared silently at the man, his dark brown eyes confidently returning his gaze. He looked back to his son, who had also been looking at the physician. As he did so he saw a spark of hope deep in his eyes and watched as the boy's face began to slowly creep into a weak smile.

****

"We must do something" said the exasperated voice of Centurion Appius Tolero, his left eye covered with a roughly cut patch which barely hid the angry red scar that ran across the remnants of his eye socket. "There must be something we can do?" he asked of the men sat around the table, each of whom sat shaking their heads.

"It's typical of that son of a dog" spat Bassano, his teeth grinding. "Rufus, what can we do? You're the clever one amongst us. If I had my way I'd march up to that pompous prick and stick my sword through his guts" he added without moving his eyes from a spot on the table in front of him.

Rufus shook his head slowly. Since the return of the army, the city had been pre-occupied with clearing the dead from the streets as the plague took a hold on the common people. Each day another bout of coughing citizens was evicted from their homes by landlords who didn't want their other tenants catching the pestilence. The merciless eviction had seen many of the families of the soldiers from Bolae left to starve in the streets, their possessions stolen or simply left behind as they were beaten from their rooms. They roamed the streets until their bodies gave in to the coughing and shaking fits that wracked them, dying in the gutters of Rome where stray dogs chewed at their gnarled limbs. The stench of death was upon the City and the people locked their doors to it and avoided contact with anyone unless it was absolutely necessary. To make things worse the heat and humidity had given way to thunderous rain, the water splashing into the streets in sudden torrents before disappearing to return hours later. The heat of the previous month had left the ground hard and bare and the sudden heavy rain had seen great rivers running down the hills of Rome, filth and detritus cascading to the lower parts of the city and creating a greater stench than the dead bodies of the previous days. The people of Rome were hard-pressed to understand the heat, the pestilence and now the thunderous rain. Augers and mad witches read the signs, watched the patterns in the lightening and Rome was afraid. Gossip ran riot, the gods had abandoned them, the vestals had broken their vows and the sacrifices were not being closely observed.

Every day a new reason for the weather and the pestilence was roaming the streets making the populace nervous.

Rufus had returned from the campaign to find his smallest child had succumbed to the sickness, dead before he returned home. Bassano looked at his friend and noticed the hollow look in his face. He turned to Tolero and shook his head with a flick of his eyes towards Rufus. Tolero nodded as he slid from his chair and stretched his back, groaning as he reached high above his head.

"Well, they think it's legal to take away our spoils after we put or lives on the line? We'll see how legal it is when we turn up at the next Senate meeting and demand our money" he said as he glanced at Rufus and shook his head again. Placing a hand on his shoulder he nodded to Bassano and turned to leave the room.

"I'll get the lads together tomorrow and we'll stage the first protest in the forum just after mid-day when the market is busier. A bit of disruption will do the patricians good. Lucius Decimus will take our case to them, and he has sworn to veto every motion they want to pass for the next few days until this matter is resolved" he added as he disappeared into the corridor.

"Rufus" cajoled Bassano, nudging his friend gently. "I know the pain you are going through" he said, a grimace coming to his face. "I know my son was a soldier and not an innocent little lamb, but you must end your grieving and come back to your senses." He knew the words were harsh, but he also knew his friend. A jolt would kick start him back on the path to helping the soldiers get what was rightly theirs. Rufus seemed not to hear. He sat, motionless, looking at the table without blinking. Bassano shook his head and stood, the chair scraping loudly on the thick tiles of the floor.

"I'll leave you then" he said with a frown. With no reply forthcoming, he strode from the room and closed the door behind him passing a slave who bowed and handed him his cloak.

****

"Command?" Marcus said incredulously. "Me?"

"Yes, you are raised to commander for this campaign though we cannot infer the title of Tribune officially as the two Tribunes are absent" replied the council, the candle to the god Mars flicking brightly as he stood staring at the three men sat across from him. "The Volsci have taken the town of Ferentium and by our reports we understand they have set up strong defences and the King of Ferentium has gone over to their side. With the agreement of the other two tribunes you have been given a force of twelve hundred men and three hundred horses to re-take the city." The Senator picked up a heavy tablet and scanned the contents before continuing. "The Hernian ambassador will be here in an hour and will give you the full details of the city and its defences. The soldiers are being drafted as we speak, but you may choose your own officers as you see fit." He scanned the list again, squinting at the letters as his eyesight was obviously fading. "What does that say?" he asked the man next to him, who smiled and held the tablet up to the light. "Three weeks rations and march within two days" he said with a warm smile at Marcus.

Servilius Ahala was a well-respected patrician with strong family connections to the Furii clan and Marcus was sure that his father's old friend had gained him this commission, his first in command for Rome. He nodded at the square jawed man, his large frame hidden under the many folds of a thick white toga with a thin red stripe. "Who do you think you will take as your officers Camillus?" asked Ahala, his eyes glinting as he spoke. Marcus had been summoned to the meeting only hours before and had been taken aback by the sudden promotion that the Senators were giving him. He nodded as his mind ran through the names he might include, Potitus and Scipio for certain, but he needed at least four more men, good men who would rise to the challenge that the short campaign would bring. As he named his two friends to Ahala the Senator nodded respectfully, but Marcus could see he had clearly given it some thought himself and so he decided to leave two names blank so that the Senator could suggest opportunities for his clients. "I believe Aulus Virginius is available and still in Rome, he has three seasons' experience and will add greatly to the campaign" he added. "And Marcus Postumius Albinus Regillensis" he said as he leant his head to one side and added "I cannot think of others at the moment and would welcome any suggestions you worthy gentlemen may have."

Ahala beamed at Marcus, his shrewd eyes appraising him for a moment before he turned to his fellow Senators with raised eyebrows and then returned his gaze back to the new Military Tribune. "I suggest the first officer is Titus Elva" he said firmly, naming the great grandson of Rome's first Consul after the fall of the Kings. "He will offer good advice as well as sound judgement of tactics, though I hear you hardly need that" Ahala added. "For the second I suggest Publius Licinius Calvus Esquilinus. The man is old and wise and served well as an officer in my command recently" he said, turning back to the Senators. "It will also get him out of the city and stop that fool Manlius traipsing around like his lap dog. With a few good campaigns under his belt it would be good to get the man to put himself forwards for Plebeian Tribune, if you understand my meaning, Camillus?"

Marcus understood exactly what Ahala was asking and he wasn't happy about it. Calvus was at the heart of many of the plebeian demands for improved social conditions in Rome and many of the Senate disliked him, seeing his clever plans as yet more erosion of their own power. Placing himself between the two sides could be dangerous. He had also heard that his old friend Manlius had become the voice of the plebeians and had reignited his own political career by helping to resolve the issue of the pestilence that had engulfed the city. The people were calling for Manlius to be voted to the Senate and he was being hailed as a great saviour by the poor, but he also knew that many thought the new-found power had gone to the man's head, his Virtus had grown into arrogance Mella had said, something that Romans despised. Nodding to Ahala he said firmly "then it is agreed. If the orders are written I will get my man to take them immediately."

"One more thing Camillus" Ahala said before Marcus could leave. "You should know that we are sending a delegation to Veii tomorrow, led by your brother Lucius" he said, his tone flat as he scrutinised Marcus's face. Seeing the question forming he continued "you are aware that for years now we have had peace with Veii. The augurs have completed a number of sacrifices and on my orders a delegation was submitted to read the Sibylline Books." At this Marcus turned to fully face the three men, his attention wholly on Ahala. "The books state that we must visit the city of Veii and ask them a question. If the answer to the question is not as the books predict, then we will declare war upon them for their blatant infringements of the peace treaty we have held with them, as is our legal right. Before you return, Camillus, we may have declared war upon Veii."

*

*

*

*

Chapter 20

The long marching column snaked across the countryside behind him as Marcus sat on his large chestnut horse drinking from a water pouch. Wiping his mouth with the back of his hand he passed the pouch to Scipio who took it gratefully. Marcus looked at his friend and smiled. The man had grown, his short brown, hair still cut in the military style, framed his intelligent eyes and broad nose. Turning, he watched the men stride past and nodded to the Centurions who saluted as they marched by their officers, the low cloud of dust turning their tunics a dusty grey as they marched relentlessly to aide their Hernian allies.

The ambassador from Hernia had given Marcus a series of details explaining the layout of the town and the defences as he had seen them days before. Marcus had laid the defences out on a table using the wooden fort and soldiers he had been given by Gaius Javenoli some years earlier and discussed options and ideas with his six leading officers, all of them delighted at the opportunity of an early briefing on the attack to come. Marcus had found himself appraising the officers as they spoke, some clearly trying to impress him with their tactical knowledge and others silent as they tried to find their place within the group. The quietest of the new officers was Calvus, who seemed distracted and angry at his appointment. Indeed Calvus had spoken very little in the three hours since the force had left Rome and seemed to be avoiding Marcus whenever he could.

"Scipio, what do you make of Calvus?" he asked quietly as his friend stoppered the water pouch and handed it back across to him.

"I guess he isn't happy about being here" he replied candidly. "It seems he likes his own company and keeps himself to himself, though I have heard he is an able commander in the field and the men he commands respect him." Scipio waved to a Centurion who saluted with great aplomb as he and his men walked past. "I get the sense that he has issues beyond this campaign to deal with Camillus" he continued. "From what I hear he was leading the legal challenge to the issue of Bolae for the men and I suspect he is very angry at being ordered out of Rome at a time when he was creating a good name for himself. Remember Marcus" he added, using his first name quietly to emphasise his point "he is a leading plebeian and has an axe to grind."

Marcus knew that the words spoken by Scipio were true. Calvus had been removed by the Senate for just the reasons he had speculated, to keep him out of the Bolae debate. Marcus wondered if the Senate were afraid of his logic and power with the people or simply wanted to remove him because he was an upstart and by removing the stone from their sandal they could walk more freely until another stone lodged in its place. He took a deep breath before turning to Scipio. "Another half hour and we will reach the ford by the village of Anitio. Let the men rest there" he commanded as he patted Scipio on the forearm and smiled to him. Nudging his horse forward he set off backwards towards Calvus, who had just appeared amidst the fog of dust from the marching men, his soldiers singing a bawdy song at which Calvus was smiling broadly.

****

The forum jostled with people, an angry mob swollen by the ex-soldiers who had fought so well at Bolae. A burst of laughter came from a group of twenty men as a female slave dropped her basket and screamed as a man slapped her backside when she leant forwards to pick up the fruit she had been carrying. Across the flagstones by the steps to the shops another group called loudly for the Senate to repay the spoils they were owed, a great cheer coming from the other men mingling in the crowd nearby.

"Where are the Senators?" called a voice.

"Why are they denying our claims?" another shouted as he raised his arms above his head, throwing them down theatrically and shaking his drunken head. A scuffle by the Temple of Saturnus suddenly turned everyone's attention to the far-left corner of the Forum, men striding out across the flagstones as the noise went from cheering and cajoling to angry shouts and the dull sound of men fighting in hand to hand combat.

Manlius grinned, this was what he wanted, anarchy. The Senate would have to listen now that the people were taking matters into their own hands. That fool Postumius had avoided his demands to meet him and to challenge his actions against his brother, but now he would have to deal with the anger of the people. He took a hold of the back of a burly man's tunic and, grunting, he yanked him back into the mob of men behind him, laughing as he did so.

"Hold your fists Quintus" he called to the man's angry features as he let go of the woollen cloth and grinned at his blood-spattered face. He was pushed from behind by the throng of newly arrived men, the braying anger rising to a cacophony of abuse as the two groups stared at each other. Manlius ignored the shoving and stood with his hands on his hips, his heart thumping in his chest as he attempted to calm his appearance.

"Sergius" he called, pointing to the man surrounded by his bodyguards who was attempting to cross to the Comitium in the northwest corner of the Forum where the day's meeting to discuss the issue of Bolae had been called by the plebeian tribunes Lucius Icilius and Lucius Decius.

The bodyguards closed ranks, Sergius' frightened face scanning the crowd to see who had called his name.

"Here Sergius" called Manlius as the crowd dutifully parted to let him step forwards. "This act is illegal" he called to a great cheer from the men around him as a stone flew over his head and clattered into the armour of one of Sergius' bodyguards, the man wincing at the pain as he fell to his knees.

"Stop that" bellowed Manlius as he swivelled to face the angry mob behind him, "we will have a peaceful protest" he called as he grimaced at the mass of men pushing forwards towards their ex-prefect. "Sergius" he said again as he turned back to the man. "See the men who fought and saved your life at Bolae? See how angry they are? Would you consign them to a cold winter with no food, no warmth and see their children die?" he asked as he raised his arms and held the prefects gaze. "These men want what they deserve from the campaign, Sergius. That is all" he stated. One of Sergius' bodyguards shoved the short stocky man two places to Manlius's right in an attempt to clear the way to the Comitium. The soldier simply shrugged at the bodyguard, a full head taller than him and then swung a punch at the man, connecting squarely on his nose with a dull thud as the taller man stepped backwards attempting to duck from the swinging arm.

"No!" said Manlius as he stepped into the space between the two men, the bodyguard stepping forwards with murder in his eyes. "Let them through. The people will judge you Spurius Sergius, as will the gods. Do your duty as a Roman citizen and support the men of Rome who die for our liberty" he shouted as the small knot of bodyguards pushed forwards, Sergius hidden in their midst as best he could. Blows rained on the bodyguards as Gatto pulled Manlius away from the growing tide of pushing men and grinned at him.

"Good words" Gatto called over the noise as his face cracked into a grin. "Just like the old days" he added with a deep belly laugh as Manlius was swept along by the tide of men as it turned towards the Comitium, the open air public meeting space.

****

Calvus had greeted Marcus with a friendly, yet guarded, smile. As they had discussed the soldiers and the march it had been clear that Calvus didn't truly want to engage with Marcus in anything other than superfluous conversation and so Marcus had said his farewell and returned to the front of the column where Mella was discussing the Scorpions that Potitus had brought with them on the campaign.

"How many do we have?" Marcus asked as he reined in alongside the two men, Scipio a few horse lengths ahead.

"Thirty" replied Potitus "each with the new range finder I added after the attack on the baggage wagons."

"Excellent, and how many bolts?"

"Each Scorpion has ten bolts to throw, though several have yet to have their iron tips put into place" he shrugged "we just didn't have time to add them before we marched. The blacksmith has the design and is confident he can forge them within a few hours" he finished, his white teeth showing as he grinned at the thought of the weapons.

"Good" Marcus responded, "I think we will need them" he added with a faraway look in his eyes. "It strikes me, Potitus, that we could make more use of weapons such as the Scorpions" he said "to thin down the enemy before we set the spears to them. If we can cause confusion in the ranks of the enemy phalanx and break them up we can send our maniples into the gaps and slice through them" he said with a wicked smile. Potitus and Mella looked at their commander, his steely gaze staring into the distance.

"Thinking ahead, Camillus?" laughed Potitus as Scipio appeared next to them.

"As usual" said Mella.

"What?" Marcus replied as he looked at the three men smiling at him. "I was just saying, that's all" he said with a grin.

"You are right" Scipio said. "The phalanx has a particular strength, but its weakness is that once the tight formation is broken it is easy to rip through the heart of it. The spears are unwieldy and can obstruct the men around them if the formation is lost" he added "and the men don't train as well with their swords, relying on the strength of numbers in the phalanx to do their job".

"But here" Mella waved a hand "we will not face an army, we will face the walls of a city" he said with a shrug as he looked at Scipio "not a phalanx."

"True" replied Marcus. "I cannot think of any siege that has ever been more than a waste of time for Rome. In fact," he added as he looked at the faces of the three men watching him "I cannot remember any siege that Rome has ever been involved in ending favourably except for the siege at Bolae" he added glumly. "How *did* Postumius get those gates open?"

"Trickery" said Mella before any of the others could reply.

"What?"

"Trickery" he repeated. "He had spies in the city before the attacks and he had them open the gates, simple as that" he said with a perfunctory shrug.

"Well, we don't have that luxury so we need to think of other ways to get inside without throwing all the men at the walls and hoping for the gods to be on our side" Potitus said. As the men fell into a silence Marcus's mind went through the options the officers had discussed before they left Rome. Each officer had moved the blocks of soldiers and placed them in various positions around the City, unsure where the defences were stronger and arguing their own idea for attack. Marcus had listened but said nothing, praising some thoughts and questioning others. He had taken to the new leadership he had had thrust upon him with energy and confidence, his thoughts running through the prophecy he had heard the old soothsayer Antonicus say to him those many years before and wondering if the words were finally coming true. He found himself instinctively reaching for the wooden Eagle he wore around his neck as he shifted on his horse and looked back at his friend Potitus.

"Potitus?" he asked as a thought came to him. "The thing about walls is that they are higher than the men, so we need to hide from their arrows behind our wicker screens. How could we build a structure which would make us higher than the walls so that we are looking down at them?" he asked as his friend pursed his lips and turned his head to one side with a quizzical look.

****

The Comitium had been filled with wooden benches, some standing three rows high on strong wooden platforms to hold the volume of men who were expected to join the debate, other men simply standing on the dusty ground as befitted their status. The day had passed the mid-point and still people were arriving, filling the space with noisy chatter and calling across to friends they had not seen in days due to the pestilence which had kept most people indoors. The area had been cleared of the filth from the heavy rain and the standing water removed the previous day.

"Bloody rabble" Postumius said as he shook his head angrily and looked to his right. "How can they expect to change the decision of the Senate?" he added with a huff as he shifted on his bench and turned to face Publius Cornelius Cossus. The Senator's robe loosely fitted his frame after he had spent five days with the sickness, dragging himself from his house to the debate to support his friend Postumius.

"They have a legal right to challenge" he said in his deep voice, his dark hair oiled forwards to hide a receding hairline. "Yet as I understand it Ahala has removed the head of the beast and sent Calvus off to Ferentium with Camillus" he added "so we should have no problems as long as that fool Manlius does as he is told" he almost growled the last sentence. Postumius looked to his friend with a momentary stare.

"Have you paid him off?" he whispered, lowering his head conspiratorially, a fresh rush of hope coming to him.

"Not as such, but let's just say he has a reason to keep quiet" smiled Cossus as he nodded to his friend.

Postumius grinned. Maybe today wasn't going to be as bad as he had thought. He had already spent the majority of the spoils from Bolae paying off his debts and buying new favours. His latest dealings with the new magistrate Lars Herminius Aquilinus was particularly interesting and opened up a new source of revenue for him that might prove very lucrative. He sat back with a measure of satisfaction and his eyes scanned the crowd. Where was that fat fool Javenoli? There was no sign of the Senator and so Postumius turned his attention to the crowd, scanning the soldiers, many of whom were staring at him with loathing. Deep in the rows he saw Bassano, his angry postulations drowned out amongst the noise of the other soldiers, all shouting at the Senators to start the proceedings. Postumius shook his head as he sighed and looked to the skies, the gods were truly looking after him, he thought as he gripped the prophecy Marcus Furius had given him and thought of the truth of the words held on the small tablet he kept on him at all times, yes, these words were true and he would lead Rome, he thought to himself with a self-satisfied smile.

A bell rang, the thick clapper making a dull sound as if the bell had a crack which stopped it from ringing truly. The men in the stands fell silent almost at once, a few remaining voices coming to silence as a hush fell over the proceedings. A priest stepped up onto the Rostra prepared for the speeches, his hood covering his head and spots of blood showing down the front of his robe. He held up a knife and a silver bowl, a few drips of red blood falling to the floor and landing at his feet.

"Minerva, Justitia" he called, his voice loud and clear. "We ask for your judgement over these matters, give us the strength of wisdom in our words and justice in our hearts for your people of Rome." A murmur went around the crowd as numerous men set to mumbling their own private prayers. He moved to the right and placed the silver bowl on a plinth which stood under a small wooden cover. Beside the bowl were three candles which the priest proceeded to light, requesting Minerva's wisdom, Justitia's justice and Apollo's authority. Once the ceremony was complete, the priest turned and left the Rostra as the noise grew from the excited crowd.

A knot of white clouds moved slowly across the sky as the buzz of the men below started to cheer as they watched the two plebeian tribunes step up onto the Rostra, their robes marking them out as the leaders of the plebeians. They quietly stepped to the left and sat on the two crudely carved wooden chairs, almost like stools, that were placed for them at the far end of the platform. Immediately behind them walked Ahala and a taller man named Fabius Vibulanus, his dark hair neatly oiled and his long nose protruding from a thin face. A series of cat-calls came from the crowd as these men turned to their right and were greeted by jeers from the soldiers sat in front of them. Postumius shook his head again, exasperated at the behaviour of the plebeians

*

*

*

*

Chapter 21

"There" pointed Calvus, his finger aiming directly at a small copse of trees in the distance. "Good spot, sir" replied the soldier on his left, waving four of the Eques forwards, their bright tunics and long blades flashing in the hot sun.

"Chase them off and see where they go" Calvus shouted as the four men set their heels to their mounts and the beasts kicked up a swirl of dust as they galloped into the distance. Marcus reined in next to Calvus. "More scouts?" he asked.

"Yes" came the monotone reply. Marcus watched the two horses burst from the copse and disappear over a low rise as the four Roman's headed after them.

"Volsci?"

"I believe so" Calvus said as he turned to look behind him at the long snake of men who were marching across the flat, dusty ground. "It seems they are intent on watching us but do not wish to engage us in the open ground" he added in his quiet-spoken, almost humble, voice. Marcus nodded but did not reply as he watched the horsemen clear the rise and wheel away to their right to follow the Volsci scouts.

"Calvus" Marcus said as he looked at the elder statesman of the plebeian council, a man ten years or more his senior and with several campaigns under his belt. "Tell me, why do you hold your tongue in our meetings and why do you stay apart from the other officers?"

Marcus had spent some time discussing the issue of Calvus with Scipio and Potitus, but as usual it had been Mella who had suggested that Marcus simply lay his thoughts at the feet of the man himself and gauge his reaction. What could be the worst that could happen, he had said, the man had nowhere to hide and whilst he wasn't being disruptive it made no sense for Marcus to treat him differently to his other officers.

Calvus turned in his saddle and waved away the soldiers who sat around them on their horses. "I wondered if you would want to have a personal moment" he said as a resigned frown came to his face. As the men walked their horses to fifty paces away Calvus nudged his horse forwards and Marcus came alongside as they walked slowly towards the head of the column of marching men, the bright golden Eagle banner reflecting in the sun. Calvus glanced to his commanding officer and appraised the younger man.

"Camillus" he said, "Rome is a fabulous city, but one with a problem" he continued to look at Marcus, seeking signs of agreement or disagreement in his body language. None came so he continued. "The city grows fast and men who have had families in Rome for hundreds of years, such as myself, call her home. In fact we have Rome in our blood as much as men like yourself and countless of my kin have died for her in much the same way as your kin have. But the problem is that we have no say in how the City is run, we cannot command an army such as this" he waved his hand nonchalantly at the troops away to their right. "What is there for us to do Camillus but to be the puppets of the state, called to campaigns with our soldiers, our spears and our blood?" He frowned and shook his head. "I once thought that I could earn glory from being the spokesman of the people, building a reputation as a man of words, able to speak clearly and passionately whilst also remaining humble and deferent to the gods. But, Camillus, I was wrong. To gain glory you must be from the highest ranks of the patrician families, be *chosen* of the gods, not just be their servant. There is no other way to gain Virtus in this world" he shrugged. "This" he said, as his voice rose slightly and his arm circled to his right at the marching men once again "and every other campaign I have fought in has shown

me that leading men is easy. But they are fickle Marcus Furius Camillus" he said, calling his

horse to a stop with a clicking of his tongue and a slight pull on his reins. "That" he pointed

to the front rank of men, the golden Eagle carried aloft "Eagle is a sign that a god has chosen

you to lead these men and they follow it because they think you are favoured. If you are

favoured, then they may be too. That is the logic of the common man." He smiled as he

watched Marcus, his eyes betraying no emotion as he looked across at the golden bird

glinting in the dust of a thousand marching men. "And that favour" he continued "could only

be given to a Patrician. Look what happened to Dentatus" he added, Marcus's brows closing

momentarily as the thought of the reference came to his mind. Calvus saw this and smiled.

"You see Camillus, you do not understand the significance of the man" he said, taking a deep

breath and patting his horse's neck as he nudged it into a walk again. Glancing at Marcus he

continued as Marcus walked his horse silently beside him.

"Dentatus was a great soldier. He won more phalera on his own than a whole army could do

and he was a great champion of the people. They loved him and he was voted plebeian

tribune. You know the stories?" he asked.

"Indeed" Marcus replied, his eyes still watching the marching men but his attention totally on

Calvus, who seemed to have been storing all of his words for this one meeting.

"Well, Dentatus was the peoples' hero and was voted the peoples tribune" he smiled at the

thought. "My father was his Aedile" he added as he glanced to Marcus, who nodded, though

it was clear that he had not known this. The role of plebeian Aedile had been introduced

many years before as an assistant to the plebeian tribunes following the sessation in which the

plebeian armies had moved to the Mons Sacer and refused to fight for Rome. It was an

administrative role, but it carried very little real power, unlike the Tribune role which could

veto any Senate act.

"Dentatus rose like a giant amongst men, Camillus. His Virtus shone like a star and he started many of the reforms in the plebeian council that we have to this day. But there was a problem, Camillus" he said as he looked away to his right at the dust where the men marched. "He was not a patrician and the gods did not favour him. He burned fast and bright, but his light was snuffed out as a candle in the night" he said, his tone falling flat as he said the words. "You know how he died?" he asked, his eyes searching his commander.

"Assassinated" Marcus said, his voice expressionless.

"Hmm" replied Calvus. "The patricians did what the enemy could never do" he added, falling into a silence as his horse trudged on quietly. Marcus looked at the man, seeing by his face that his thoughts were wrapped in some personal battle.

"The assassin of Dentatus was never found, Calvus" Marcus said after a moment's silence. "It could as easily have been a beggar looking for gold as a patrician looking to remove him for his challenge to the Decemvirs" he said as Calvus raised an appraising eye and glanced across at him. "Though many people do believe there was some deceit in the death of an honest man" he added.

"But the point, Tribune, is that as a plebeian he gained a level of power that came too close to the power of the Senators and he was removed, as one would remove a fly from one's soup" he added. "He was sacrosanct, but his death went unanswered. Yes, there were calls for a public enquiry but they were dismissed by the Senate, another nail in the man's coffin, another hero of the people sent to meet his gods." He shifted on his horse so that he faced Marcus. "And do you know what the people said? They said that he must have fallen out of favour with the gods. And *that* became his legacy, not the great work as a citizen and a soldier, not his support to Rome, but the fact that he fell from favour with the gods." He shook his head slowly as he breathed a long, drawn-out, breath.

"Rome is more dangerous than this" he said as he nodded towards the army, his suggestion clear. "In some respects, I enjoy the freedom of the road" his face almost smiled as his eyes narrowed at Marcus "but I wonder when it will be my turn for the gods to become angry with me and turn off my light" he added with a strange stare at Marcus.

Marcus wondered what the veiled meaning of the final comment was as Calvus turned his gaze forwards to see one of the four horsemen ambling over the rise ahead of them.

"The will of the gods is unknown Calvus. As many good patricians have died as good plebeians in strange ways at the heights of their careers, whether that be military or political. If the gods have a path we must follow it and we must observe the laws and the functions of the rituals that they use to send us signs. Such things are as it has always been and always will be" Marcus replied, the absolute belief in what he said bringing a smile to Calvus' lips.

"Ha, Marcus Furius" he laughed "but the thing is" at this he pulled his horse to a stop and turned to face him "that the interpretation of the gods will can only be taken by a patrician. How do we know that the patrician *really* understands and interprets the signs as the gods will? There is no proof until after the events have taken place and clever men can re-interpret the signs and agree what they really meant. Now" he narrowed his eyes as he spoke the next words "a prophecy is a different matter."

Marcus fixed Calvus with a blank stare, feeling his heart jump in his chest at the mention of the word 'prophecy'. Calvus stared at him, looking for some sign that he had taken the meaning of the words, but nothing came. Smiling more broadly Calvus kicked his horse into a walking motion, the beast snorting and flicking its tail in annoyance at this stop-start journey.

"let's say, Camillus, that a prophecy had been made in which a plebeian was to become a great leader of Rome. What do you think the Senate would do with that information?" he asked as he rubbed at his thigh.

Marcus took a moment to think, knowing that if the information fell into the hands of some of the more unscrupulous patricians they would do everything in their power to remove the man. He decided to answer the question with another.

"And what if a patrician had heard a prophecy in which he was to become a champion of the people and to give the plebeians a voice in Rome?" he asked, the question causing Calvus to frown quizzically and to cock his head to one side as he considered the question, his eyes showing that his mind was working through a number of thoughts.

"Interesting Camillus" he responded, a smile growing across his face. "If this *prophecy*, if there were such a thing, were to gain public knowledge then the man in question would be in a very dangerous position" he said "and would probably end up in a similar position to Dentatus, snuffed out before his light shone brightly enough to change the course of history and the lives of the people of Rome for the better." Calvus's head dropped as he continued to consider the question before he turned his gaze back to Marcus. "Of course there are ways such a man could influence change, but by simply being seen as a friend of the people this causes problems in itself. Look at your friend Marcus Manlius" Calvus said.

Marcus considered the point. Manlius had gained a following in Rome for his sudden championship of the plebeian cause, especially the call for the loot from Bolae to be returned to the soldiers. It had given him a new level of status that many thought was already going to his head as he paraded around the forum waving his arms theatrically and calling for changes to the laws to support the common soldier. Marcus had spent many hours discussing the issue with his brother Lucius and between them they could only see a sudden end to Manlius and his bravado. In many ways it was exactly as Calvus had been saying, his star was shining but it may soon be snuffed out of existence. Marcus noted that Calvus was still looking at him waiting for an answer.

"Manlius is a good, honest, man" he said, weakly, knowing that, in truth, he did not believe his words.

"Manlius is growing power hungry" came the reply. "He has the patrician greed in him" he said with a level of hostility that Marcus caught and narrowed his eyes at Calvus.

"Apologies Camillus" came the quick reply as Calvus noted the mood change in Marcus's face. "There are many old opinions I must" he took a moment to continue "refrain from verbalising" he finished as he sat forward and stroked his horse's ears.

Marcus grunted acceptance of the apology and took a deep breath, the words of the prophecy ringing in his ears *'the eagle will be a true servant of the people'* and *'remember the plebeian poor soldier'*. He looked back to Calvus, who was watching him from the corner of his eye as their horses walked slowly towards the distant ridge, the rhythmic clopping of their hooves the only sound Marcus could hear.

"I would be interested in listening to your debate on how to solve the issues you mention, Calvus" Marcus said after a momentary silence. "We seem to have time on our hands" he added with a faint smile, unsure if the older man would give him the benefit of his wisdom. Calvus looked across at him with a frown on his face, which quickly changed to a blank, stoic, look as his eyes betrayed the quandary running though his mind.

****

For the second day in succession Rome was awash with people going about their daily routines without fear of the pestilence which has kept them housebound for weeks. The deaths in the streets had almost completely passed and the markets were now full as the warm weather and thunderstorms abated to ease the population's fears. Thousands had died over the last few weeks, with funeral smoke a constant sight on the horizon and pyres burning as loved ones wailed into the night at the untimely deaths of their kin. The rains seemed to have cleared the streets of the pestilence that had haunted them.

Postumius's son Megellus stood with his father in the forum, the shops to his left as he looked up at a statue of Apollo killing the Cyclops, a crude statue which the senate were to replace in the coming winter. Crowds of people shoved and called at his father, ex-soldiers swearing and cursing him as they turned and saw their old commander crossing the space from the Curia Hostilia, his bodyguards jostling everyone who came close enough to be dangerous out of the way.

"Megellus" called Postumius, his grin so wide that Megellus thought his face would split. "Here" he called as two burly bodyguards cleared a path between the two of them, a knot of men scurrying away before they were caught by the fists of Postumius's guard. Postumius smiled and placed a hand on his son's shoulder as he steered him into the safety of the guards. "Such a good day" he said as he glanced up at the sky, mostly blue with some heavy clouds in the distance which suggested more thunderstorms later in the day.

"The Senate have passed the law and Bolae will not be re-populated as that fool Rufus requested" he beamed. "It seems the city has already fallen into enemy hands, though they won't be getting many treasures from it as I did" he half laughed as his son looked admiringly at him. After a few minutes silence Postumius stopped and gripped his son's arm tightly, drawing a deep breath as he did so. "Ah, Megellus" he said, the boy quickly glancing around at the faces in the forum who seemed to have stopped to see which senior Patrician was clearing the way through the crowds. "To think I could have lost you" he said with affection and a shake of his head. "The gods are smiling on us Megellus. Our family will soon gain the glory as our cousin Aulus Postumius Tubertus did" he added with a faraway gleam in his eye, a reference to a distance cousin who had received a triumph after beating the Aequi. "You, my boy, will be the generation that brings out family line great glory" he said looking deeply into his eyes, pride burning from every pore of his body.

A bodyguard knocked into Postumius who wheeled on him with an angry shout before he realised the man's nose had been bent out of shape, the blood already splattering to the floor as three stout ex-soldiers yelled curses and sent fists flying into the other bodyguards.

"Give us our money you dog" called the shortest, his scarred face and patch covered eye contorted into a mask of rage as he launched himself at his ex-commander. "You thief" he shouted as he was butted by the bodyguard with the broken nose, his head cracking with a dull thud as the shorter man's forehead turned a sharp red from a mix of his own blood and that from the broken nose of his assailant.

Postumius grabbed his son's shoulders, forcing him behind another guard as he yelled at the men to get them out of the forum. More men appeared some with stones and clubs as Postumius's jaw dropped, his bladder suddenly feeling very full as he watched the gang of men stride across the forum menacingly.

"Stop this" came a strangled yell as a white clad man, his arms aloft as he stepped from the crowd into the melee that was being created by Postumius's bodyguards as they beat the three attackers who had waylaid them. "Now" he yelled louder, Postumius seeing it was Marcus Manlius, his angry face turning to the attackers. "We will have peaceful demonstration" he said loudly as the men around him looked at him with loathing and spite written across their faces.

"He owes me six months' worth of bronze" called the eye-patched man, his finger jabbing at Postumius as he held his other hand to a thick bruise across his forehead covered in blood. "I want my money" he yelled as he stepped forwards to the angry shove from the blooded bodyguard.

"Come on dad" said the man next to him, his face scratched and blood across his tunic.

"Yes" added Manlius, "go" he ordered, as a series of grumbles came from the men around him. "It will do no good" he called, turning in a circle to face the angry crowd "to fight in the streets. Our cause is true and the Senate cannot deny it" he said as Postumius turned to stare at him.

"Your cause?" he said incredulously. "*Your* cause? You were not at Bolae Marcus Manlius. You were not there when these men turned on their master against their sworn oaths" he stared at the short man as his son dragged him back from the bodyguard. "There is no *cause* that concerns you Manlius" he said forcefully as a stone thumped into the chest of the guard two men ahead of him, the man falling to his knees with a loud grunt as the stone clattered onto the cobbles. Around them people started to leave as they could sense a sudden change in the hostilities surrounding them. Manlius looked around at the crowd, "who threw that?" he called, roughly pushing the men closest to him to get a closer look at the faces behind them in the crowd. "Who?" he called again as twenty defiant faces stared back at him.

"Guards" came a sudden yell and a rush of men cascaded into each other as they attempted to move out of the forum as quickly as they could as the sound of men running across the forum came from behind Manlius. Postumius stepped forward, his bravery suddenly doubling as his attackers ran from the scene.

"You, Marcus Manlius had better watch out" he said, jabbing a finger into the man's chest and snarling at him as he spoke. "These plebeians you mix with will be your death" he said as he gripped his son by the arm and looked across at the newly arriving men led by Aquilinus. Aquilinus appeared at a run with some thirty men, paid thugs from the street gangs he had called to arms as soon as he heard that there was trouble in the forum. Each man stared at the almost empty space around Postumius, his bodyguards bleeding and one man on his knees gasping for breath. "I came as soon as I heard there was trouble commander" he said as he came to stand next to Postumius, his eyes glancing at Manlius uncertainly as the two men

stared at each other, Postumius angry and red-faced but Manlius calm and almost smiling.

"You should stay away from crowds Publius" Manlius said with a grin. "They could be the

death of *you*" he said as he turned and walked away with a shake of his head.

*

*

*

*

Chapter 22

"Seems like they have locked themselves in, Sir"

The Centurion turned with a shake of his head as he looked back at the city of Ferentium. The

thick walls stood fifteen feet high and were topped in sections along their length with a

wooden structure behind which the defenders were standing, their long spears erect against

the skyline. Marcus frowned, his mind working through ideas and options as he studied the

layout. All around were deep ravines which made it hard to approach the city which stood on

a small hill surrounded by two shallow tributaries of the river Tiber, their fast-flowing water

flashing in the sunlight. Guards were shouting abuse at the Romans as they arrived and

started to set up a marching camp in a spot to the west which Calvus had scouted earlier. The

city was impressive, though not as large as Marcus had first thought. The front wall was, to

his eye, some three hundred paces along the front edge and another four hundred at the sides

with only two entrances visible from where he sat.

"Ditches?" Marcus asked as he turned to the Centurion.

"Strangely none, Sir. They obviously think the walls can keep us out on their own" he

grinned as he spoke.

"Call the officers to my tent as soon as it is ready please Regillensis" he said to the Centurion with a friendly pat on his shoulder. Marcus Postumius Albinus Regillensis had a quick mind and a calm nature in battle, both traits that were proving useful already. So far, he had been everything Marcus had expected of him, his soldiers were drilled well and his competitive nature meant that he volunteered for many of the forward scouting actions. Marcus smiled as the Centurion trotted off to find the officers.

"Want me to go and scout around the city" said Mella, sat on a horse to Marcus's left, his bronze helmet with a blue feather dusty after the long ride to the city. Marcus continued to look at the city for a moment before he replied.

"Yes, I think we should go and have a look, Mella. Fetch Potitus would you, I think it would be good to get his engineering mind to look at those walls."

****

The door opened with a loud creak, its hinges bemoaning the weight of the ten-foot-tall doors cast in thick bronze with scenes from ancient battles, soldiers dying on spears, ancient phalanxes standing firm against hordes of invaders and a serene sky filled with gods looking down from the clouds, grapes and honeyed nectar in hands, as the humans died in the scene below them.

"Impressive" said Ambustus under his breath with raised eyebrows to Lucius. "Must be worth a thousand Ases" he added.

"Three" came the reply as Lucius could not take his eyes from the door, its finely polished scenes clearly crafted by a great artist as the light picked out the vibrant colours of the bronze and highlighted faces straining mid-fight.

Ahead of them the delegation that had met them at the crossroads to Veii entered their council chamber, the cool air drifting out of the room as the door slowly groaned open. Two elderly men, one a soothsayer, had met them a day before to respond to the message sent to

the King of Veii from the Roman Senate. The two men had said little, but they carried a

candle in a wooden box which was a sign of the treaty between the two states, its light

maintaining the peace that the treaty promised. The elder soothsayer had confirmed that the

King and his council would greet them in the city, but that they would have to leave their

small party of guards outside the city walls. After agreeing to this Ambustus and Lucius had

prepared their mounts and entered the city behind the two Veienteine ambassadors.

The room was large and cold, the darkness punctured by a number of big, shuttered, windows

around the room which threw shafts of light into the space illuminating the thirty or so men

sat in a semi-circle around a raised dais on which was sat the King.

Lucius glanced around the room spotting numerous frescos and paintings, some in gilded

frames, the gold dull in the low light as his eyes began to adjust to the dark interior. Away in

the corner a well, its old stone circular walls clear, stood in stark contrast to the newer

elements of the building, a relic of older times. The floor was a mix of elaborate flagstones,

thick and heavy but rubbed smooth with the passage of thousands of feet over their surface

and the walls were, mostly, whitewashed to give as much light as possible. Behind the King

was an iron gate, the spear tops painted gold, which held a statue that Lucius couldn't make

out in the darkness beyond the ironwork.

The ambassadors stopped and supplicated themselves on a reed mat before their King,

stretching their arms long as they knelt and mumbled words that neither Lucius nor Ambustus

could understand. After a moment, they were called forwards and Lucius looked up at the

King of Veii for the first time. He sat on a throne, its high back visible behind his head, ivory

coloured orbs atop the two ends with sculptured snakes winding around the thick oak. His

hands were spread over the rails as his arms rested along the thick wood, another orb sitting

proud at each end. Lucius noted that the legs of the chair continued the snake motif and that the floor of the dais was comprised of thick oak boards with more snakes carved intricately into the wood, each snake winding its way to the kings throne as if the serpents were attracted by his magnitude.

The man himself wore a thick red robe, the edges frayed with gold. He wore a long beard and his eyes were heavy lidded as he stared down at the two Romans, his gaze moving from one man to the other. His nose had been broken many years before and was twisted slightly to the right, but it made his features all the more striking. As Lucius awaited the next steps of the formal greetings he nodded to the king and dropped to one knee on the mat, as did Ambustus. The soothsayer, his long beard tied with a piece of string to keep it away from the flame, brought the candle of peace forwards and placed it on the floor in front of the king, his mumbling words clearly a prayer to intone the gods to welcome the guests and help with the discussion to follow.

One of the seated men to Lucius' right hand side now stood and stepped forwards, placing a silver dish with the motif of a pair of writhing snakes onto the floor. He knelt and raised his arms to the sky, looking up at the ceiling and said "Juno, mother of all, hear the words to be spoken and guide our judgements. Let the guests speak freely without fear and let our great king give his judgement with your will." At this he dipped his finger into the blood in the silver dish and twisted to wipe two lines across Lucius and Ambustus' faces. He then turned to the king, and bowing, he did the same, the blood dripping into the man's thick beard as he looked impassively at his guests. As he stood and returned to his seat Lucius glanced across at the faces of the men sitting watching the proceedings. The majority of them looked at him with cold stares, their distrust and hatred of the Romans written across their expressions. The soothsayer now reappeared carrying a small table, its surface covered in a red cloth with a finely sown picture of two birds in flight clearly visible as the centre-piece. As he placed the table beside the two guests a slave, his brown tunic and thick leather neck brace, stepped across and placed a silver tray with a wine flask and two silver goblets on the table, hiding one of the birds from view. The soothsayer waved his hand as if to ask the Romans to help themselves as the slave left and another appeared with a silver bowl of fruit which was placed across the remaining bird on the table. Lucius knew the formal greetings must come before the pouring of wine, so he smiled at the soothsayer and nodded his gratitude as the seer smiled back, his eyes tired but his smile appearing genuine. Lucius glanced to Ambustus, who nodded his reply and Lucius took the lead in the greetings.

"Friends of Rome" he said lifting his head to the king as Ambustus placed the small casket he had been carrying onto the flagstones in front of him. "Great King" he said, his head bowing at the words "I am Lucius Furius Medullinus and this is Fabius Ambustus, ambassadors of the City of Rome." He leant across and picked up the casket, its jewelled top set in a silver mount as he opened the box and took out a purple cloth, the fabric containing something which made the king squint as he looked to see what gift the Romans had brought him. "We ask your gods to listen to our meeting and to help us to speak freely and for Justitia to help guide our discussions." At this a murmur came from his back, which he ignored.

"Great King we offer this gift as a measure of our friendship and respect for you, your people and your great city" he added as he unwrapped the gift and placed it into the hands of the soothsayer. The gift was a silver and gold snake, articulated so that the body moved, slithering as a snake might do, the gold and silver etched into fine scales along its back and with two fine emerald eyes which seemed dark and menacing in the light of the room. Lucius watched the king's face for signs of acceptance, but none came, the man seemed uninterested in the gift as it was passed to him by the soothsayer.

Lucius looked around. At this point in the proceedings it was customary for the guests to have the wine poured for them and for chairs to be brought forwards, but nothing happened as a stony silence descended into the room. Ambustus cleared his throat lightly as Lucius returned his gaze to the soothsayer who was looking at him with a puzzled frown as if expecting Lucius to speak.

"Great King" he said, his face stoic as he sensed that now the formalities were over it might be best to start the discussion. "Our Senate has asked us to come as ambassadors to discuss our treaty and renew the vows we took, vows of peace and vows that we will not support enemies against our friends." He looked at the king before continuing. "These vows were sworn before the gods and are legally binding for all."

"You make it sound as if you have an axe to grind Medullinus" said the soothsayer, his voice deep and confident as he stepped forwards and looked down on the still kneeling Romans. "Tell us why you really came here this day and what it is that you *Romans* want from us" he added with a tone of spite. Lucius took a moment to glance to the king and then back to the soothsayer. The king was looking bored, his face a mask of weariness as he sat motionless on his throne. Lucius looked to Ambustus, who shrugged and nodded. Turning back to the king Lucius continued.

"Attacks on our roads and our armies are increasing and we have reason to believe that some of the people of Veii have been involved in these attacks" he started.

"Proof?" said the soothsayer, talking over Lucius again and distracting his attention. Again, Lucius glanced to the king and back to the face of the seer, who stared at him impassively with wide eyes as he awaited his reply.

"Prisoners from this City who attacked our army, shields bearing the cities colours and testimonies from settlements where..."

"Where are these prisoners you speak of" said the soothsayer, his head bobbing as he looked around the room and shook his head. "What proof is there that these were not bandits who simply painted a wooden shield with the colours of our great city?" he asked over the stupefied Lucius, his anger starting to rise as he looked at the man stood in front of him and again to the king on his throne.

"We have sworn deputations" he started as Ambustus held out a scroll for him to open. "But words can be written by anyone without recourse or legal footings if the person who made the claim is not here to speak the words of treachery" the seer added with a puzzled look as he stared through Lucius.

"Great King…" Lucius started to say as he turned his face away from the soothsayer and glanced back at Ambustus.

"The king will listen and speak when he has decided, Romans" the soothsayer said, his lack of the use of the guests name showing his disregard for them. Lucius looked to Ambustus and stood, as a small gasp came from the men of the Veienteine senate, some chairs scraping on the flagstones as men thought Lucius might be making an aggressive move. A soldier stepped forward, his sword half-drawn. Lucius looked at the soothsayer.

"If I am addressing an augur and not the great king of Veii I will stand, a Roman ambassador kneels before no ordinary man" he said loud and clear, his voice rising as he turned to face the old man who was now smiling at him. "The proof is there" he said throwing the scroll to the floor "the prisoners died after making their confessions. I put it to you that you harbour our enemies from the Volsci and you aide them in their attacks on our convoys. I also put it to you that…"

Again, the soothsayer spoke over Lucius, his voice low enough to be heard but also infuriatingly calm. "We understand the prisoners were killed by Roman hands. Murdered by assassins whilst in their bonds." He shook his head at these words, a murmur coming from the senate behind Lucius. Lucius frowned, he had been played well by the clever soothsayer, his calmness giving him a sense of authority which Lucius had lost as soon as he stood. Taking a deep breath, he regained his composure before speaking.

"You are well informed" he said with a smile, his voice lowering and his mind racing. "Such things happen in war" he said as he glanced to the bored looking king before continuing. "It is our legal right under the treaty to ask such questions of our '*friends*' and it is legally binding for you to answer truthfully. Such things are as it should be." He turned back to the king, who dropped his head to avoid eye contact and picked up the snake as if suddenly interested in the fine detail of the carving along its back. "We ask the questions under a vow of peace and under the candle of the gods. We await your reply." Lucius took a step back and Ambustus stood and moved next to him, their bodies rigid as if they had said their final words.

The soothsayer stepped forwards and poured himself a goblet of wine from the jug on the table, sipping the white liquid and smiling. Ambustus twitched at the breaking of custom and lack of respect shown by the man, his narrowed eyes and broad smile clearly cajoling the Romans into some kind of action. After taking another sip, in which the silence grew and the tension in the room became almost unbearable, he spoke again.

"This" he said, kicking the scroll with the outside of his foot "is of no consequence. It means nothing without the men to accuse us standing here and proving they are from the city. Also" he added as he placed the goblet down and turned his face to the men of Veii "there is no case for us to answer to if you cannot control the bandits who raid your Roman roads because you are too weak or too arrogant to keep them away from your lands. You Romans grow fatter on your conquests and your schemes to conquer *all* the Latin delta. How do we know that this isn't just a scheme set up by your warlords to break the peace to which we have adhered for so many years? How do we know that you are truly the peaceful ambassadors you say you are?" He stared at Lucius as if expecting an answer to his questions, his head cocked to one side slightly as he frowned at both men for a moment.

"As Apollo, Mars and Justitia are my witness, under the vows of the treaty, the people of Rome have borne no arms or treachery to your people" Lucius said his voice low and respectful.

The soothsayer looked to his king, who flashed a smile before replacing it quickly with the impassive face he had worn throughout the conversation.

"You turn up at our door with stories of treachery and deceit, claiming that our people are attacking your armies. Yet you bring no proof that we can use to help us to make a decision. You bring tales of woe, how your armies are attacked by small raiding parties" he shrugged. "I cannot understand why a few men would attack a full marching army. Tell me Roman, why would this happen? You say we are loaning troops to the enemies of Rome. Painted shields" he looked around the room with a grin, his arms rising as he circled the room with his eyes, his teeth visible as his wide grin split his face. "Painted by any number of farmers who have had a bad harvest and need money so turn to banditry. Everything you say leads us to conclude that Rome is looking for reasons to remove the treaty and start to wage war against our lands. Here" he pointed to the candle "the candlelight burns strong every day and has never gone out. What reasons do you really hold for your coming to our city, Roman? Is it to challenge our hold on lands to the north so that you can feed your expanding population? Tell us, Roman, what you want from us."

Lucius took a slow breath and turned to the king, addressing him directly. "Great king of the mighty city of Veii. Tell me that this man speaks your words and I will respond. If not I demand, under the terms of the treaty, to discuss the issues we have in private." He finished with a look of anger at the soothsayer, who simply smiled back at him as if he had paid him a compliment.

The king took a deep breath and let out a heavy sigh. He glanced at the senate around him and then back to the two Romans stood below his dais. His eyes suggested he was thinking through what to say, but no words came from his mouth as he looked, again, at the gold and silver snake in his hands.

"A poor debate" the king said, his voice high and lofty as he pursed his lips, the bottom lip extending as his left shoulder lifted into a quick shrug. "I expected more from what I hear is such a fine orator and general" he added, his eyes narrowing as he looked at Lucius. "And you Fabius Ambustus" he glanced at the stocky soldier "the first man to charge his Eques into a phalanx of soldiers." He made a laughing sound as he said the words. "Such stories of glory you Romans dream up as you conquer all the *little* towns and cities surrounding us. We wondered when you would start" he added as he lifted the snake to the light. "This is pretty" he said "but is no gift for a king" he said as he stared at Lucius, his eyes boring into him as his jaw stiffened. "Here" he said, throwing the snake to Ambustus "you keep it. I want nothing from Rome. We have done none of the things you claim and I have no more to say to you. Take them out of my sight" he said as he stood from his throne and moved away to the right to leave the room. As he stepped from the dais his long red robes brushed the box holding the candle, which teetered before falling forwards, the wax of the candle spilling onto the flagstones as a loud gasp came from one of the senators behind Lucius. The candle fell from its housing and rolled to Lucius' feet, the candle flame stopping with a dark wisp of smoke coming from the wick as the red light extinguished. Lucius looked from the candle to the soothsayer and smiled.

"It would appear that the gods have spoken" he said as he turned on his heel and stalked from the building, a smiling Ambustus following at his heel.

*

*

*

*

Chapter 23

"Here and here" Potitus said, moving a troop of wooden horses to the side of the wooden fort Marcus used to display the city of Ferentium, its walls surrounded by stones and dirt to portray the layout and contours of the ground. "These are the best places to locate an attack as the ground is level and will not obstruct the machines" he said with a nod of approval to the table on which the scene was set.

"The main attack points will be here" he moved a wooden block with a carved phalanx of men to face the left-hand corner of the city "and here" he moved another to the right of the main gates. "The cliffs here are impenetrable and this area" he placed a thin stone across a hand-smoothed area of sand "is too marshy from the river to get a good foothold, we would be slaughtered attempting to cross the area."

Marcus appraised the layout and could see the logic of the assault pattern. "Calvus?" he asked, startling the man stood two places to his left. "What do you think? Is this sufficient?" Calvus grimaced at the scene and stepped a little closer to the table as two other officers moved out of his way to allow him access. "Assuming the assault plan remains as you discussed I think this cover position from those tower things" he looked at Potitus with a grin "is the key to getting close enough to the walls to get over them and open the gate. Whatever happens we need the gate open." He paused as he held one of the wooden horse figurines in his hand and looked back to Potitus. "Explain how these things work again please Potitus. I need to be clear on the way that they will support the foot soldiers before I fully agree." Potitus nodded. Rome had never used siege warfare properly, preferring the full-scale attack or to call the enemy out into a set-piece battle. Over the years, many of their enemies had simply locked themselves in their cities and sat back to await the summer campaigning months to end and the soldiers from Rome to return to their own city. Since discussing options with Marcus on how to support the attack and how to neutralise the threats of the archers and slingers on their vantage positions on the walls Potitus had come up with a tower, some twenty feet high on which two men could stand and use either bows or even a Scorpion. He had set to work designing the tower and had used Marcus and Scipio, who seemed to have a canny ability to see the problems with every design, to redevelop the machine before he committed some of his newly formed engineers (some craftsmen and carpenters from various units) to create the structure. The structures were nearing the stage at which the wooden ladders could be added to the frame of the tower and Potitus had felt the same thrill he had gained when creating the Scorpions from Marcus's original design.

Potitus took a handful of sand and spread it on a clear space on the table, smoothing it over as he spoke. "The walls are here and fifteen feet high" he drew a picture to represent the walls, with an archer crudely shaped on the parapet. "If we attack here" he drew a few men rushing forwards "then we would expect to lose men at all points until the wall." He smoothed the sand over again, leaving only the picture of the walls and its defenders intact. "But if we place a tower here" he drew the twenty-foot-tall structure "and give covering fire," he drew an arrow, "then the defenders are in a vulnerable position if they stay upright to defend the wall. This allows the men to get closer and place the ladders, whilst also supporting them from above with our own arrows, so that they can get up onto that parapet" he said.

All the officers nodded at the logic of the idea.

"I've never seen anything like it" said Calvus as he looked to Potitus with a measure of respect in his eyes.

"The Tribune gave me the idea" said Potitus unassumingly. "All I did was turn his thoughts into something we can use" he smiled.

"Will it work though?" asked Regillensis who had offered to lead the attack on the walls, his face earnest as he knew the chances of failure for a wall attack were high but the glory of success for the officer in charge could outweigh the danger.

Potitus looked to Marcus, who shrugged. "We won't know until we try" he added "though I must say the idea of covering fire to support the attack will go down well with the men."

Calvus clicked his tongue as he clenched his teeth. "Fire arrows?" he said as a thought came to his mind "Will they cause problems?"

"Yes, Scipio thought the same so I've added some water buckets to the tower and have two men assigned to douse the wood with water if they attack with fire" he said, his brow creasing at the thought. "Maybe we need more water close to the towers though just in case" he tapped his chin with his finger as he nodded at thoughts running through his mind.

"How long until the time is up?" Marcus asked, breaking the momentary silence that had come to the campaign tent in which the men stood.

Regillensis walked to the tent entrance and looked up at the sky. "Within the hour" he called back as Marcus glanced at the men around him.

"Men, prepare your soldiers for the assault, you have your orders. Scipio and I will attend the main gate to see if they have decided to surrender. When they decline we will roll up the *assault towers* and once they are in position we will start the attack. Three waves as planned. If repulsed, we will fall back and review the strategy." He looked at the nodding faces of the officers with pride. "Has Fasculus come back yet? He asked nobody in particular, to which the reply was in the negative. "Then let's get ourselves prepared gentlemen, we have a city to take.

****

Fasculus stood looking up at the short climb to the city above him, the steep rocks smooth and showing no obvious hand-holds. He'd crossed the surprisingly deep stream and reached the rocks below the city with ease, but, as he had expected, there was no easy way into the city from this location. He shook his head as he stared, shielding his eyes from the strength of the sun, at the walls above him. The city wasn't on a high plateau, but the rocky cliff at this side gave it a clearly defendable position which didn't seem able to be attacked, the distance from his standing position to the top of the wall was probably seventy or eighty feet. Marcus had asked him to scout the rear of the walls for any opportunities which they could use to approach the city from anything but the front elevation, but so far, he had found none. He shifted his sword across his hip as he stepped onto the lower rocks and looked around for tell-tale signs of any entrances or access point being used by the people of Ferentium. Again, there were none, no secret trail, not hand holds worn away over years of scaling the wall to meet a secret lover. He grinned at the thought as a call came from above him, he'd been spotted. Turning he raced to the river's edge, hoping it was far enough away from arrow fall as he heard the unmistakable twang of bow strings. Without glancing back, he reached the water and stopped, turning to see what was happening on the walls. He could still see the bucket and wheel at the top of the wall, used to bring fish or rocks or other goods into the city by this back wall, but so far, he saw no other way in. An arrow slapped into the ground ten yards from him so he stepped back, up to his shins in the water, as he craned his neck to search the wall for any other openings. Nothing. The lifting gear might be able to hold a man's weight but it would be a painfully slow process to drop men over the wall by rope if they wished to attack the Roman's rear. Still, he'd better inform Camillus that he needed a couple of guards in this area just in case, he thought as he waded into the cold water and headed back to his horse standing munching the thick grass on the other side of the stream.

****

"Surely the gods favour us" asked Ambustus as he and Lucius mounted their horses at the gates of Veii, his eyes roving the surrounding area for points of weakness as Lucius had asked him to do before they entered the city.

"It is clear to me that they do" Lucius replied loudly as the guards looked to each other nervously. The news of the candle falling at the slightest nudge by the king's robe had spread rapidly and the soldiers of Veii were already apprehensive as the Romans left the city.

"Be gone" called the soothsayer, his beard blowing in the strong gust as the gate opened, a dusty hue spreading quickly into the inner space of the city entrance.

"This city is safe from Roman desires; the old prophecy will keep us safe from any mortal act" he said cryptically as Lucius furrowed his brow in reply. Just as he was about to ask what the old man was talking about a soldier stepped forward and slapped his horse's rump with the flat of his sword, sending the animal into a springing leap at which Lucius gripped the reins strongly and leant forwards lest he get catapulted off its back. A great laugh came from the guards as the horse bolted out through the open gate, quickly followed by the angry shouts of Ambustus as he chased after his commander.

****

Fasculus had reported his findings to Marcus and was disgruntled to find that he had to choose two men to return with him to guard the rear of the city. Despite his protestations Marcus had simply ordered him to return to the site within the hour. As he sat stuffing bread into his mouth and grumbling his displeasure he suddenly thought of a way to deal with another of his problems, a wide grin coming to his face. "Ha" he chuckled to himself at the thought. It wouldn't be popular, but he decided he needed to do it. Standing he walked directly to the Tribunes tent and asked for a moment with Camillus. On entering Marcus looked up from a deep discussion on the Scorpions with Potitus and waved Fasculus over to the table.

"Yes Centurion" he said, giving Fasculus his old title despite the fact that he held no rank in this small force.

"I have decided to take Felix from the third cohort with me" he stated as he saluted and looked away into the corner of the tent, a curl coming to his lips as he continued "and Mella" he said quickly, glancing at Marcus to gauge his response.

"Mella" replied Marcus and Potitus at the same time, both men turning with quizzical faces to Fasculus.

"Good man, Mella" he replied. "Good soldier, good in a scrap and has good eyes. He would be useful, Sir" he finished, his eyes returning to the top corner of the tent as he watched his senior officers look to each other with frowns across their faces from the corner of his vision. He coughed "if I could have the order slip please, Sir" he stated, clicking his heels together in his best Centurion stance.

"Very well" said Marcus. "But Fasculus, if I hear you and Mella have been causing problems I will have you busted back to latrine duties for a month" he added, a half smile coming to his lips.

"It's just that it's about time we had the space to talk to each other, sir, that's all. And as I say he's a good soldier" he added as he stiffened his neck and looked up again into the corner of the tent.

Marcus grinned and wrote something into a wax tablet, pressing his ring into the wax before sealing the order. "Just don't kill each other, save that for the enemy" he said as he handed the tablet across.

"Yes Sir" came the stout reply.

****

The sun had descended across the middle of the sky, the heat already dropping from the noon of the day as Marcus and Scipio stepped up to the space in front of the gates of Ferentium, just out of arrow range. In his hand Marcus held the small javelin which he would use to declare war on the city should they decide they did not wish to surrender to his forces.

A man appeared above the gates, his dark hair cut short and as much of his leather armour as they could see was covered in bronze bravery discs, awards from many previous battles. Scipio nodded approvingly at the man.

"City of Ferentium" called Marcus "The allotted time for discussion is at hand. What is your decision? Will you surrender your arms and liberty to Apollo, protector, and Mars, war-bringer, in the name of the people and senate of Rome?"

A silence fell as the man atop the wall and two new arrivals shook their heads and laughed at the two Romans below them.

"You cannot take these walls Roman. Go home and give your woman the benefit of your *little* spear" he called to a great burst of laughter from inside the city.

"Almost humorous" said Scipio as Marcus grunted in response.

"Then you leave me no choice than to declare that we, the people of Rome, will take this city and enslave all who bear no arms against us. We will, as is our legal right, kill anyone who bears arms against us and claim this city and its lands as our own". With that he stepped forwards and threw the javelin frontwards, its nose dipping and skipping along the dry, hard ground before it came to a stop just before the gates. Before the javelin had landed Marcus had already turned and walked away from the gates, adjusting his helmet and striding purposefully towards the awaiting army. With a wave to Potitus he smiled to Scipio "I am going to enjoy this" he said.

Potitus called to the officer in charge of the towers and the seven horses tied to the lifting mechanism were whipped forwards, their snorting causing the men on the wall to look away to their right with questioning gazes.

"Hold there" called a soldier as he held the reins of the horses, another soldier using a long pole to guide the tower as it started to lift into and upright position. Potitus had created a large wheelbase on which the towers were to sit, the only way he could move them across the ground he had said. As the towers began to appear the defenders came streaming to the walls, their puzzled calls growing as the structures appeared to be rising from the ground.

"Look at the fear they bring" said Scipio, a grin splitting his face.

"Only fear of the unknown" replied Marcus "but it gives us an advantage and we must use it" he said as he turned and called to the men to keep the strain on the left rope. Slowly the structure lifted, men rushing to the base, removing chocks which held the structures in place, changing grips on the rope and calling instructions to each other as they dragged the tower higher. Potitus appeared at Marcus's shoulder.

"She's beautiful, isn't she?" he said, a wax tablet full of notes on the movement of the machines in his hand. He whipped out his stylus and quickly mumbled "more weight on the right base" as he wrote it into his notes.

Scipio nudged Marcus and pointed at the tower as it landed with a bump on its broad-based wheels, the remnants of a commandeered wagon. "It looks enormous" he said as the legionary in charge went around the base checking the wheels and hammering wooden stakes into the fixing at the side of the tower. Marcus moved across and looked at the machine, his admiration clear in his eyes. The tower was essentially a wooden platform on wheels with two ladders surrounded by a series of planks to keep the soldiers inside safe from arrows or slingshot. The wagon-base had been adjusted slightly to give a firmer base via additional planks of wood which gave it stability. As he walked around the base the legionaries were attaching ropes to the front via two large metal rings which had been attached to the reinforced base planks. The tower seemed sturdy, but the frame was light and Potitus had already voiced his concern that for true stability it needed bigger beams and a broader base, but in the current situation it should work just as they wished it to. Potitus and Marcus had been discussing how they would move the towers into position without losing too many, if any, men. They knew that any men pulling the machines would make easy targets for the defenders at the wall and that, as Scipio had pointed out, if the defenders rushed the machines with cavalry from the gates they would be easy prey to such a small, fast, attack force. Potitus had decided that a small force of a hundred spearmen should guard each of the towers and that the tower should be pulled forwards into position by thirty men with another thirty covering them with shields and wicker screens. It was risky, but represented their best chance to get the machines into position with the minimum loss. With a wave of his hand Potitus sent the wicker shields forwards. Two hundred men picked up the four feet high barricades and rushed forwards, an archer helping to carry the heavy shields which would sit as close to the walls as possible and provide covering archery fire.

Marcus stepped forwards as the men looked expectantly at him. Taking a white robe from one of his messengers he donned the garment, covering his head in the robe and stepping up to the first tower, now ready to be dragged forwards. He raised his hands and turned towards the men, all faces watching him.

"I call on Mars to give these towers his strength. I call on the sacred rites of our laws to be upheld in accordance with the laws set down by Apollo and I ask for the safety of our soldiers and the smiting of our enemies" he said as he stepped forwards and waved the orderly with the chicken's forwards. Two birds were clucking loudly in the cage he dropped to the floor as he handed Marcus a handful of scented cake, moist despite the warm day. Marcus had frowned when he realised that he had not requested an augur for the small force he led but nevertheless he was well aware that the men would expect a patrician to complete the ceremonies for the battle. He nodded to the orderly who undid the catch on the cage and the first chicken leapt out flapping its wings, a good sign, thought Marcus as he crumbed the cake and let it fall onto the ground, both birds instantly swooping onto the food at his feet. The second bird scratched wildly, kicking dust back in the direction of the walls and he heard a murmur go around the watching men, another good sign. He smiled, he needed no more answers from the gods. He looked up at the closest soldiers, many holding amulets or tokens of luck as they awaited his verdict, those closest already smiling as they knew the portents were good having seen many such readings over the years.

"We will kick down the walls and smite the enemy, it is written" he said as a great cheer rang out through the Roman lines, spears rising and falling in unison as the noise echoed off the walls of Ferentium. With a wave of his arm the phalanxes started to move into their formations and the army of Rome lined up to face their enemy.

As he removed the hood and handed it back to the orderly, who was struggling to catch the chickens, Narcius appeared and saluted the officers, Calvus striding behind him, and said "Scorpions ready, Sir. We will be in position in three minutes and can provide cover as detailed."

"Excellent. Just remember, don't waste those bolts we don't have that many" replied Potitus as Marcus greeted Calvus's arrival.

"These tower machines are very interesting" he said, looking up at the wooden structure which was now starting to be pulled forwards as a cheer came from the Roman phalanxes lined up facing the walls of Ferentium. He turned to Marcus "Your tactics are" he narrowed his eyes "different" he said. "In a good way" he instantly smiled as he let out a low laugh. "These things" he waved a hand at the tower, looking up at the structures as they moved slowly forwards "could offer Rome a major advantage if they work as we expect." He watched as Narcius stepped forwards and berated a legionary for not pulling as hard as he should be, cracking him with his vine cane and seeing the other legionaries nodding their approval at the punishment of the lack of effort by the man being chastised. "I will join Narcius in *supporting* the men" he laughed as he slapped Potitus on the shoulder and stepped forwards.

"He's changed" Potitus said with a look to Marcus.

"We had an open and honest discussion" Marcus replied. "He has many views on many things and I have to say that I was surprised at how persuasive his arguments are. In fact, we discussed a great many things" he said cryptically as his eyes watched the towers creaking forwards now that both had been manned and were ready to move.

"Time to get in position and see how this game plays out" he said with a wide smile to Potitus as he moved across to his horse.

*

*

*

*

Chapter 24

The alleyway was dark despite the warm sunlight of the mid-afternoon as Manlius stepped out of the darkest shadow at the approach of the thin man, his bald head glistening in sweat as he laboured up the steep hill. The man's look of surprise, and fear, made Manlius grin as he held up his hands to show he was not a bandit or murderer.

"My friend, I am not here to harm you" he said, his face cracking into a smile as he stepped into the alleyway. The bald man backed away and glanced over his shoulder to see a thick-set man with a deep white scar across his chin step out from behind him, how had he missed the man, he cursed to himself.

"What do you want, *friend*?" he asked in a quavering voice, gripping the pouch attached to his belt. He glanced over his shoulder again, seeing that the man behind him had not moved.

"To talk" came the reply. "I am Marcus Manlius, you must know me?"

The bald man squinted and stepped closer. "My eyes are not as good as they once were" he said as he squinted at Manlius and craned his neck as if he was trying to make out the face of the man. "I know of you, but what do you want of me Marcus Manlius?" he asked.

"I understand you have details of a meeting between your master and Publius Postumius" he said as he stepped forwards, the smile friendly and warm but a harsh tone in his voice. The bald man stepped back again, the unmistakable collar marking him as a Verna, a slave born into a household and so valuable property. The slave gripped the pouch more tightly, Manlius seeing the action and raising his hands to show he still held no weapons. "All I want is the date."

The slave, his old face wrinkled, took a deep breath. "If master finds out" he mumbled.

"Who would tell him?"

The slave glanced again at the man with the scar leaning on the wall. He narrowed his eyes, he knew that man, he had seen him at the master's house. "Him" he said, pointing. "He works for my master" he said, his eyes wide and mouth open as he turned back to Manlius.

"He works for me now" said Manlius as he leant back against the wall and looked over at the sweating slave, his spindly legs showing a dark tan from his hours outdoors. "You have nothing to fear. I only want the date of the meeting and we will be gone, you will never see or hear from us again".

The slave gulped, sweat dripping from his temples onto his cheeks as he considered his next steps.

"I know Ahala well" added Manlius. "Don't worry, I have no hatred towards him and will not harm him in any way" he added, hoping that this would help the slave to come to a judgement.

The slave looked around him, looking up at the high walls of the alleyway and leant forwards. "The second night after the full moon" he said quietly as Manlius patted him on the shoulder and handed him a thick silver coin, at which the slave gaped and bit the silver to check it was real before nodding and rushing off up the hill on his thin gangling legs.

****

The towers seemed to take an age to reach their positions, the men of Rome standing watching as they were dragged slowly into the predetermined places Potitus had had dug into flat ground. At one point, the right tower had lurched dangerously as the wheels hit a large stone and the force of the pulling men had caused the wheel to jump as the metal binding creaked against the dark grey rock.

Marcus sat looking at the scene, the city directly in front of him with its naturally defensive topography. To the right and left were steep slopes pitted with ravines which offered no attack opportunities, the rear falling to a steep cliff also held easily defensible ground. The only option was a frontal assault as they had planned. He had set the line out in three columns of men, each a deep mass of spears, with the few Eques he had at his command ranged on his far right but close enough to respond to any cavalry charge from the gates of the city. He looked up at the sky and nodded, he had plenty of the day left and he hoped this first assault would give him a measure of success in his first command, though his heart beat fast in his chest as he contemplated the thought. Regillensis and Narcius were standing in the centre ground, their ladders at the ready with the storming parties, who had been drilled for hours in the necessities of scaling the ladders and holding the narrow walkways above the city before moving en-masse to open the gates. Marcus would close the gap to the gates once the men were over the wall and he would lead the entry into the city with his Eagles once the gateway was cleared, with Calvus close behind with the second wave. He bit his lower lip as he thought through the actions, seeing it in his mind's eye as it played out, looking for errors, changes to tactics and ways to make the attack more effective. Nothing came to his mind as he watched the arrows rain down on the towers and the men pulling them, the heavy shields starting to fill with bristles as each missile landed. So far, no Roman men had fallen. Scipio and Virginius held the remaining forces that would close in as soon as the gates were held by the attacks from Marcus and Calvus.

A sudden rush of movement came from the left-hand tower as it jolted and shook for a few seconds, the men pulling it dropping the rope and turned on their heels to race away as the archers behind the wicker screens stood and launched arrows at the walls. Marcus took a second to realise that the tower had reached its position and he saw the two men rush from the wicker screen at its side into the safety of the structure and start to climb the ladder, the first man carrying his bow and quiver full of arrows and the second struggling to lift the heavier Scorpion up the steps. As they did so a flurry of arrows landed on the men rushing from the scene, one man falling with an arrow through his leg, the scream coming seconds after Marcus saw the man hit the dust. He stretched his neck to see if the fallen man was moving as a low cloud of dust grew across his vision where the majority of men were racing from the tower. A cheer went up as he saw the figure dragging his leg, his teeth clenched as he limped at great speed back towards the Roman line, arrows thumping into the ground all around him. Without thinking about it Marcus found he had kicked his horse forwards, digging his heels into the animal's side and shouting at it. Potitus called something to him, but it was too late, he had made his decision. He bent low on the horses back, two hundred yards closed to fifty in a few heartbeats as the soldier twisted as another arrow hit his shoulder, knocking him to the ground as a great groan went up from the Roman lines. Marcus knew that this first action was critical to the motivation of the men. To see every man safely back from the tower would be a great boost to them, so he yelled at his horse to speed up, waving the reins wildly as he approached the soldier, his face screwed in pain. As he cleared the front line of soldiers he saw faces turn to him, their calls to their comrade turning to cheers as he raced forwards. As he approached the man, his arm stretched out towards him, he remembered something his brother Lucius had said to him years before, *the soldiers want to believe their leaders are favoured by the gods, if you get the opportunity to prove it is so, then do it, but to die doing so would be stupid.*

Was this a stupid act? He reined in as an arrow thumped into the ground next to him, the soldier's pleading face strewn with tears which drew long lines down his dust-covered face. "Quick" he called "Give me your hand, can you jump?" His horse swivelled as an arrow flashed past its ears, the noise of the cheering Romans growing as Marcus leant over and gripped the man's arm, hauling him to his feet. Another great cheer came as Marcus realised that the Scorpion atop the tower had sent its first bolt into the defenders, clearing a section of the wall and giving him vital seconds as the defenders suddenly ducked at this new threat.

"Quickly" Marcus called again, his teeth grinding with the effort of trying to lift the man, whose leg seemed normal with the exception of the dark wooden shaft through his calf, the amount of blood covering the leg almost non-existent. The legionary hauled his leg forwards with his loose arm, the shaft of the arrow in his shoulder bouncing as he did so with a huge grunt and his teeth grinding in pain.

"Good man" called Marcus as he half lifted the soldier across the back of his horse, his mount turning and snorting at the new weight. Kicking hard Marcus steered the animal back towards the troops at a slow trot and he sat up with a prayer to Fortuna that she would keep them safe.

With the words of Lucius in his ears he turned to the soldiers who stood cheering and he waved a hand, calling loudly "the gods are with us" as he closed on the rows of men, the cacophony of noise growing louder as he closed the ground.

The soldier called his thanks as he was dragged from the back of Marcus's horse and taken away by medics, his grateful calls drowned by the cheering of men. As Marcus waved to the soldiers Calvus appeared at his side and frowned at him.

"You could have got yourself killed" he said flatly, his angry reproach evident in his eyes. Marcus took a deep breath. "A calculated bit of theatre" he lied "see how the men cheer now. They will see that the gods favour us" he said through deep gasps as he sat as tall as he could on his horse.

Calvus shrugged but laughed quickly "Well, either way your action moved all the archers to the left wall as they saw the Roman Tribune charging at them, and that allowed the tower on the right to get into position without incident. A calculation?" he said, "or just a rush of blood?" he smiled.

"The gods must surely be smiling on us all today" laughed Marcus as he turned to the sound of the Scorpions thumping their bolts into the defenders. "Time to attack?" he asked as Calvus sat on his horse watching him, his scrutinising look causing Marcus to feel uncomfortable at the gaze.

Calvus smiled and turned to look at the scene. The defenders were now intermittently ducking to avoid the bolts and arrows from the Romans and the bolts had caused havoc with the thick line of men who had rushed to hurl their arrows at Marcus. With a quick glance at his sword, which he tapped three times before lifting it from its scabbard, he smiled back at Marcus. "Yes, I think now is as good a time as any, Tribune" and he set off back to his position in the line as Marcus waved to the trumpets to call the ladders forwards.

****

"I won't condone violence" Manlius spat as he turned on the two men standing in front of him, their faces red with anger after the last hour of bickering.

"You don't understand what it means to us. You patricians are all the same" came the angry retort from Bassano as he ground his teeth at Manlius, his chest stretched as he stood with his fists balled at his side.

"So, you will hit me? You will take out your anger on the man who is trying to help you?" he said with a snarl as Rufus stepped between the two men and lifted his arms.

"Come on you two" he cajoled "this isn't helping."

"No" pointed Bassano, raising his voice to a shout "*He* isn't helping. What has all his postulating achieved? Talk, talk, talk but no action. My son is dead because of that bastard, his family living in their rich house with the money that *we* gained" he turned and shook his head as he kicked at a stool sending it skittering across the floor of the room. "*He*" he said again with malice in his voice, jabbing his finger at Manlius "doesn't understand our plight. Why is he here anyway?" he said to Rufus, his eyes red rimmed with the fury that was bursting from within him.

"I asked him" said Rufus, standing tall as he looked at his old friend, the tired face and hollow eyes looked even worse than the last time they had met. A short silence filled the room before Tolero stood and gripped Bassano's arm. "Come on, sit down" he said gruffly, his one good eye flicking from Rufus to Manlius.

"I tell you again" Manlius said as Bassano sat heavily onto a long wooden bench "Postumius and Ahala are planning something and we need to know what it is. They connived to get the Senate to agree to Postumius's challenge regarding the spoils from Bolae and they paid the priests, I am sure of it" he said as he looked at the floor with a shake of his head. "Whatever they are up to we need to know" he added after a moment.

"How?" replied Bassano as he slapped the table in front of him with the palm of his hand. "Tell me" he said without looking at Manlius, "tell me how you know this. If you have proof we can take it to the Plebeian Tribunes" he added with a hopeful look to Rufus.

Manlius sat, his breathing heavy as he leant forward, his elbows on the table. "I have no real proof" he said slowly with a shake of his head. "They seem to be one step ahead of us at every turn" he added as he glanced at Rufus.

"This is getting us nowhere" Tolero said, his anger rising. "I'm with Bassano, we take this into our own hands. The Plebeian Tribunes are useless, the law is on the Patricians' side and we have nothing we can do to regain our rewards" he said as he sat back with his arms folded across his chest, flecks of spittle white in the corner of his mouth as he spoke.

"And do what?" Manlius said with a shrug. "The law must be followed if you are to get compensation" he said. "I have spent days paying people to get me information, to get a crack in their armour where I can punch my knife" he said, using a phrase all the ex-soldiers would be used to, "but so far, nothing" he said, his exasperation written across his face.

Bassano stood and looked to Rufus with a shake of his head, glancing to the three men behind him and finally to Tolero. "That settles it Rufus" he said, waving away his friend's hand as he beckoned him to sit. "These meetings are of no use, all they do is twist and turn my mind making me feel like an ant under the Patricians' sandals" he turned to Tolero.

"Are you with me?" he asked as a grin split the one-eyed man's face and he stood clasping forearms with Bassano. "Rutilus? Felix?" he asked to two of the men behind him, who both did the same, gripping his forearm tightly before he turned to the last man. "Amitus you had better stay with these two, you weren't at Bolae and you can support the families if our actions go wrong" he said with a stiff nod.

"What actions" shouted Manlius as he stood and stared at the men in front of him, his eyes searching every one of the men with a measure of fear and urgency.

"Plebcian business" spat Bassano as he produced a mock smile to Manlius and turned his face to Rufus, who remained motionless staring at the table.

"I am sorry my old friend, it must be done" he said placing a hand on his shoulder before turning and striding from the room.

"What are they doing?" Manlius called, looking at Rufus and Amitus as the room emptied, "What are they doing?"

*

*

*

*

Chapter 25

Narcius grunted as the ladder shuddered under the weight of several heavily clad legionaries above and below him, the thick wood bending precariously as the man ahead of him slashed into the arm that attempted to push the ladder away from the wall.

A scream to his side made him glance to his right, a sudden fear that the man might crash into him and knock him from his position dispelled as the blur of a body disappeared into the empty space below him, a thick crunch the only sound as the man hit the ground.

"Keep moving" he called, his hand attempting to grip the ladder as well as the hilt of his sword, his shield tied across his back. The attack had been swift, the towers creating a space into which the first ladders had run, the first cheering men scythed down as they reached the top of the walls without any resistance. The defenders had spread out as soon as the ladders arrived, several points being attacked at once to thin their lines. A sudden spray of blood washed into Narcius's vision, his blinking eyes quickly focusing as the head of the defender above him was jerked backwards with such force that he didn't have the time to see anything other than the eyes of the man who was snarling at him simply disappear into a cloud of red as a bolt went straight through his face.

"Now" he yelled "Go" he screamed, battering the man above him with his shoulder as he attempted to scramble up the last few feet to the top of the wall. Finger nails scratched his leg from below causing him to swear and scream louder to move faster as his legs pumped to get up the last steps. The man ahead of him was over the wall, *three* he said as he clambered onto the cold stone and slid on his thigh to jump to the parapet, its wooden boards already slick with blood. No *two* his mind told him as he saw the body of the first man over the wall falling into the space to his right, into the city. "Line" he called, trying desperately to grip his shield and set his feet into the slippery footholds of the wooden floor. A clang told him the next soldier was over the wall and preparing to get into position behind him. The walkway was only two men wide and Narcius gripped the leather shoulder pads of the man behind him, dragging him into the line to face three snarling defenders. "Hold this line Eagles" he shouted as he grinned at the approaching men, their long swords flashing as they crept towards them. He heard cheers behind as he turned quickly to see several places where the Romans had gained the wall, the sudden thumping sound of a thousand marching men closing to the gate coming to his ears. This was what he lived for, he thought as he grinned at the first defender to swing his long sword at the front line of *his* First Century of Eagles. The legionary in front of Narcius simply swivelled his shield as the attack came and ducked into a short stabbing reach, taking the man in the rib cage with a great heave of air before he grunted as he twisted his sword and returned to his stance, a perfectly executed movement, Narcius thought. The defender didn't have time to grunt as he fell to his knees and was knocked over the parapet by another defender, his eyes screwed tight against the pain as his blood leaked onto the floor in front of him.

'Come on" roared the man in front of Narcius, clearly enjoying his first battle.

"Steady, lad" Narcius said through a wide grin. "Remember your training. They come to you, you stay ready and get under their sword arm" he said slowly as the next defender, using a two-handed grip, stuck his sword straight out in front of him. Narcius had time to look into the city, the walkway to the gates was ahead of him and the gates almost directly to the left at the bottom of the steps. He smiled as the legionary ahead of him sliced into the thigh of his attacker, ripping a long slice deep into his muscle. As the man buckled under the pain, his lungs screaming, the legionary simply rocked back on the balls of his feet and butted his shield boss into the man's face, knocking him senseless and shoving him over the drop into the city, his arms circling wildly before he fell.

Narcius turned to the wall searching for Marcus and waved his sword in three wide arcs before turning back to the defenders streaming up the walkway. "Forward" he called "to the gates" and he shuffled along behind the two legionaries in front of him with his shield held firmly across his body as another defender fell to his death ahead of the moving tide of Romans.

**

Marcus felt the exhilaration of the run, his legs hammering out the staccato rhythm of the short steps as the soldiers moved en-masse towards the gates, the Centurion calling his men to stay in line. From his position in the front line he could see the two towers to his right and left covered in tiny pin-pricks where the arrows of the defenders had been wasted. He grinned at Potitus' ingenuity and then focused on the gates ahead of him. Narcius had given the signal that they were moving for the gates and Regillensis had finally gained the wall to the left of the gates, his task was to clear the walls so that the Roman archers could take positions from which to fire into the city itself. Marcus smiled at how easy it had been so far, his glance to the skies followed by a mumbled invocation to Fortuna.

"Fortuna smiles on us today, Sir" came a reply from his right where a fresh-faced Centurion, his first command smiled back at him as he jogged along effortlessly. The young man's eyes flashed with a mad glint, his grin showing his exhilaration. Marcus glanced at Quintus Fabius, the third son of one of the more pre-eminent families in Rome who his father had asked him to add to his army to 'blood' the lad as a favour to their family. So far, he had been an excellent, though often drunken, junior officer who had taken to being off the leash from his family with verve.

"We're not done yet Fabius" replied Marcus with a smile as he glanced forwards again "but the goddess does watch over us. Just keep your head down and stick to your training" he added. Ahead the walls were starting to show Roman helmets as the archers sprinted from their wicker screens to climb the ladders, their speed across the ground impressive compared to the steady trot of the more heavily armed foot soldiers. Marcus knew that it was now all about timing. The speed of the attack on the city had been their advantage, the defenders not expecting either the towers or the sudden onslaught as they thought they were safe behind their walls. The column of men was starting to slow down as it approached the gate, the sounds of sandals thumping the floor and metal clanging on metal getting louder as the men tightened up in their approach to the gates.

**

Narcius leapt from the last step, fanning out into the space as several well-armoured defenders rushed at him and his men. "Close the line, keep it tight" he yelled as a small legionary stepped forwards to hack at the spear of a tall man, his bronze helmet with a long nose-guard surely a relic of some Greek ancestor. A bump at his shoulder told him another man was in line, then another. He grinned and glanced to his left, the gate was surrounded by a column of spears, death written in their shining iron points. Narcius knew that spears were no use against his maniples, their ability to quickly attack, break into small groups and surround an enemy with speed would soon overwhelm them. He glanced right and then above to check that no other threats existed. To his right were the town houses, a series of wide roads running away into the distance were crammed with soldiers marching towards them in deep rows, spears held in the air to traverse the narrow junctions.

"Speed lads. Speed" he called. "Maniples" he yelled, the veins appearing in his neck as his throat hurt at the cry. "Now!"

Instantly a series of groups of men split from the line, each group of eight sprinting to form a small knot of shields bristling with swords. The spears of the attackers crossed each other as they followed their lines of sight, each man unsure which Roman to aim for.

"Attack" called Narcius as he stepped forwards, batting a long spear away as it jabbed slowly at him, the face of a boy no more than fifteen years of age almost crying with fear as he stepped into the gap between his spear and shield and punched his sword into the boy's neck, the soft tissues exploding as his head was whipped around. Kicking the falling body Narcius didn't have time to feel the warm blood on his arm as he parried another spear, the movement coming from the man's shoulder telling his trained eyes exactly where the tip would go. Again, a flick of his shield and a punch forwards with his sword saw the defender fall as two men either side of the, now dead and falling, man also fell to their knees under his Eagles onslaught. The gate was now only three men away as Narcius heard the first clatter of wood on stone as the rear line scrambled away from the attack on the gate. Within a heartbeat some men stood with hands in the air calling for surrender and mercy and others rushed away, scrambling in any direction where there was a clear space, fear and panic taking control.

"Clear the space, set the line and get these idiots out of the way" yelled Narcius as he whirled to see the mass of defenders quickly settling into a line across the entrance to the inner city some fifty yards away. "And get that bloody gate open" he screamed as the first Ferentian slammed into one of his men. He whirled back at the oncoming column and shuddered, he hoped Marcus had reached his position.

"Hold the line men and then when the gates are open we run" he shouted to the men around him who were setting their feet into a low stance and settling their shields to form a barrier.

**

"There" said Fasculus, his position mid-way up a tree just beyond the line of the river giving him a clear sight of the back of the city.

"Where" whispered Mella, his arms clinging to the thin branches.

"See where the bucket lands, its darker. How did I miss it?" he said with a shake of his head.

"Felix" he whispered back down to the ground as the man looked up and waved. "Go now, fetch the Eques, at least a hundred" he said with a grin.

"I might have got you wrong after all" smiled Mella "though I wouldn't put a bet on it" he laughed as Fasculus smiled.

**

Marcus let out a deep breath as the gate shuddered, a small cloud of dust moving at the base of the thick wooden doors as they started to slide outwards bringing a great cheer from the Romans, some of whom leapt forwards and sprinted to the gap carrying hammers and long wooden stakes. As the doors reached half their aperture he saw that Narcius and his men were struggling to hold their position, the front line visibly buckling under a great weight from the phalanx of spears driving into them from the defenders.

"Halt" he shouted as he heard Calvus repeat the order from behind. "Scorpions" he called as he glanced to Fabius, his mouth split into a wide grin as he turned to look over his shoulder.

Marcus hoped his planning had been meticulous enough. He glanced back at Narcius, the back of his men now clearly visible as the gates were fully open. Six Romans on each side of the gates were hammering stakes into the ground to hold them open, their work rate tremendous, arms thumping up and down, the clatter of the hammers indistinct in the noise of the fighting beyond the gate. Behind him Marcus heard the legionaries moving aside as twenty men rushed forwards with the Scorpions and their bolts, the heavy breathing sounding ridiculously loud compared the sounds of battle from fifty yards ahead. Potitus appeared behind them as Marcus stepped forwards.

"Sir" said Fabius, his eyes bright and eager as he touched Marcus's forearm. "May I step closer to see? I've heard such good things of..." he glanced, a wicked smile on his face, at the men hurriedly setting up the machines. Thinking nothing of it Marcus tapped his shoulder "come then" he said as he stepped up to Potitus.

"This is a masterstroke" Potitus said as he walked along the line of Scorpions, each legionary carefully placing the legs and checking the machine was set sturdily into the ground. Marcus looked at the gates and smiled. "Scipio gave me the idea" he said with humility. "You know what he's like with details. As soon as he said that the gateway could be our sticking point I had to find a way to clear it. I hope Fortuna looks over us and this is that way" he said as he turned to look at the gates, Narcius glancing anxiously over his shoulder as the Roman Legion came to a standstill outside the city gates. Marcus saw Regillensis shouting orders to the men remaining on the walls, though he couldn't hear what he was saying. He chided himself for not thinking through this part of the plan well enough and ground his teeth at the thought that his officer might be swamped by the defenders if the bolts didn't do their work quickly enough before Regillensis could give the signal.

"There" yelled Potitus, causing Marcus to jump as his mind was so focused on the gates. Potitus was tapping a point on one of the Scorpions as a soldier struggled to latch the bronze fitting into its housing. "Quickly" he added, his voice sounding frustrated rather than angry.

Marcus looked back at the gates, three of the hammer wielders had joined the beleaguered line of Narcius, grabbing shields and swords from the dead at their feet whilst three had run back towards the waiting army. Marcus made a mental note to praise the three men's bravery and give additional duties to the other three.

"Are we ready?" he asked to Potitus.

"Yes sir" he said as he stepped across the first Scorpion and tapped the wooden legs. Marcus noted that each Scorpion had a small wooden eagle tied to a leather thong around the bronze sighting plate. At the sight, his mind went to the prophecy and how the Eagle would lead Rome. This was his destiny, he thought, as he turned to the gates and called for the trumpets to sound retreat for Narcius, the blare cutting through the dull clatter of metal on metal from ahead of them.

"Load" called Potitus as Marcus watched the Roman force begin to peel away from the defenders. The men had strict instructions to run right or left at the gates, each man informed that if he ran straight towards the Roman line he would be cut down by the death-bolts of the Scorpions.

Marcus found himself holding his breath as the defenders chased the Romans to the edge of the gate, their screams and cheers as the Romans ran sounded loud in the silence of the thousands of Romans standing watching the scene. Two of the Ferentians grabbed the gates and pulled manically at them, kicking at the long stakes to loosen them in an attempt to urgently close the gates. Calvus appeared at Marcus's shoulder and stood in silence, his arm tapping his sheathed sword as he mumbled some quiet prayer.

"Now" Marcus mumbled at almost the exact second that Potitus called the order to fire.

**

The Ferentian leader, Sossimedes, was from a long line of wealthy Greek aristocrats who had founded this city many centuries before. His deep black hair, oiled into curls, jolted as he stopped and stared at the scene outside the gates with wide eyes. His victorious men had cleared the gates of these Roman fools with their strange machines, *a trick*, he spat, and not worthy of a true soldier. He shook his head as he kicked at a dead Roman, the man's helmet covered in a deep red smudge where his blood had run from his veins. His eyes roved the ground outside his city. Why were the Romans not attacking, they had the advantage? He stepped forwards and called out "Roman's come to your deaths we have fine spears which will strike you and send you to your worthless gods." A great cheer of laughter came from the few hundred men standing in the narrow gateway, their spears at the ready.

Sossimedes knew he could hold this gateway for hours with this force of men and smiled, then his face fell into a frown at a line of men with three legs. No, it wasn't men, what was it? A strange thudding sound came to his ears before he felt a sensation of flying, his legs leaping into the air, he saw his feet rising as he hit a man behind, a sudden searing pain bursting through his chest as his eyes went black.

**

The first bolt hit the king, striking him dead centre in his chest and forcing him twenty paces backwards as his body collapsed into itself at the force of the bolt which had thrown him from his feet. Another thump, then another as more bolts ripped into the spearmen standing in the doorway, their mangled bodies disappearing into the mass of confused men who were tumbling in great swathes, a sudden sound of screaming and fear rising from the gateway. Men ran, some out of the gate, others backwards into the city, but whichever way they went they screamed.

Marcus stepped forwards, squinting up at the walls to Regillensis, his archers raining arrows into the men below and the line of swordsmen holding against the strong-willed defenders. Looking back at the gates Marcus was fascinated to see lines of men still standing in deep rows despite the carnage in front of them. They simply didn't know what to do he told himself as he looked to Potitus, his efficient machines pumping arrow bolts into the mechanism and firing three bolts per minute. He watched a long brown streak as it disappeared into the ranks of men, a slice appearing in their midst as the front men fell under the death arrow.

A movement on the wall caught his eye as a grinning Regillensis waved his sword back and forth energetically. "Attack" Marcus shouted without a moment's hesitation gripping his sword and pointing it forwards, his legs running as Potitus called the Scorpions to halt and hundreds of men raced forwards from the Roman lines, charging at the gates of the city. The younger legs of Fabius outsprinted Marcus as the man screamed at the retreating line of Ferentian soldiers, many of them dithering as they dropped their spears and looked wildly around them for places to hide. Several legionaries were already in the gateway, the ornately carved stone standing silently as the screaming of men reverberated and echoed off the short archway. Marcus followed Fabius, a sudden sense of foreboding coming over him as the younger man launched his elaborately decorated long sword at the back of a fleeing defender, the sword slicing into his shoulder as the man fell screaming to his knees. Fabius had kicked his sword free and was hacking at the man's head by the time Marcus reached him and gripped his shoulder.

"Quintus" he said between deep breaths. "He is dead. Here stay by my side" he added as the young man's blood-spattered face stared vacantly back at him before he seemed to recognise who it was.

"Camillus" he said, his voice low before he nodded and grinned. "My first" he said with a mad look in his eye as Marcus glanced at the pulped head of the defenceless man at his feet. With a nod, he stepped forwards. "Come on" he said. "We need to get to the elders before the men completely wreck the city".

Stepping past the gory mess Marcus stood tall and took in the scene around him. Everywhere was in panic and chaos, people rushing headlong into alleyways and doorways, Roman soldiers attempting to grab loot and Ferentians rushing to either defend their homes or simply to stay alive by whatever means they could.

"Narcius" called Marcus waving his sword at the first spear who was attempting to create a line of soldiers which would maintain some sense of an ordered approach into the city. Narcius heard the voice but took seconds to scan the surroundings and locate his commander. Marcus strode across, pushing two rushing soldiers back with a snarl as their excited faces changed to fear at his angry expression.

"Cover the gate, make sure no-one leaves and find Scipio. Tell him to get three sections into each of those roads" he pointed beyond the hurrying and fighting soldiers. Ahead of them were three distinct roads radiating from the entrance to the city, each wide enough for five men to march abreast. "Set guards at every road intersection and build a holding pen for any prisoners outside the main gate. I want this place locked up tighter than a money-lenders purse" he smiled as he patted Narcius on the shoulder. "And" he added with a wide grin "great job" he said, Narcius's returning smile showing his appreciation. "You can tell me all about it later." As he finished Virginius appeared through the gate and saluted, his men coming to a stop as Narcius called out orders to the Centurions and started to organise the lines.

"Virginius, with me" Marcus said as he turned to see Fabius stood behind him watching the men forming into lines. "Come on, we need to find the city council" he said as he moved across, stepping over the dead men strewn across the entrance, and waved to a troop of men that Narcius had singled out and sent across to him. "With me" he called as he strode away towards the central of the three roads ahead of him, moving slightly to his right as he spotted a small knot of Romans fighting furiously with a group of defenders, the defenders appearing to be getting the better of the fewer attackers.

As the men of his Eagles closed ranks Marcus edged them forwards, a wall of shields five men wide and six deep stepping into the gap in front of the road. The defenders saw the approach and an anguished cry came from the men at the front, some of the rearmost fighters turning and disappearing down the well cobbled street at this new turn of events.

"Disengage" Marcus called as he stepped forwards to the relief of one of the Roman legionaries, his arm covered in a patchwork of criss-cross red marks where he had fought for his life. Marcus stepped into the gap as a swinging sword came straight for him, the edge of the blade crystal clear in his vision as he focused on the nicks along the cutting edge, the red blood dripping along the blade and the white fingers clenching the sword hilt. The man was screaming, his eyes almost closed as Marcus dropped his weight to the right, lifting his shield with his left forearm and feeling the blade clatter along the edge of the wood. Instantly he saw his target, the man's thigh was directly in front of him and he drove his sword straight through it, the muscle giving little resistance as the short sword punched through and rattled along his thigh bone causing the man to scream as he crumpled to the floor. At his left shoulder, Virginius hesitated, a look of surprise on his face as Marcus glanced quickly to him and then pulled his sword free before pushing his shield forwards into the falling body of the man. With a kick into the defender's face Marcus quickly drove the point of his blade into the face of the screaming man, his sword arm still swinging the long blade he held up in the air as he struggled and twisted to gain some leverage.

"Don't hesitate" Marcus roared at Virginius without looking at him, flecks of spit coming from his mouth as the lust of battle took over him. "Keep up" he called again as he stepped forwards with a shake of his head, his junior officer clattered from behind by a legionary who apologised but pushed him forwards again to keep up with the commander. Within three steps the Eagles had cleared the line of defenders and Marcus stood and looked around again. Narcius had worked his magic and a clear line of soldiers was setting up by the gateway, Scipio directing parties in various directions. Looking ahead into the roadway Marcus could see the larger town houses further along the street, knowing that the city square was beyond them he set out again, calling his men into their line and setting the pace. At his shoulder Virginius bumped his shield with Marcus who looked angrily at him and then took a deep breath.

"Sorry Virginius" he said as his eyes glanced left and right at movements from the houses, soldiers rushing out with armfuls of loot or dragging a woman by the hair, the screaming and sounds of fighting loud in the air. Marcus knew there was little he could do the stop the looting or rape until he got to the elders and gained a formal surrender, the death of the king was a blow he hadn't expected so early in the fight. "Just keep up with the men, take second line if you wish and keep your shield high" he added with an appraising look at Virginius' long blade, the metal a foot longer than any of the Eagles around him. He remembered how clumsy the long blades were in these tight battles and smiled across at the man as he gritted his teeth and visibly raised his shield.

Two Ferentians burst from a doorway, one with a large axe, the blade chopping into the shoulder of the soldier two places to Marcus's right and dragging the man to the floor, his sword hand gripping the wooden handle of the axe as he screamed a deep throated curse at the Ferentian as he twisted the man in front of him to be despatched by a thrust to the throat by another legionary, the axe-man's angry yell cut off instantly as his blood splashed onto the wooden doorframe as if his voice had somehow been trapped in the blood that left his throat.

"Keep moving" Marcus called as the remaining Ferentian was sliced across the face with a quick thrust from the Romans, his head whipping to the right as he was caught by a quick parry and then a thrusting punch into his ribs. As the men in the second and third rows stepped over his body a series of kicks and sword thrusts made sure he was dead and of no danger to those further back in the Roman line. Marcus nodded approvingly at the efficiency and training of Narcius's men.

The small force of Romans came to the last house on the road, the light of the city square ahead of them. With a glance over his shoulder, Marcus saw Scipio had sent a sizeable force of soldiers to follow behind him, the Romans marching quickly along the grey cobbled stones with hard, cold, faces as they moved quickly to his rear. As they stepped into the square it was clear that some of the earliest of the attacking Roman forces were still fighting running battles with the defenders, but here in the large square the defenders were more than holding their own.

After ten paces Marcus called a halt, his quick eyes scanning the scene and a wealth of scenarios coursing through his mind as he contemplated their next move. He couldn't make out any distinguishing marks of nobility in the large phalanx of men who stood their ground in front of a small temple, the colourful statues looking down on the scene with their godly smiles and serene faces.

"Virginius take the next hundred men and close those two roads" he said as he whipped his sword around at the entrances around them. "Keep everything that faces the gate clear of any defenders he said again as Virginius saluted and stepped backwards with a relieved smile, his voice calling to the men arriving behind him. He turned to the legionary to his right "find me a trumpeter" he said as he stepped forwards and looked right and left, calling to a number of Romans who had arrived from various alleyways and ordering them to get into the line.

"Romans, disengage" he called into the fray ahead of him, the majority of the men stepping back quickly as their training had taught them, but some taking a moment to hear the instruction and falling to the slices of the spears or swords of the defenders. "Disengage" he called again, stepping further forwards as the Romans edged backwards to a few calls from the blood covered Ferentians.

Within moments the square was a mass of men moving into positions, the defenders lining up twelve men deep in two phalanxes, the front line bristling with eight and twelve-foot-long spears behind thickly painted wooden shields, the colours creating a bright barriers across the square. The Roman force was more than double that of the Ferentians as the soldiers appeared from all the roads and alleyways leading to the square, Scipio instantly setting up lines to face the defenders once he saw Marcus and his soldiers in position. Marcus took another deep breath, his eyes scanning the phalanxes, the helmets dull in the shadows of the tall buildings behind them and the sun shining into his face. 'A tactical advantage to them', he thought, if they knew they had it. He waved to Scipio and called him across.

"Is Calvus here?" he asked without taking his eyes off the rows of men in front of them, the impasse suddenly causing a silence which was spreading across the city, a few screams and the unmistakable clamour of fighting coming from deep in the roads somewhere behind Marcus.

"He's with Narcius at the gates" Scipio replied, his quick intelligent eyes roving the ranks. "I don't see a leader" he said, his head moving right and left looking for the feathers which stood proud from the helmets of the leaders of the city.

"No, neither do I" he replied. "Let's see if they have one" he added with a grin as he stood tall and stepped into the space between the Roman shields and the Ferentian spears.

"Men of Ferentium" he called, his voice strong and loud as he looked slowly along the line of faces who were staring at him, some with fear and others with hatred. "Mars the war-bringer has spoken and you have lost your city" he said, his sword rising slowly and pointing to the sky as a few faces followed the movement into the heavens. "Your cause was surely unjust and your gods have deserted you" he said with a small bow of his head to show the sorrow he felt. "I am Marcus Furius Camillus, appointed by Rome to seize this city, and in the name of Apollo, Mars and the Senate of Rome I claim her as our prize."

Voices rose in the Ferentian ranks, a sudden cacophony of deep groans and shaking of heads, some angry at the loss and others defiant. Deep in the ranks a scuffle broke out as one man was clearly trying to rush forward and attack the Romans.

"I promise leniency to any man who throws his spear to the ground and surrenders" he called as the heads of the spear bearers glanced to their comrades around them. "Any man who drops his shield will suffer slavery but not be put to death" he shouted as he moved to his right and looked at each face in the crowd in front of him, his silence causing many to mumble to their fellows, the hubbub of noise growing as each second went by.

"I will speak with your leaders and take your surrender" he called as a greater clamour grew amongst the soldiers, some throwing their swords to the floor with a metallic thud. Marcus stood for a long moment, unsure that his words were understood or were being well received as the phalanxes bristled, some soldiers calling for surrender and others calling for attack.

"Move the men into a wider line" Marcus said to Scipio as they awaited the response. "I think they have lost their leaders" he added "they must have been with the King at the gate" he shrugged "and leaderless men can do dangerous things."

He stepped forwards again as Scipio turned to the men behind and started to issue orders, the moving Roman army causing a sudden flurry of Ferentian soldiers in the front line to drop their spears and rush forwards with arms in the air. Behind them other men growled their anger at the cowards who had given up, but the number of men throwing their weapons to the floor grew.

"Hold there, kneel" shouted Marcus, bringing his sword out in front at the surprised faces of the weapon-less men rushing forwards, fear appearing on their faces.

"Kneel" he shouted again as the first men knelt. A sudden panic gripped Marcus, the space in front of him full of men, some of whom he could see had come to a standstill unsure what to do, and he realised he was in the no-man's land between both armies, it would be easy to rush him.

"Kneel and we will take your surrender" he shouted as the Roman line took a step forward to be closer to their commander. A moment's silence descended and Marcus could hear the blood coursing through his veins as the first Ferentian men knelt, their faces full of fear. Behind them a clattering sound rose amidst a deep groan from the soldiers of Ferentium as more men simply threw their spears to the floor and called for mercy as the Roman lines cheered triumphantly at the kneeling ranks of the soldiers.

*

*

*

*

Chapter 26

Small pockets of resistance and fighting lasted for an hour as groups of Ferentians attempted to defend their homes and stood against the Romans in the narrow streets of the city, the cobbles running red with blood. Marcus had returned to the gates where Scipio had been detailed to set the defensive lines with Narcius, both men standing looking at the heaps of bodies spread across the entrance to the city, the walled doorway seeming to frown at its downfall.

At his approach Scipio waved him across. "That's the king" he said as he pointed to a bearded man with dark oiled hair and a white face, his eyes open wide as he stared up into the sky with a look of surprise. Marcus looked down at the dead body, a bolt still attached through his chest and a deep red, almost black, thick pool of blood underneath him.

"Look at this" Scipio said as he stepped across numerous mangled bodies, the bolts still either in the men or having passed through them, their rich clothing and armour marking them as the nobility of the city, it looked as if the bolts had ripped through every noble in Ferentium by the number of richly clad men lying dead at his feet. Scipio pointed to two men joined together by a shaft of wood, the bolt having skewered them through the stomachs. The front man's face was screwed in the agony of death but the man at the rear seemed to simply be asleep, his calm face a parody of the man attached to him by the bolt. Scipio laughed mirthlessly "looks like they were lovers and it was his first time" he said with a shake of his head at the pained expression on the front man's face. "These things" he said, kicking the bolt that protruded from the men "are lethal" he said. Marcus looked at the death around him, and took a deep breath.

"This space was ideal for them" he said pointing to a Scorpion bolt, his appraising eyes looking at the scene. "If they had more space we would not have hit them so hard. We were lucky to get the king in the first shot" he shrugged "and then the nobles simply stood like a chicken at a sacrifice waiting for the inevitable to happen." He turned his head slowly around the scene as a scout appeared and reported to Narcius, his wide mouth starting to curl at the corners at whatever news he brought.

'Narcius, detail some men to clear the bodies and line up any of the nobles in a separate pile, it would do us well to give them a decent funeral, and we don't want the gods to be angry with us" Marcus said with a grim smile.

Scipio glanced at Marcus as Narcius wandered across. "Camillus, sir. You have to see this" he said with a toothy grin which caused both Marcus and Scipio to frown at him as he turned and marched out of the blood-spattered city gates.

****

The six Senators sat around the low table, sweetmeats and milk-soaked breads laid out on the surface in various dishes of silver, one with a gold effigy of Apollo emblazoned on the side. "It's a question of taxation" Javenoli said as he stuffed a date into his mouth and chewed the soft fruit noisily. Spitting a seed into a bowl he continued. "The reserves are dangerously low despite the state's share of the spoils from Bolae, our debts exceed our income and the city continues to grow. Without something to bolster the reserves we cannot spend any more money on the roads or bridges" he shrugged slightly as he reached for another date, his eyes quickly searching the other senators for signs of agreement.

"More taxation though, Gaius" replied the bald-headed Cicurinus, a droplet of milk running down his chin as he wiped it away with a small cloth. "The people won't like it" he said exhaling deeply with a shake of his head as he took a grape from one of the bowls and bit into it. "It will give the plebeians another thing to veto as well."

"Without additional income we cannot support the building programme" Javenoli added "unless one of you men has a better plan for gaining some quick income?" he asked. A silence fell as the faces of the men looked to one another and shook their heads.

"Taxation or less war" replied Ahala, his lean face and light brown eyes looking at Javenoli with a smile. "It seems that one follows the other like a love-sick puppy" he added with a guarded expression.

"But it's a puppy we cannot feed" Javenoli replied with a thoughtful expression on his face.

"War is inevitable Ahala, you know that. The Latin delta is full of cities and trumped up kings who want to take our lands now that we are growing stronger than they are. With every passing day, we grow closer to war with Veii maybe that will solve our crises?" asked the lined face of Atratinus, his face alert at the prospect. "A war with Veii may be useful, it would help with two of our problems at least" he added as he glanced to Ahala "assuming we won of course."

"We will win" Ahala almost growled as he looked through his dark eyes at Atratinus. "Veii has only one defence, its walls. If we can scale them, then she will fall" he added with certainty.

"I doubt we can scale those walls, my friend" replied Senator Fidenas. "They are thirty feet high and ten feet thick. It would take all of the men in Rome to attack them and overwhelm them. I believe we need a new tactic to overcome Veii, storming the walls will not work" he said, his thinning hair oiled across his low forehead.

"Good men will storm any wall" Ahala replied, his face set into a stern grimace.

"I disagree" Fidenas said as he shifted on his couch to look directly at Ahala. "For twenty years we have had peace with Veii and in all that time they have built and rebuilt those walls. We do not have enough men to get over them" he shrugged "and the Etruscan alliance will surely come to their aide" he added with a small nod of his head. "The Capenates are spoiling for war" he said with a gleam in his eye as he looked to Ahala and smiled.

"The Capenates are a bunch of old toothless women" Ahala laughed. "I fear my own mother-in-law more than I fear a thousand Capenates" he added to a ripple of laughter from the assembled men.

After a short silence Javenoli coughed slightly, his hand moving to his lips as he did so. 'Gentlemen, what have we decided with regard to the financial situation?" he asked, his eyes wide as he lowered his head to drink from a silver cup with a picture of Hector being slain by Achilles, the men stiff and crude in their poses.

"Another war tax will be difficult to pass through the plebeian council, as I said" Ahala replied, his anger clear in his voice.

"Why so?" Javenoli answered. "Surely they understand the issues at hand. Without the tax, we cannot afford to continue to fund the basic equipment for the Legions and to support the improvements we need in the roads."

"They see only what they want to see and they don't trust those in charge of the funds" Atratinus added as he lay back on his thickly padded reclining couch, its soft blue cushions arranged to support his back. "We need a new tax" he said with a sense of finality "not another grain tax or bridge toll that we spend more money administering than we gain from collections."

"A tax on the poor would give us plenty of funds, there are enough of them in the streets" Javenoli replied with a shake of his head. "I agree Atratinus, a new tax, but what? And how do we find compromise with the plebeians?"

Atratinus shook his head as he considered the problem. As he began to speak a booming knock came from the door, three loud bangs which made each head turn towards the doors as they swung inwards.

A well-dressed female slave appeared, her woollen Chiton long and flowing with a thin cord belt around her middle and elaborately braided hair sitting on her shoulders, all of which suggested she must be a favourite of the master of the house.

"Master, a messenger" she said, her face looking to the floor as she spoke, her eyes glancing quickly to her owner as her full lips curled.

"Send him in" Ahala said quickly, a flush coming to his cheeks at the glance from the slave and the raised eyebrows from Atratinus, his smile showing an element of jealously.

The slap of sandals on the floor announced the messenger, his dusty clothes and untidy hair telling of the long ride he had undertaken to return to Rome at his best speed. Bowing he searched for Ahala, the senior of the group and leader of the Senate. As he stepped forward and bowed he handed across a sealed and covered tablet, the brown leather clean and bright against the dust of his clothes as he removed it from the shoulder bag he had swung across his body.

"Sir, news from Lucius Furius Medullinus. He asks for your time in attending to the matters in the message and I am asked to return with any orders at your command" the messenger announced as he stepped across and handed the leather-bound message to Ahala.

Ahala sat up straight and took the message with a nod and a serious frown as the five men around him also sat straight and looked to him with fervent glances, their eyes greedy for the information he held. Ripping the seal and scanning the message Ahala's eyes narrowed, his eyebrows pinched and his lips curled two or three times before his face looked up at the men around the room.

"Gentlemen, it is war. Veii has snubbed our ambassadors and ridiculed our city" He turned to the men around him with a gleam in his eye "it is time to make them pay for their insolence."

****

Marcus stood with his hands on his hips, a broad smile across his face as he watched the small convoy of men traipsing across the path through the ravine, the grinning face of Mella at the head of the small force.

"What exactly is happening?" Scipio asked as he wandered across to Marcus and stood watching the procession of men and horses.

'It seems Mella found a few fugitives from the city attempting to escape with quite a lot of treasures" Marcus smiled in reply, his eyes scanning the convoy coming towards them.

"This has been a good campaign Marcus" Scipio said in a low voice with a rise in his eyebrows. "The senate will be pleased that you have retaken the town within the three weeks it set." He considered Marcus for a long moment, the dark hair and muscular frame complemented by his good height and bright intelligent eyes. "My father says you should run for Censor. Now would be a good time."

Marcus turned to his friend, his warm face full of pride at the quick defeat of their enemies. He smiled. "Maybe" he replied as he placed a hand on his friend's shoulder "but what use would I be in planning roads or bridges or even in administering the public morals" he laughed as he said the final word. "What do I know of such things?" he added.

Scipio looked to his friend with a frown and a slight shake of his head before speaking. "You are perfect for the role" he said with true meaning. "You have a dignity born of your heritage as well as high moral standards from your training as *the* Camillus" he said with a grin, which Marcus returned. "And" he continued "the people will respect you because of your military record, your dignitas and your clear thinking. I would think that within your eighteen months in the role you would make a few changes to the administration of Rome which would benefit *all* of the people." Marcus looked at his friend and smiled. Both men had spent many hours discussing the issues of Rome with Calvus; Scipio arguing for a strong paternalistic and military based state, but Calvus interested in forms of government and shared Republic which, he stated, were true to the original founders of Republican Rome in which they lived. Without a true and democratic Republic, Rome may as well appoint another king, he had argued. Marcus had been swayed by the arguments of both men, though his head told him that the more testing and difficult road was that described in Calvus's argument. The words '*all of the people*' also struck a note in Marcus's mind as his thoughts went to the prophecy and the words '*the Eagle will be a true servant of the people. He must be a patron of the people.*' Would the role of Censor help him to achieve his destiny? He looked to Scipio, his eyes bright as he spoke "You may be right, it is something I must consider when we return to Rome, which I wish to do as soon as possible. Detail a guard of three hundred men to hold the city, Virginius will command until the Senate decide on our next steps" and with this he strode forwards towards Mella who was less than a hundred paces from the entrance to the city.

*

*

*

*

Chapter 27

Aquilinus looked at the document again, his bright eyes scanning the words and numbers quickly but efficiently. Everything looked in order and he smiled at the seal of Cicurinus before he placed the vellum in a leather holder and handed it to the slave who was standing waiting across the desk from him.

"Take this to the Quaestor and have him deliver it" he said, his eyes already moving to the next wax tablet on his desk, the pile had grown in the past two days since the levy for the army to attack Veii had been given. He looked up as the slave exited the room, the ornate door closing slowly as the man disappeared. Aquilinus sat back in his chair and pinched the bridge of his nose, the headache was coming back again. He closed his eyes, screwing them tightly and then releasing them to stare at the wall ahead of him as his eyes focused on the small table which held two Greek vases, each covered in battle scenes from the siege of Troy. At this distance, he couldn't make out the individual figures and he shook his head with a deep sigh. He cursed his father's weak eyes and considered for a moment how the man had been almost blind before he reached his fortieth birthday. He had the same curse. Sighing deeply, Aquilinus rose from behind the desk and frowned at the pile of work awaiting his signature.

"Wait" he called, rushing to the door as the chair behind him rocked on its legs at his sudden movement. "Salvator" he called to the slave who was donning his cloak by the main doorway. "I will take the details to the Quaestor myself" he added as he strode across and held out his hand for the leather pouch. "Fetch me two of the guards" he said as he gripped the leather and weighed it on his hands, his mind racing through how he could use the war against Veii to maximise his political career.

Within a few minutes, Aquilinus and two thick-set bodyguards were turning past the temple of Saturnus, the lofty statue of Saturnius Mons looking down on his people behind six thick columns, each column ringed with flowers from the recent festival. Despite the early hour, the forum was busy with people doing their daily shopping or listening to oration and poems along the recesses of the old shops. Aquilinus smiled at the youthful faces listening to an old bearded man who was attempting to recite Homer, his high-pitched tone not doing any justice to the epic poem.

"Aquilinus, over here"

Glancing to his right he saw that Tribune Postumius had called his name and was waving to him from a sandal maker's stall, his small retinue included his son and his wife, her thick stola a very light blue with a darker blue Palla over her shoulders and a small retinue of slaves and bodyguards. Postumius had turned out to be very well connected and was the current hero of the victory over Bolae and Aquilinus knew the man could be extremely useful to his career.

"Tribune" he said as he strode across to Postumius, the bodyguards growling at the crowd to get out of their way as they did so. "My lady" he said, nodding at Postumius's wife, "Sir" he said to his son as the young lad smiled nonchalantly back at him. "A fine day for meandering through the crowds" he said as he looked to Postumius and then to the sandals he held in his hand.

"Gallus surely you have some better quality than this" Aquilinus said to the small dark-haired stall holder with a wink as he raised his eyebrows to Postumius. The small man grinned toothlessly and disappeared under the table, dragging a heavy sack into view and rummaging into the contents as Postumius smiled and placed a hand on Megellus's shoulder.

"Here master" said the stall holder as he held out two pairs of sandals, each cut in soft leather with thick soles, the leather ties holding the pairs together. "From Carthage" he said as he looked at the two men appraisingly, his mind working through what he could charge for them. "Goat leather, beaten six times to soften them and then the stitching is done by virgins under a candle to Juno." He nodded firmly as Postumius took one of the pairs of sandals, his head nodding as he felt their weight and handed them to his son.

"Master will grow into them and they will grace his feet making him fly like Apollo" the seller said as he tried to embellish the goods. Aquilinus glanced to Postumius and smiled before looking to the stall holder and saying, "one eighth of an As for both" at which the man, as expected, made a guttural sound as if he had been stung, his breath sucking deep between his clenched teeth. "I have five children to feed, Master" he said, his eyes flicking to Megellus and back to Aquilinus. "Quarter As for the two is the best I can do. No more or I won't be feeding my poor babies tonight" he said as he shook his head and waved his hands theatrically, his eyes twinkling as he told the lie. Aquilinus half-laughed. He had made it his business to know most of the stall sellers as his role included handing out the licences for trading. Gallus was a good man and had more bastard children than Aquilinus could remember, his drinking habits and carousing were legendary amongst the stall holding community.

Postumius glanced to Aquilinus, who seemed to be enjoying the bartering, something that Postumius didn't understand, he was happy to pay the going rate, though these new sandals were definitely a better quality than the ones on the stall.

"Tribune?" Aquilinus asked as he inclined his head to the stall holder "do you have a deal?" he added.

"Yes" said Megellus firmly before Postumius could reply, a laugh coming to his father's face as he fingered the soft leather of the sandals.

"You grace me with your custom, Master" said Gallus as his face split into a wide grin, his black beard oiled into short curls making the yellow teeth appear unreal as he smiled at the men and held out his hand.

"The boy knows his mind" Aquilinus said as Megellus paid the stall holder from his own purse and the small group left the stall, the ladies falling behind the men as they set off across the forum.

"It is important for the youth to understand the value of money and to be able to converse with the plebs and traders" Postumius replied. "The city grows every year and without the essential skills of managing the people, he will never rise to command a legion as his forebears have done" Postumius said haughtily as Aquilinus feigned his brightest smile.

"Very well put" Aquilinus agreed as he smiled to Megellus, who had his father's stride, the chest lifted and eyes looking arrogantly at the crowds as they were jostled out of their way.

"Are you out on official business?" Postumius asked as his eyes flicked to the leather pouch in Aquilinus' hand.

"Yes" he replied "a draft for the Quaestor for the Veienteine campaign. It seems that the soldiers are still upset regarding the issue of Bolae" Aquilinus said, raising a hand slightly as he knew Postumius's part in the matter "but these orders require each man to call to arms or to be exiled from the city" he added with a brief smile as Postumius nodded his reply.

"Each day I receive petitions from the plebeians demanding their spoils" he said, his face momentarily downcast before he looked up with a smirk.

Before Aquilinus could reply a call came from a small knot of men in front of the small party and they came to a stop, the bodyguards suddenly becoming tense as they surrounded their masters, Postumius gripping Megellus and pulling him closer to his side.

"Publius Postumius, where is my money" called a man with a greying eye patch on his face, his dark hair lank and greasy as if it had not been washed or combed for days. "I demand retribution for the blood I gave on the battlefield, for the brothers I lost in service to Rome" he called as several men appeared wielding thick clubs and short daggers.

"Run and get the Quaestor" Aquilinus whispered to his slave, the man disappearing into the crowd within seconds.

As Tolero spoke, he shifted the eye patch slightly and set his feet firmly as if he were about to run at Postumius. Aquilinus, with a confidence born of years of ordering men around in administration stepped forwards and placed his hands on his hips.

"Who are you men to make this demand?" he said, his eyes scanning the brutes who blocked their path as the crowds parted to a discreet distance; enough to be out of harm's way but close enough to watch the ensuing action with interest. "What right do you have to stop a Tribune of the people?" he added as Tolero stepped forwards, his eyes boring into Aquilinus.

"I have the right of a soldier to his spoils from battle. I have the right of a man who has bled for his city and seen his brothers die for its glory to receive that which is owed to me" he growled as a fleck of spit dripped onto his lower lip.

Aquilinus, his blood up, stood his ground as he looked at the man in front of him with disdain. "The law stated that the Tribune was within his rights and the Senate agreed" Aquilinus started to say before Tolero, his hands moving like lightning, punched him square on the nose, the straight arm punch taking the Patrician secretary off his feet as his face erupted in pain and he fell unconscious onto the floor. Two bodyguards jumped forwards, one grabbing Tolero by the arm and the other kicking out at him as the man, his years of military training making his actions instinctive, wheeled the grip of his attacker and placed one guard in front of the other, one of the men behind him glancing a blow with a wooden mallet across the leather skull cap of one of the guards. Both men went to the floor as Tolero yelled "You owe me Postumius" and turned back towards the Tribune, whose face drained of colour at the sudden turn of violence.

One of the bodyguards grabbed Postumius and moved him behind the remaining guards as he stepped forwards and rained blows at Tolero, the two men grappling and cursing as they whirled in a small circle, the attackers moving around to loop Postumius's party.

"Father?" Megellus said, his strong voice bringing Postumius back to his senses and his wife screamed at the men to leave them alone.

Postumius gripped the arm of one of his attackers as he wheeled his club above his head, the heavy toga around his arms restricting his movements as he did so. The attacker grinned at him before Postumius smashed his elbow into the side of the man's head before stepping forward and pushing him to the ground as a bodyguard moved in front of him and pulled a short dagger from his calf-length sandals, the metal glinting before a red spray of blood and a scream from the assailant told him that he had plunged the metal into the man's thigh.

"You need to get home" Postumius called to his wife and son, almost pushing them backwards as the men in front of him closed ranks on Tolero and stepped forwards again, Tolero's brute force knocking a bodyguard to the floor with a sickening thud of his leather thong-bound right hand, the gritted teeth and hate in his eyes turning to Postumius as soon as the guard fell to the floor.

"Halt!" called a voice as a sudden gap appeared in the crowd and the broad striped toga of the Quaestor appeared with a small retinue of men, each armed with a sword. "Halt in the name of the Senate and people of Rome" he called as Tolero glanced to him and back to Postumius. "Come on" Tolero called as he moved towards Postumius, his eyes challenging anyone to stand in his way. Postumius placed his feet into the stance of a Greek wrestler and smiled confidently at Tolero as two bodyguards stepped in front of him. Although inside he was shaking with fear he smiled at Tolero, knowing that the Quaestor could action criminal proceedings against him for brawling in the forum and attacking a Tribune and seeing instantly that the arrival of the Quaestor meant that the fight was almost certainly over. "I know you Tolero" he said, pointing a finger at the advancing man "and you" he said looking to Tolero's right "and others" he added as he marked each man with a stare. "You will be brought to justice for this, all of you" he added as Tolero swung a dagger at the face of one of the bodyguards, the man ducking its arc and swinging a punch at the body of Tolero, who simply moved aside as the movement missed.

Tolero laughed loudly as he gripped the arm of the bodyguard, stepping low and across the man as a thick wooden club connected with the man's skull, a sudden cracking sound splitting the air as his hair turned crimson and he fell with a thud to the flagstones. As Tolero raised his dagger and lunged forwards at Postumius he was grappled to the ground by two more men, each of them grunting at the force of Tolero as he struggled to gain purchase on the smooth flagstones of the forum.

The Quaestor appeared and shook the dagger from Tolero's hand as two more of the attackers were grappled to the floor by the newly arrived men, one taking a dagger in the arm and screaming curses at the attacker before smashing the hilt of his sword into the man's temple and knocking him senseless before collapsing himself. Tolero shook himself free and whipped his blade in a circle, the blade catching the Quaestor across the forearm, his blood spraying into Postumius's face.

Tolero grunted as he was clubbed by a thick-set man, his bloodied face testament to the blows he had taken in defence of Postumius.

"Tribune?" the Quaestor said through gritted teeth as he gripped his bleeding arm "Who are these men?" he asked with wild eyes.

"They are dead men" Postumius replied with a smile as he looked to his son.

****

"No Camillus" Ahala stated firmly, his eyebrows raised and his mouth turned down at the edge of his lips. "The" he looked again at the tablet, the smooth wax covered in scrawled words "*Scorpions?*" he asked with a frown "are simply too expensive for the state to develop. Should you wish to continue to utilise them for your own small force then we are happy to sanction that use." As he finished he raised a hand as Marcus looked as if he was about to speak. "I don't doubt that they are particularly useful and that they served a purpose in the attack at Ferentium, but I don't see how they will be of general use to our forces." At this he turned to the aged man on his right and gave him a quizzical look, the old man nodding his agreement.

Marcus fumed at the lack of foresight from the council but bit his tongue. He knew it would come to nothing if he continued to ask for funds to develop more Scorpions and so he nodded his assent and placed his hand over the wax tablet he had brought to the meeting, closing the top cover and standing with a nod to the two Senators sat across the table from him. Thanking the Senators, he turned to leave before Ahala spoke again.

"Camillus, will you be putting yourself forward for the vote for Tribune for the assault on Veii?" he asked, his companion sitting straighter as the words were spoken. "Rome could use someone with your undoubted skills and good fortune" he added as his face took on an impassive look.

"I have decided to run for Censor, Senator" he replied. "I also believe my brother Lucius has put himself forward for the role and so I will take a step to the rear for the moment" he said with a nod of his head.

"Shame" replied Ahala before looking up and smiling. "I hear your good lady wife is with child" he half asked, half stated before adding "congratulations" as Marcus nodded back to his question.

"Our thanks, Senator" replied Marcus as he nodded again to the two men and turned to leave the room. On closing the door Scipio, who had been waiting anxiously outside, rushed across.

"Well?"

"They said no"

"What? Why?"

"Money, I guess" shrugged Marcus "Lucius says the treasury is bare despite the treasures we returned to Rome and the spoils from Bolae. If they had only changed their minds and repopulated Bolae they could have sold the prime land and made enough money to fund the next seasons horse and some armour. It's no wonder the plebeians..." he started before Scipio shut his words off with a loud *shush*.

"The issue is closed then" he said loudly as a few heads turned towards the two men, some eyes squinting as the line of men waiting to see the Senators looked at them and listened to their discussions.

Marcus chided himself for letting his voice mouth some of his thoughts in such a public arena. Without thinking he had nearly spoken support for the words of Calvus, something that he knew would create him a number of political enemies, something he could not afford if he were to run for Censor. Glancing around he smiled warmly to Scipio and clapped him on the shoulder before speaking in a semi-whisper which he knew everyone in the room would hear. "Ahala and Cicurinus did say that they would be delighted if I were to run for Censor though. They think that the public morals would be served well by my knowledge of the sacrifices and rituals as well as my skills with finances" he smiled as the two men headed for the doorway.

"Excellent" said Scipio "and I am going to ask to run for junior Tribune in the siege against Veii" he added as Marcus half laughed at his theatrics. Heads turned at both statements and Marcus could see some of the older Patricians nodding heads and tapping their fellows on the shoulder with a glance towards the two younger men as they left the room.

****

An hour later Lucius arrived at Marcus's door, the slave allowing him entrance and taking his travelling cloak.

"Lucius" exclaimed Marcus, his wide smile beaming at his brother, "it is a joy to see you. Livia" he called "Lucius is here."

Marcus's wife appeared, her flowing robes draped to the floor as she greeted Lucius and waved for the slaves to bring drinks and sweetmeats for the guest. After a few pleasantries Livia had made her excuses and left the two men to discuss politics and war as they always did, Marcus beaming at her as she kissed him softly on the cheek before leaving.

"A fine woman" Lucius said as she left "father did well for you there young Camillus" he laughed as Marcus's grin split his face.

"So, what news?" Marcus asked after a second or two of silence.

"I have been offered the second in command for the attack on Veii as I expected" he added with a satisfied nod of his head as he picked up a wooden cup and poured some of the house wine from their father's vineyard in Tusculum which had been left by a slave.

"Excellent. And the Tribune, not Postumius?" he asked as Lucius grimaced for a second.

"Flacus" replied Lucius with a frown.

"No? How?" came the quick reply.

"Probably bought it" Lucius said with a short exhalation of breath. "After the fracas with the Capenates a few years ago I thought he would never command again" he shook his head. "Nearly a thousand men dead and lucky to escape with any measure of honour" he continued as he tipped back the cup and drained the wine. "This is good" he said with a surprised expression.

"I had it watered with fruit juice and lemon" replied Marcus "to take away the acid and make it milder" he smiled.

Lucius nodded as he re-filled the cup and sipped it again admiringly. "You must write down the measures so I can do the same" he said. "Flacus is a fool and everyone knows it" he added as he looked to his brother. "With him in charge I will be running the army without the glory of command" he said glumly.

Both men sat in silence for a moment before Marcus replied.

"How is the levy coming along? Are you near strength?" Marcus asked.

"From the latest report, we have nearly three thousand men, so over two thirds of strength. With Ambustus as master of the horse we will soon have more than enough Eques. You know, ever since that damned charge on the phalanx at the three crossroads the man has attracted every glory-hunting Patrician in the city and Latin Delta" laughed Lucius. "I wouldn't mind if it had been his idea" he said with a shrewd look to his younger brother.

'A moment of luck on my part" Marcus replied with a knowing smile.

'Luck plays no part in it *Camillus*" Lucius said with a smile. "Luck is when good planning and timing come together" he added. "When you have the gods on your side" he added as he cocked his head and looked to his brother "then such things are called fortune, and you, my brother, have the gods smiling on you."

Marcus felt uncomfortable, as he always did when the prophecy and its words were discussed. "I still don't see how the prophecy will be my destiny, brother" Marcus said honestly. "The Eagles are not yet leading Rome, they are a small force and have little control, never mind *five times*" he added. "And the *barbarians*?" he asked with a shrug of his shoulders.

Lucius smiled at his brother as he sipped from the cup. "I am sure that in ten years brother, you will be telling me exactly how this prophecy has worked in our favour." As he placed the cup on the table he turned back with a measure of urgency in his face which made Marcus look at him eagerly. "Have you heard about Tolero?" he asked as Marcus shook his head and frowned, his brows creasing.

"It seems that Tolero and several others attacked Postumius in the forum and demanded payment from Bolae" he said quickly, wetting his lips with a smile at the wine cup. "Yes" he said as Marcus's blank expression told him the news had not yet reached his door. "They attacked Postumius and his family in the forum, and from what I hear they tried to drag the clothes from his wife's back and killed two of Postumius's bodyguards before Structus, you know the Quaestor?" he asked before continuing without stopping "came to his aid with several guards and arrested Tolero and his men. To make it worse Tolero sliced Structus across the arm with a dagger, it will be his death" he finished with a shake of his head.

Marcus sat with his mouth open at the news. "And Bassano? Was he there?" he asked.

"No Bassano was not there but I hear he has petitioned the Senate and been refused. Tomorrow the leaders, including Tolero are to be publically crushed in the Curia. They deserve it!" he stated with finality as Marcus sat back in his chair and took a deep draft from his cup.

"Bassano won't like that" he stated. "Have the Plebeian tribunes vetoed the act?"

"No, from what I hear the two men have been quiet on the subject but the old soldiers are bitter and are calling for a sessation for the Veienteine campaign."

"No" replied Marcus. "Why have I not heard of this? I was at the Senate meeting earlier today!" he said with a shake of his head. Lucius shrugged and placed the cup back on the table.

"Tomorrow will be a difficult day" he said as he looked at his brother. "Postumius seems to be charmed. Anything he touches seems to turn to profit and anyone who opposes him seems to come to grief" he added with a frown as he looked to his brother. "It is no wonder the man believes that the prophecy of Antonicus was about him."

"Then maybe it is" laughed Marcus as he sat back in his chair.

"Don't say such things Marcus" Lucius said as he tapped the edge of the table three times and mumbled some words to avert the evil eye. Marcus smiled at how superstitious his brother had become, but said nothing.

*

*

*

*

Chapter 28

Taking the final turn Bassano closed his back to the wall and took a deep breath, the odour of urine from the narrow alley hitting his nostrils as he screwed his face against the smell. As he waited he was sure that nobody had followed him, but he needed to be certain.

Five minutes later he was on the move again, taking the dark alley towards the Quirinal Hill and skirting the drainage ditch which ran along the length of the lower slope. Within two minutes he had found the location he had been given and sat behind a wall across the road watching for movements within the house. A small shutter opened in the door, the orange light of a candle flicked across the square viewing portal, a pair of eyes became momentarily visible in the shadow before the light disappeared. Moving quickly Bassano, crossed the street and knocked four times on the door, his eyes never moving from the street around him as his breathing quickened in his chest.

"Salve friend" came the disembodied voice as the viewing hole opened slightly and a fearful eye peeked out.

"Tolero" said Bassano as he edged closer to the wooden door eager to get inside the house. The sound of a metal bolt rasping along its housing screeched into the night as the door jerked open and Bassano slipped inside, the heat of the house hitting his cold skin.

"Welcome Centurion" said the man with the candle behind the door. "We thought you weren't coming" he grinned, his smile showing that he was pleased Bassano had arrived. "In there" he pointed with the candle, the flame flickering as it moved and the strong smell of the cheap tallow pervading the small entrance hall.

Bassano moved into the room and blinked as several candles lit the room, the light almost hurting his eyes after such a long time in the darkness of the streets.

"Centurion" said a number of the men, many of them standing as he entered, some clapping him on the shoulder and grinning at his arrival, others more sullen but nevertheless pleased to see him.

Nodding to the men and gripping the shoulders of one or two of his old comrades Bassano, looked around the room. "So Amitus" he said, sitting on the end of a bench as several of the men shoved each other to move along to make space "what is the plan?" he asked to the bearded man at the head of the table, his bone handled dagger positioned in front of a small devotion candle which was placed in the middle of the table, a smell of lavender coming from the oil in the rustic bowl next to it.

Amitus glanced at the men around the table, his eyes dark in the half light. "Tomorrow at dawn Tolero and Rutilius will be taken to the Curia" he started as a low grumble came from the seated men. "Postumius will deliver his speech condemning them for attacking a Tribune and a Quaestor and then they will start the process. Darcius" at which he nodded to a short man with a bald head and thick eyebrows "says the sacrifice is to be completed by the Flamens and the ceremony will take ten minutes so we need to act before that time. Any later and the gods will not be pleased" he added as several men fumbled with rue sprigs or other talismans to their favourite deities, some mumbling a quick prayer to avert the eyes of the vengeful gods.

"We can't get them out of the gaol tonight?" Bassano asked, his eyes staring at the leader of the meeting.

"Unlikely Centurion" Amitus said. "They have several guards and are in the deep pit at the Tullianum and the ropes and wheel have been removed. To get them out we would need a small army and a lot of luck" he added solemnly as his head shook slowly from side to side.

"Then tomorrow it is" Bassano said. "And what is the exact plan?" he added as he looked at the faces of the men around the room, all of them ex-soldiers from the Bolae campaign.

****

The sword arced but Postumius simply stepped inside the arm of his attacker and punched his sword through the breastplate of his assailant, the man melting into the background as he fell. Another attacker lunged forwards, his face split by yellowed teeth and narrowed eyes, the shout indistinct in the noise of battle. The man's spear was tipped with a rusty point, and as Postumius wafted the heavy iron aside with his shield he shook his head at the lack of preparation the soldier had given to his weapon, surely such a man should have been flogged for his lassitude. The spear rose in the air as the face of the enemy turned to surprise and then to fear as Postumius strode forward, his thighs strong and thick, like Achilles he thought, and dispatched the spear holder with a thrust through the heart, grinning at the man's scream as he fell to the dusty earth. Several more attackers appeared, some falling back with fear in their eyes, others running forwards for glory, or death.

"Master." The voice was low and respectful but loud enough to wake Postumius from his deep sleep. As the final attacker thrust his spear towards Postumius he smiled as he opened his eyes to see the dark room of his bedchamber.

"Is it time?" he asked, his senses bringing him to the present as he blinked away the happy thoughts of his invincible dream.

"Yes Master" said the slave as he placed a towel next to the bowl of steaming water on the pedestal near the bed.

"My armour?" Postumius asked.

"Gleaming brighter than the morning sun in summer" smiled the slave, his head nodding at the hours he had spent deep into the night polishing the brass and oiling the leather of Postumius' Tribunes' uniform.

Postumius grunted as he sat up and took a sip of the cool water handed to him by the slave, the cold liquid waking him as it hit his tongue and took away the dryness of the night.

"Excellent. Light another candle to Mars and tell the cook to boil eggs, I fancy eggs before I go out today" he said, the slave nodding as he placed a garment on the bed and bowed as he stepped backwards towards the door.

"And hot bread" Postumius called, a grin coming to his lips as he considered the day and what it would bring.

The house woke soon after Postumius, the slaves working the fires and adding oils to the lamps. Postumius strode around the house, his energy growing as the sun began to creep over the horizon. All he could think about was the spectacle of the day, the deaths of the men who had attacked him in the forum and how right and proper it was that they died in full view of their plebeian supporters. Soldiers needed order and punishment was the best way to gain order, he thought to himself.

He shifted the wax tablet which he had placed on the table in front of him and mumbled the words as his slave rolled the boiled egg and began to remove the shell. "People of Rome. Citizens, Senators" he said in a low voice as he considered changing the words to place Senators ahead of the citizens. He knew his speech would be the talk of Rome for many weeks and it had to be perfect if he were to raise his case to move into the Senatorial ranks. "Senators, Citizens" he said with a curt nod "the gods have decreed the punishment for these men. Men who swore an oath to Rome and to their fellow soldiers and then broke it" his shoulder twitched as his mind went through the action of throwing his right arm out theatrically at this point to increase the effect of the words, a grin coming to his face.

"Father" came a sleepy voice as Megellus entered the room, his hair still tangled from his sleep and his eyes showing his excitement as he strode into the room, his face set into a firm smile but his stoic posture attempting to show his stature as a patrician of Rome, even to his father.

'Ah, Megellus" Postumius said, kicking a chair away from the table with his right foot and motioning for his son to sit. "These eggs are cooked to perfection" he said as he pointed to a wooden bowl filled with the small white, shell less, objects. "You and mother must be ready for the sacrifices, it will do you good to see the augurs and priests at their work" he said as he continued to read the words on his tablet whilst munching on a chunk of bread he had torn from the small loaf in front of him, the steam rising into the rapidly lighting room as the sun continued to rise above the houses outside.

"Will it be" Megullus asked, his eyes looking to the table and then to his father, who had stopped eating and turned to face his son "horrible?" he finished.

Postumius contemplated the question, one that had not crossed his mind as to him the fate of the men was of their own choosing and the punishment was as befitted the crime. He looked to his son, the small mouth set in a fixed demeanour as he tried to appear brave. War made men hard, Postumius thought. They saw death and destruction every day, becoming almost immune to the smell and sights of it, however terrible they were. Yes some men struggled to come to terms with the worst atrocities, often drowning their nightmares in endless nights of debauchery and drunkenness, but this was the way of the world, life was hard, the gods were fickle and could turn your success to failure in the blink of an eye. He looked at his son again and smiled. "Yes Megellus" he said. "It will be horrible to see a man crushed under the stones." He placed his hand on his sons and smiled at him. "You must understand that the gods have decreed this action and the punishment is fitting for the men who attacked us in the Forum and tried to kill us." He picked up an egg and placed it in the small bowl in front of Megellus and nodded for him to eat. "When you are older, my son, you will look back on today and what you see and you will know that it is right for us to smite our enemies and to put fear in their hearts. The actions decreed by the law must be carried out in the manner of the punishment, however terrible it may seem to your young eyes." He considered his son for a moment as the boy sliced the egg into three pieces and placed one of the slices on a small chunk of warm bread before starting to eat it. "Death comes easily but we choose the manner of our death by our actions and our choices" he said as he looked into his sons eyes "the gods decide our fate and we play our part in determining the timing and manner of our successes and failures" he said as his sons eyes opened with wonder at the words. "These men are the stones in the river that tumble as the water rushes over them, wearing them to grains of sand whilst Patricians stride the river with the favour of the gods" he said with such conviction that Megellus's mouth fell open at the words.

"Today will be hard my son" he said "the deaths of the men will be terrible, they will scream and cry, the crowds will wail and gnash their teeth and the bodies will be like nothing you have ever seen. But, Megellus" he said as he reached across and placed his hand on the boys shoulder "you must sit tall in your seat and look down on these men as grains of sand being washed away by the river as you stand proud across it, your grandfather and great grandfather and all the generations of the Postumii standing beside you. You will be strong my son, I know you will" he said, his own deep brown eyes reflecting back at him from those of his son.

****

Marcus felt the pang of guilt that he felt every morning when he saw the beggars in the streets, some missing limbs, others blind but most emaciated due to lack of food. He strode past two men too weak to raise their bowls and shook his head, their Greek features suggesting they were mercenaries who had fared badly in some recent campaign. The streets were quiet as the sun was only just starting to rise above the hills, the dawn chorus of birdsong still fresh in the air.

'These beggars should be cleared from the streets Camillus" Regillensis said as the two men headed for the Curia, their thick cloaks billowing in the strong breeze as a small retinue of attendants and slaves followed behind them. "When we are Censors we should take it as our first act to clean the streets of these men" he said as he shook his head at another beggar in a pile of his own urine and faeces, the stench filling the doorway in which he lay.

"I agree" Marcus said with a wrinkled nose as he moved past the man quickly. "We need to be elected first though" he laughed as Regillensis laughed with him. "I think we should also look at how we can continue the building of tenements for the soldiers, they need houses and there are too few in the city" he added as his eyes looked to the sky. "We will be very early" he said to his partner as they started to cross the Vicus Cuprius, the high sided buildings giving way to lower dwellings with the high walls of the richer families.

"Better to be early so that we can greet all the Senators and tell them of our plans to rid the streets of the beggars" Regillensis replied rubbing his hands as he turned left and started to climb a short steep rise.

Out of the corner of his eye Marcus saw a movement which momentarily confused him, the sudden flash of light disappearing almost as quickly as it had come. Turning his head he suddenly stopped, causing Regillensis to turn and stare at him.

"What is it?" he asked as he frowned at Marcus, who was looking into an alleyway to his left. Marcus didn't answer but stepped to the entrance to the alleyway as two of their guards stepped forwards and stood shoulder to shoulder with him.

"Probably nothing" Marcus replied as he squinted into the darkness, the alley suddenly seeming cold and empty as the road behind the houses rose away into the gloom.

"Come on then" called Regillensis as he set off up the rise his sandals slapping on the cobbles as the slaves hurried behind him.

****

"That was close" whispered Felix as he took a cloth bundle from behind a wooden box, the old wood soft and covered in mildew.

"Too close, but a good omen that Camillus didn't see us" came the reply from the man crouched next to him in the darkness, both men starting to breathe again now that the men who had suddenly appeared at the entrance to the alley had moved on.

Felix untied the straps and loosened the cloth to reveal several swords and a large spike, the wooden shaft only a foot long. He grinned as he re-tied the bundle and passed it to Bassano, who hefted the heavy bundle and stood, his eyes still peering into the light at the end of the alleyway. "Let's get moving" he said as the two men set off up the hill behind them "we need to have the men armed before the sacrifices start".

****

Postumius looked at his armour, every curve shining in the lamp light and each leather tie polished to its best. He nodded approvingly as he half-smiled at the slave, his head bowed but eyes searching for approval.

"Good" he said, to the obvious relief of the tunic wearing slave who bowed and moved to the door taking a thick brown cloak from the peg and handing it to the door slave who would fasten it across his master's shoulders.

"Don't be too long" Postumius called to his wife, who was fussing with Megellus' hair which seemed to have a mind of its own despite the thick layer of oil that had been applied. "The sacrifices will start within the hour and the punishments will be twenty minutes after that" he added as he walked across to the room in which Megellus was pushing firmly at his hair, which obstinately refused to lie flat.

As he turned to leave Postumius felt something knock against his foot and heard a dull clunk as a knee high jar of oil toppled and landed heavily on the floor, the oil gushing into the hallway as he stepped quickly away from the glutinous liquid, his eyes filling with rage as he almost danced backwards from the thick tide of yellow oil.

"Who left that there?" he yelled, the slaves pulling back from him and fear coming to their faces.

"Master" supplicated a female her body laying flat against the floor, her hair dark against the light marble and her chest heaving with obvious fear.

"Get it cleaned up" he yelled as his wife stood and moved across, fear in her eyes that her husband might lash out at the expensive slave.

"Wait Publius" she said, her voice almost tearful as her hands clasped together and she followed her husband towards the door. "You cannot go now" she half cried, her voice low and demure despite the anguish it held. "The omen" she exclaimed as she glanced at the oil and then held out her hands to Postumius, the rage still showing in his eyes. He glanced at her before looking to his sandals, the clean leather showing no traces of oil.

"Don't talk such nonsense" he replied as he shook his head and pointed at the prone slave girl "and get her to clean up that mess before she does any more damage to the house" he said, his eyes falling on his wife and his face softening. "I'm sorry my love, you know I don't believe in old women's tales, I've seen too much death to think that spilling oil in the house is an omen of bad luck." Postumius kissed his wife on the cheek as he spoke, her fear still evident in her face as she looked at him. "Be quick, and don't be late" he said as he turned to the door and clicked his fingers for the guards to take positions ahead of him as the door opened to reveal three more thick-set ex-soldiers waiting in the street outside.

****

"The crowd is bigger than I expected" Regillensis said with a modicum of fear in his voice as he and Marcus stared from their seats on the raised plinth erected for the Patricians to watch the executions.

"Why so?" replied Marcus. "This is the biggest spectacle the Plebeians will have before they leave for Veii, I'm surprised the whole city isn't marching down the hill to see this" he added with a shrug.

Regillensis smiled and nodded to Marcus "there's Atratinus, Camillus. Don't forget he offered personal funds to rebuild the lower docks by the temple of Aesculapius" he added in a quiet voice "use that as a starting point for his vote" he said with a light touch on Marcus's arm. The two men had discussed which Senators they should approach to discuss votes in the coming Censorial elections and Atratinus was a key contact that they needed to get on their side.

"Right, see you later" Marcus said as he stepped forwards with purpose towards his man. As he moved forwards, he saw the shape of Postumius rise from the steps to his right just in front of Atratinus, a knot of guards moving back from the steps as Postumius started to climb them. Seeing Marcus move purposefully towards him, Postumius mistook the beaming smile as a mark of respect and returned the smile warily and held out his hand as Marcus approached. Taken aback by the sudden action Marcus took the hand and shook it vigorously as Postumius looked at him with an interested expression.

"Well, Marcus Furius Camillus I am surprised to see you here so early" he said quite loudly as his eyes glanced to the Senators who were milling around the platform "though I am delighted to have your attendance" he quickly added.

'It is a sad day, but the law is the law and the gods must be appeased" Marcus said with humility as Postumius nodded, again surprised at how friendly Marcus was being. Before he could speak, Senator Atratinus moved across and slapped Postumius on the shoulder, his beaming smile extending to Marcus as he shook hands with both men and exchanged pleasantries.

"You two *commanders* exchanging old war stories?" he asked with a welcoming smile as Postumius turned to the older man.

"Indeed" replied Marcus, his mind racing to see how he could use this moment to ingratiate himself with the Senator "though Publius Postumius is the hero of the hour, his hammer blow to Bolae is an example to us all" he said magnanimously as Postumius looked to him with a quizzical frown before accepting the comment graciously.

"I hear you did well at Ferentium too?" the Senator asked as he moved his hand to his leg, the old ache starting again. Noticing the movement, Marcus smiled and suggested "Let us sit and discuss the campaign, I am sure Publius has more important matters to attend to on this day than listening to our chit chat" he said with a tilt of his head and a smile to Postumius, who simply nodded his assent and bade the two men farewell as he moved away to the rostra to check the position for his speech.

****

The rope strained as Tolero, his thick muscles cold from sleeping on the hard floor of the Tullianum, gripped the metal cage which was hauling him from the prison, the small light above him from the hatch into the pit growing larger as he moved towards it. He growled and bit his lip, the stubble on his chin catching his teeth as he swallowed, his throat dry and coarse. His mind whirled through a series of thoughts, how to escape, how to get a message to his family and how to die if all else failed. He had discussed the issue with Rutilius in the dark of the pit when the ghosts of the dead were roaming and moaning in their minds. In the total darkness and they had both agreed to die in silence as a protest against Postumius and his actions. Better to give the crowd a poor show as a mark of honour and strength than to die screaming, they had both agreed. He blinked, closing his eyes as the light burst into his vision as soon as his head appeared above the hatch to the pit, his grip getting tighter on the metal as he did so.

"Step clear" came the voice of the gaoler, his keys jangling as the metal cage came to a halt. Tolero was chained in three places and it took a few moments to release the chains and re-tie them so that he could not escape, the heavy metal falling to the floor as the final clasp bore into his ankles and he winced at the pain, already seeing a thick red welt appear where the manacles were rubbing his leg.

"Here" said a dark-haired youth, the muscles in the right arm much bulkier than those in his left, suggesting he was a blacksmith. Tolero moved across, shuffling as the heavy chains restricted his movement and slumped onto a wooden bench as the youth glanced to him before moving back to help haul up the cage with the other prisoner in it. Tolero grimaced as he rubbed at his eye, the patch still in place but loose as he had not thought to tighten it in the total darkness of the pit. He clenched his fists, feeling the muscles tense as he did so and releasing them with a deep breath as he looked up to see his friend appearing from the hatch from the Tullianum, his eyes screwed up against the light before they opened and glanced around as if seeking a way to escape. Tolero smiled, he had done just the same as his head had appeared into the light. He felt a sudden dread that there was no escape, a cold fear coming to his body as he shivered suddenly and felt an icy sweat come over his body. He shook away the dark thoughts and set his eyes on Rutilius as he was ushered across to the bench.

"You two stay there" said the youth as he turned to move away.

"Where else would we go?" Rutilius replied with a gruff laugh as Tolero grinned back at the est. The boy ignored them as he helped the older man to remove the wheel that attached to he rope and allowed the metal cage to descend into the prison. After a few minutes the two nen were given a small wooden bowl of water to drink and a chunk of bread covered in an olive paste, which Tolero found was actually quite tasty and asked if there was any more. After the guards had stopped laughing they simply dragged the two men to their feet and started the short walk to the Curia, the chains dragging along the floor with a metallic chink at each footstep.

"Keep your heads low you bastards" the older gaoler said. "The people don't want you looking cocky in front of their gods" he added as Tolero spat at him and received a thick ear for his actions.

"I'll come back and haunt your dreams" Tolero said with a manic laugh as the gaoler grinned back at him. "Had worse curses" he said in reply "and there ain't one of them come true yet" he added with a shrug and a yank at the chains which caused a surge of pain through Tolero's legs.

The sun was low in the sky and the day was beginning to warm up as the two prisoners shuffled into the square of the curia, the crowd had grown to a few thousand men and a few women, their light squeals at the arrival making heads turn towards the two chained men. Two drummers appeared as they entered the square and started to beat a slow pace, the thick sound heavy and melodious as Tolero and Rutilius fell into step without having to think. A few calls came from the crowd, some jeering the prisoners and some calling the names of their legions as a mark of honour. Tolero looked up as he heard his name called and searched the crowd for the owner of the voice, yes there he was, Bassano, large as life. A surge of energy ran through Tolero as his old companion winked and smiled at him.

*

*

*

*

Chapter 29

"Here they come" said the slightly bored voice of the man Postumius was questioning with regard to the new land for sale outside Ferentium. His eyes flicked up as he stood to see the procession, the drums suddenly starting as a wave of sound came from the crowds of people standing waiting in the square, a small cheer announcing that the crowd too had become bored as they waited for the spectacle to begin.

Postumius nodded to the two priests, both men rising and waving to the heralds to call the sacrificial animals forwards as they draped their white cloaks over their heads and began to move scented jars of perfume and oil into the correct positions.

Marcus stood, as did most of the Patricians on the platform, the wooden floorboards groaning slightly at the sudden movement. He stared into the distance to see the two men being hauled across the dust covered space, their hands and feet manacled as they attempted to walk as confidently as they could. His heart went out to them both, two old soldiers who had fallen foul of the schemes of Postumius. He remembered the words Calvus had said to him, that one Patrician could sentence a thousand plebeians to death with a whisper, but one plebeian could scream his lungs hoarse and his voice would not be heard. As the words ran through his mind Postumius climbed onto the rostra, the wooden stage slightly higher than the platform on which all the Patricians sat, their heads turning at the movement and many sitting back in their seats with satisfied nods.

As befitted the Patrician ranks, the rostra was positioned to face into the men of the seated older families, Postumius's back to the crowds behind him. At a point some thirty steps from the platform and in view of the seated leaders of Rome, the prisoners stopped at another wooden platform one edge of which was covered in large stones, some the size of a small child, with a thick wooden plank, solid and foreboding leant against them. The plank was three or four feet wide and six feet long, its use was clear for all to see.

Marcus saw more people arriving in the crowds as the numbers swelled, those at the front jostling for position as a series of guards strained to hold them back from the site of the execution. He glanced to his right to see Calvus shaking his head and talking to one of the plebeian tribunes, both men looking fearful but stoic in their resolve. Regillensis nudged his arm and nodded towards the rostra where Postumius now stood and turned his back on the people behind him as he cleared his throat, beaming at his son who was sitting in the front row five paces in front of his father.

"Before the Auspices are taken" Postumius began before a call came from the crowd.

"Leniency" came the shout, taken up by numerous deep voices. Postumius ignored them.

"Senators and Citizens of Rome" he continued. "The gods give us laws..."

"Leniency" came the shout again, at which Postumius stalled and took a deep breath before starting again.

"Laws which must be obeyed if men are to win honour and glory for their families and for Rome. These laws..."

"Leniency"

"These laws" Postumius said more loudly as he looked into the faces of the Patrician families, smiling at his son's dutiful face "have been broken by these men. Their attack on a Quaestor" he pointed his arm to the sky "and a tribune of the people, elected as an official of this great city..."

"Leniency."

This time Postumius could hears lictors shouting into the crowds and men shuffling as people were clearly pushing and shoving to get a better view of the proceedings.

"The attacks on our officials are against our laws and must be punished. I call on the Flamen Dialis to seek the approval of the gods…"

"Leniency"

"For the punishments" Postumius finished, clearly angry at the shouts from the crowd. The Flamen Dialis was the chief priest of Jupiter, his large frame covered in a deep brown garment which flowed to the floor and his apex, the pointed olive wood and wool head cap which was conical in appearance. The priests were never allowed in public without the cap and it was said that should a prisoner meet the Flamen on the road to his punishment then he would be reprieved for that day. As he stepped forwards, Marcus looked to the prisoners. His time as a Camillus had taught him the correct procedures for all sacrifices and auguries and he knew that the prisoners were not allowed to be in chains when the Flamen Dialis was within their sight. As expected he saw the two guards removing the last vestiges of the bonds from Tolero and Rutilius, both men rubbing their wrists as they were freed from the chains but the thick manacles remained in-situ to be used later when the men were chained under the thick board.

As the Flamen turned to the watching Patricians, a sudden movement caught Marcus's eyes, a surge from three or four rows back in the crowd abruptly swelled into a full-scale charge as several men, cloaks and hoods covering their faces surged forwards, a glint of metal telling Marcus's trained eyes that treachery was afoot.

****

Tolero had seen the priest step forwards as the youth undid the bonds, the guards behind them pressing their blades to their backs to ensure that they knew they could not escape. He glanced around looking for Bassano but saw nothing. If there was a plan now would be the time; it had to be before the sacrifices were taken. His heart quickened as he heard a movement in the crowd, a sudden gasp and a call were enough for him to whirl on the guard behind him, his head already turned towards the commotion in the crowd, and to thump him across the back of his head with the remaining metal manacle that was attach to his wrist. As the man fell, a gash across his skull telling Tolero that he would not be getting up for a long time, he whirled on the youth who had dragged him across the square, malice in his thoughts, but the youth was holding out a sword to him and grinning, his teeth white in his dark-skinned face. Incredulously he took the sword and turned to see several men rushing forwards as he heard a scream of anger from the Rostra.

****

Postumius watched serenely as the Flamen stepped forwards and bowed slowly to him, taking a step towards the Rostra. Behind the priest he saw the face of Megellus as he sat tall and proud in his chair, his eyes gleaming with pride. Suddenly two, no three people were standing, Furius was calling something and pointing before Postumius realised a great shout had come from behind him in the crowds. Turning he watched as Tolero raised a sword, his hands free and his face screwed in a scream of victory.

Guards rushed forwards, lictors pulled their axes into fighting positions as a gang of hooded men surrounded Tolero and Rutilius, dragging at them as a fist fight ensued in the space around the rocks.

"No!" screamed Postumius, dragging his ornamental sword from its scabbard and launching himself into the crowd, scrabbling at the clothes of men and dragging them out of the way in his anger. People pushed him and jostled him as he shouted to the prisoners and called for justice, but he pushed on through the throng, driven by the anger and desire for justice that coursed through him.

"There he is" shouted Rutilius "kill the bastard" he spat as his eyes caught those of Postumius, the two men locked in a momentarily stillness which signified their hatred for one another.

"No" shouted a taller man, pulling at the prisoners arm "you need to leave, to get out of the city" he said, his voice familiar.

"Bassano?" shouted Postumius as he thumped his sword hilt into the face of a man who was standing in his way, the frightened face bursting into a spray of blood as the man fell to his knees with a whimper.

Somebody knocked into Postumius as he shouted "You deserve to die, all of you. I will have your bodies half-burned and you will rot in the afterlife, never able to leave this world, your Lares scarred by your fate."

At this Tolero stepped across the prone body of a guard and pushed a lictor, who was struggling with a hood-covered assailant, into Postumius, the Tribune tumbling to the floor as the heavier man with his ceremonial fasces fell into his knees.

Tolero picked up one of the stones as a surge of people started to rush away from the square, the veins on his arms straining as he lifted it above his head and launched it at the prone form of Postumius. "As my gods are my witness Publius Postumius, I do to you what you would have done to me" he called as the stone, as big as a man's head thumped into Postumius's shoulder, denting the brass and ripping the leather clasp from the armour, the scream from Postumius sent a wave of energy through Tolero as he saw another stone smash into the body of Postumius, his legs slipping as the stone hit and the man raising his arms and face to stare with loathing at Tolero, his face a mask of pain and anger.

"You will pay for this, and your families" Postumius growled as he winced at the pain but tried to stand, his legs slipping gain on the smooth floor as his arm buckled under another stone thrown by a hooded assailant, this stone smaller but connecting heavily on his upper arm.

Tolero looked to Bassano, his eyes visible under the hood and bared his teeth. "Kill him" he said as Bassano picked up a heavy stone and, straining, launched it from no more than three paces into the breast of Postumius who had half-risen and stared at him with his mouth open as if ready to speak.

As the sickening crunch of stone on metal came Tolero had already lifted another stone and launched it as his old commander, two other of the hooded men also lifting smaller stones and throwing them at their ex-leader.

Postumius went down with a clatter, his arm breaking as a rock caught the arm he was leaning on and smashed it into a red pulp, the bone gleaming white before it disappeared under the body of the Tribune, his scream dying in his lungs as two more large rocks hit home, each making a dull clang as they bit into the armour on the man's body.

"We must go" shouted Bassano as he pulled vigorously at Tolero's arm. Rutilius stepped forwards and heaved a final rock at Postumius, his limp body not reacting to the heavy object as it smashed into the back of his neck. "Bastard" he shouted as he turned and slipped on the flagstones, seeing the space behind him almost empty of people who had turned and fled. Before he could move Rutilius was yanked backwards by an arm and turned to scream into the face of Calvus, his irate features a blur as he punched the man square on the jaw and dragged himself free before grabbing a discarded sword and racing after Bassano and the other fleeing men who were already thirty yards ahead of him.

As he picked up his knees and drove his arms into a sprint he felt a sudden jolt at his side and felt himself fall, the sword in his arm clattering to the floor ahead of him as his legs scrambled to return him to his feet.

"Hold" said a voice he knew as he turned to see Camillus standing behind him, his red face a mask of anger. "What have you done?" he said, his voice low but strong and his eyes boring into Rutilius' soul.

****

Megellus jumped from the platform, tears streaming down his face as he called to his father. A man pulled his arm and told him to get behind him as he battered a hooded figure to the floor, his sword short and wide unlike any he had seen before. The man was in front of him and pushing through the crowd who were rushing in every direction in a panic as they yelled and screamed at the sudden violent actions surrounding them. The man with the sword gripped Megellus' hand and pulled him forwards, turning his sword flat and smashing it into the face of a plebeian who was pulling at his cloak and shouting, the man's head whipped to the left as the sword hilt hit and he was gone.

Within a few seconds the screaming voice of his father had stopped and a great cheer came from ahead of him as Megellus suddenly felt his hand come free from whoever had pulled him forwards, the figure of the blue cloaked man rushing into a knot of men and slicing through them as if the gods were parting the crowd for him. Megellus blinked his tears from his eyes as he ran forwards to see the man kneeling at his father's side, his head turning to him with sorrow in his eyes and anger in his face as he twisted and leapt forwards to chase the hooded figures and prisoners who were charging across the square.

Megellus rushed to his father, the brass armour that had shone so brightly now dented and scratched, red spots on the floor and a thick pool of blood under the contorted shoulders of the man he had grown so close to over the past month since his illness. The head moved, the eyes blinked and Megellus fell to his knees.

Father" he said his voice a whisper.

"Meg..." came a rasping sound as the body of the man shuddered and a look of total pain came across his face, the mouth drooping and the eyes squinting as he tried to speak.

"Meg..." he said again, the noise hoarser.

"Father" was all that Megellus could say as his father's head fell backwards and his vacant eyes stared into the sky as a low moan of air escaped from his dead father lips.

****

"I have no fight with you Camillus" roared Rutilius as he grabbed the sword and turned to run again before Marcus scythed his legs with a kick and he slumped to the floor.

"You have attacked a Tribune of Rome for the second time and so you have a fight with all Romans" Marcus growled as he stood tall, his frame a head taller than Rutilius and stepped forwards. "Yield" he commanded as Rutilius shook his head, his eyes scanning the moving crowd around them for a chance to escape.

"You of all men know what he was like" he yelled at Marcus as he edged backwards. "You deserved your phalera, you led the men well and you deserve credit. He was a dog, born of a bitch..."

Before he could finish Marcus stepped forwards and sliced his sword across the gap between them. "Yield or I will kill you" he said with a measure of cold brutality.

"So be it, I will not yield to be crushed under the stones again. I will die fighting as my father did" muttered Rutilius in a low voice as his shoulders sagged slightly before he took a deep breath and launched himself at Marcus with the fury of a man fighting for his life.

As the first attack smashed into his sword, Marcus wheeled left and aimed a kick at Rutilius' knee. Neither man had a shield so he had to be careful not to leave his left side open. Rutilius ran at him again, his arm swinging wildly and his eyes betraying the fear he felt as he sliced his blow across Marcus's right side, the blade whipping up and back across him as he dodged left and left again. With a thud, Marcus swung his sword up and out in an attempt to get under the arc of Rutilius as the man gained his balance and chopped downwards and across his body. Rutilius's long blade scraped along Marcus's shorter sword with a long rasp as Marcus used the sound to tell him when to step into the blades slowing arc, edging his sword upwards to take away the power of the stroke. Rutilius knew was what coming and threw his body backwards to avoid the short punching movement that Marcus then sent at him, the blade slicing into his leather body armour but doing no damage. Rutilius saw the futility of his attack and turned to run, swinging his sword wildly at Marcus as he did so, the arm extending over his shoulder as his head turned to find a clear path.

Almost before he could take a step Marcus had launched himself into a two step action, blocking the swinging arm and punched his sword into Rutilius' side, the blade passing through the leather with a slight kick before Marcus leant his body into the motion, his shoulder rolling to allow him to drag the blade from the strike and prepare for the second blow.

Rutilius screamed as his sword fell from his hand, the blade reverberating as it skittered along the floor and came to a stop as the man fell to his knees.

"You're all the same" screamed Rutilius as he looked up at Marcus, gripping his side and looking at the blood that leaked from his body. His eyes flicked to the side as Marcus saw a movement from his right, the small frame striding into the gap between the two men as Megellus, his eyes cold and vacant hacked his sword into the neck of Rutilius, the ornate blade of his father glinting in the morning sunlight as it arced momentarily into the soft flesh of the grinning man, his smile his last act of defiance.

*

*

Chapter 30

Marcus heard the crying of the women before he could comprehend the second swing of
Megellus's sword, the blade slicing into the back of Rutilius' head with a dull ringing sound
as the blade slipped off the skull and hit the floor.

"Hold" he said to Megellus as the boy looked to him, his face betraying no emotions as he
turned to Marcus. "He is dead, return to your mother, I will find the others" Marcus said to
the small framed boy as he turned and called to a soldier who had just hacked the hand from a
hooded assailant, the man falling to the floor as a second soldier stuck his spear into the
man's torso, the screaming continuing as his blood flowed on to the dust covered floor.
Without any response, Megellus bent forwards and wiped the blade on the dead man's
clothes and turned to walk away as Marcus frowned at the boy as he moved.

"Camillus" said the soldier.

"Let's find them" Marcus said. "Where is Regillensis?" he asked, scanning the rostra for
faces he knew as men milled about, some with swords drawn, others visibly shaken by the
sudden violence in their home city.

"He went down there after the prisoner Tolero" pointed another soldier who had appeared,
his blood covered sword testament to the fighting he had done.

"Then let's follow him."

The three men raced across the Curia, the remaining crowds splitting as they approached,
some pointing and waving at the direction the fugitives had gone, others cowering as the
soldiers ran past. The men had headed towards the Caelian Hill, no doubt in an attempt to use
the lower valley between the Palatine and Esquiline as an escape route. The road past the

entrance way to the Temple of Jupiter was away to their right up a short steep slope and Marcus wondered if they would use this slope to double back and head for the river. As he ran he looked to the soldier to his left.

"Name soldier" he stated.

"Maximus" the said as he loped along, his easy stride showing his fitness.

"If it were me I would skirt the Temple of Jupiter and head back to the river. What would you do?" he asked as he continued to pound the street, faces peering out of alleyways as men shouted encouragement and pointed along the road. After a moment Maximus looked to Marcus.

"It would make sense" he said, visibly slowing as he turned to look at Marcus. "This road could lead to the Sisters Beam or to the flat lands beyond, but beyond that is open farmland. I would look to escape to the river and head downstream" he finished as the two men came to a standstill, the third soldier coming to stop behind them as he leant his hands on his thighs and sucked in deep lungfuls of air.

"Then that is what we will do" Marcus said with conviction as he turned to the labouring soldier. "You" he said, his smile warm but his mind telling him that this soldier needed extra fitness duties. "Return to the Curia and find Calvus. Tell him Marcus Furius Camillus needs ten men at the Pons Sublicius as soon as he can get there" he finished as the man saluted and turned to run heavily back in the direction from which they had come.

"Sir, this way" said Maximus "I know a short cut."

****

Marcus stood and looked at the bridge, the water higher than usual at this time of year as the sudden rains had followed the dry months, the water cascading down in dirty brown torrents and churning against the hulls of the small skips that moored along the sidings.

He scoured the boats looking for signs of movement, but nothing came to his vision.

"See anything?" he asked Maximus as the man shook his head and replied in the negative.

"Let's go to the bridge and see if it gives us a better view" he added as the two men strode purposefully to the wooden bridge which spanned the Tiber. People looked at them, swords drawn, some scurrying away, others standing and wondering what was happening as the story of the attacks in the Curia had not yet reached the river.

Two men appeared around a corner carrying a fishing net, the long bundles of cord over their shoulders. Marcus whirled towards the movement, the first man calling in alarm as he saw the two soldiers, the one with the blue cloak with gritted teeth and death in his eyes. With a wave of his sword Marcus called them forwards, "carry on" he said as he turned his head to the left and looked at another movement along the docks near the road to the Forum Boarium. A man had appeared and looked at them, his steps halting momentarily as he glanced to them and then continued on his way. The movement caused Marcus to focus on him, his head held low as he walked towards a deep hulled boat on which another man suddenly appeared, his hand rising in a greeting as Marcus became suspicious.

"There" Marcus said. "That man has a hood on his cloak at the back. Let's go and check him out" he said, striding forwards as the man glanced towards him again. As the two soldiers stepped towards the new arrival the man on the boat saw the movement and called to the figure in front of him, the man raising his arms as if in exasperation before turning and calling loudly towards the alleyway from which he had appeared. Three figures suddenly exploded from the gap between the buildings, their hoods still over their heads followed by a fourth, the ambling figure of Tolero, clearly worn out by the run to the docks after a night in the Tullianum and the fight in the Curia.

Two of the men stopped and looked to Marcus and Maximus as they picked up their speed and charged towards them, the taller of the two removing his hood as Tolero too stopped and stared at the approaching soldiers. Bassano stared back at Marcus, his eyes full of sorrow yet a determined look on his face.

"Hold Camillus" Bassano said, raising his right hand as the man on the boat called for them to climb aboard quickly.

Marcus ran across and stopped ten yards from the gang of fugitives, Tolero holding his side where he had been cut but grinning at the excitement of the chase despite his obvious pain.

"Let us go Camillus" said Bassano, his voice steady and with a resolute edge. "Postumius was no friend to Rome or its people. He got what he deserved" he said in a matter of fact tone.

Marcus shook his head as Maximus stepped forwards, his muscles tensing in his sword arm. "No Bassano. What you have done is wrong. The gods and the people of Rome will not allow me to let you go. Murdering Postumius was wrong and what you have done is inexcusable" he replied coldly.

A moment of silence passed as the two groups of men looked to each other before Bassano looked to Tolero and smiled. "Old friend" he said, "it seems we have no choice." He looked up, several men appearing behind Marcus and Maximus as a look of fear came to his face, the voice of Calvus clear in the still air of the morning as he called his arrival. Marcus turned and held up his arm for Calvus to wait as the men approached at a run.

"Bastards" Tolero spat, a large drop of blood covered phlegm hitting the ground in front of Maxmius' foot. "I'm done for anyway" Tolero added, his hand coming away from his side to reveal a large rent which bled out more of his life force as he winced at the movement.

"You men, go" called Bassano quickly to the hooded figures behind them as he pushed at a man who stepped forwards with his sword out. "No, go. It is us they want" Bassano said as he looked to see Calvus and his soldiers fifty yards away but striding forwards purposefully. "Go now, they will not catch you" he said as the men behind him turned and ran, the noise of their feet pounding away disappearing to shouts from Calvus and his men.

"We cannot yield Camillus" replied Bassano. "As you Patricians would say" he grinned "Nulla Spes" and he turned to the smiling face of Tolero, the two men instantly gripping the other's shoulder with their free hand and with a nod pulling their swords into the gap between them. Marcus put his hand to Maximus as he stepped forwards unsure if the motion was aggressive, though Marcus understood at once what the two old friends were going to do. Tolero laughed as he pulled Bassano towards him, Bassano grinning back as the two men thrust their swords into the body of the other and the metal protruded upwards through their backs, each man slapping the shoulder of the other and grunting with the pain of the strike. Marcus watched as the blood ran along the blades as if trying to get back into the bodies from which it had come, before both men wavered for a second, and then fell to the floor.

*

*

*

*

Chapter 31

Ten days had passed since the death of Postumius and Marcus had seen his brother elevated to Military Tribune once again, leading the soldiers off to Veii amongst great cheers from the crowds along the streets of Rome. Lucius had spoken to Marcus before leaving and discussed tactics for the attacks, asking Marcus to join him as a junior tribune, to which he had declined, saying that he wished to await the birth of his child before he set out on a campaign again.

The news from Veii was that the walls were stronger than the Romans had envisaged and Marcus sat in the forum awaiting the news from the Senate meeting which had been called to discuss the latest failed attempts to breech the stronghold of the Veientines. Marcus sat with his sandals off his feet as the warm afternoon sun beat down upon Narcius and Mella, the three men eating a cold meat lunch.

"They can't possibly leave an army to stand at Veii" Mella said with a shake of his head. "I know that the campaigning season is close to an end, but leaving men to stand outside the city will cause problems at home. Who will feed their animals? Who will reap the fields and sow the crops for next year? It can't be done" he said as he sipped a cup of lemon flavoured water that Marcus had brought with them. Narcius grunted agreement, his eyes watching the doors to the Temple of Saturnus where the Senate were meeting.

"It seems to me" Marcus said as he wiped his mouth with a small cloth "that we have no choice" he shrugged as he spoke. "If we leave the city over the winter it will store more food and water and receive additional support from their allies, by next season it will be more difficult to attack and defeat the city. In fact" he added as he sat forwards and scratched his lower leg "to my mind we need a bigger standing army, one which will be able to stop any new reserves entering the city and one which can also hold against any attacks from" he frowned as he considered the allies of the Veientines "the Capenates or even the Labici" he said.

"They are too cowardly to attack us" Mella said with a huff as Narcius smiled at him.

"Oh no" replied Marcus. "Mark my words Mella, they still have a part to play in this war. They know that if Veii falls they will have no support against our troops. For the Capenates this is a critical time. Same for the Labici and Volsci" he added with a knowing nod as Narcius waved a hand as the doors to the temple slowly opened.

All three men stood, as did a great deal of the crowd which had gathered outside the Temple to await the judgement of the elders of Rome.

Servilius Ahala stepped from the doorway, his eyes looking into the crowds who stepped forwards to hear his words as he raised his hands for them to await the remaining Senators' appearance. He caught Marcus's eyes and nodded, his face smiling as he held out a sealed pouch and raised it to the crowd, a great murmur rising from the assembled Romans as they edged closer to their leaders. More Senators shuffled forwards, many in deep conversations as they edged onto the steps around the temple, guards and soldiers ringing the lowest steps to keep the crowd at bay. After a few moments Ahala turned to the crowd and held the pouch aloft, the red-dye of the leather bright in the daylight.

"People of Rome" he said, a silence falling round the forum as his gaze wandered across the many faces staring expectantly to him. "We, your leaders, have discussed the issue of Veii" he said, a small cheer coming from some of the crowd who were instantly hushed by the larger portion of the assembly.

"We have agreed that our army will lay siege to the city of Veii throughout the winter." As he spoke a great number of people set to mumbling and asking questions as he waved his arms for silence, most of the crowd edging forwards. Marcus took a deep breath as he thought through the words he had spoken to the Senate that very morning, his argument to pay the soldiers who were stationed at Veii still going through his mind. A number of Senators had argued against him, but many had agreed it was a good solution to the problem of the farmer-soldiers who made up the ranks of the army. Marcus had been ushered from the Senate meeting once his argument had been given, the Senators would decide in private, they had said. Ahala glanced to Marcus with a smile as he raised the pouch again and shook his head at the calls from the crowd, who were finally falling silent as he stood in silence awaiting their focus.

"This pouch contains the agreement" he said as he raised the pouch higher and watched a few thousand heads move in unison with his arm. "The argument was strongly put by Marcus Furius Camillus to pay those soldiers who would stay in-situ at Veii a living wage from the Republican purse" he said with a nod towards Marcus as a number of heads turned to see Marcus standing to their left, a few cheers of "Camillus" echoing off the walls of the buildings and shops around the forum.

"And it has been agreed that Veii is a worthy enemy and must be treated differently to those of other campaigns. Their walls are strong, their resolve is strong and their hearts are strong" he continued. "But they do not have the gods supporting them" Ahala cried as he thrust the red pouch higher in the air and a tumultuous cheer rang out across the forum, the guards moving forwards as the ranks of men pushed towards their leaders as they cheered.

"People of Rome, calm yourselves" cried Ahala, his voice loud but still drowned by the cheering crowd, some calling prayers to Mars and others waving their arms as they began to shift and edge forwards.

Marcus marvelled at the people of Rome, so easily led to jubilation and excitement. Ahala, master of the crowds that he was, simply stood and held the red pouch in the air waiting for silence as the people hushed and cajoled their fellows into stillness. As the calm fell he gazed out into the throng and smiled. "We, your Senators, have agreed to pay the soldiers" he said, holding his arm aloft to stop the cheers as they started but were cut off with hushing sounds. "We have also agreed to the creation of new taxes to support the war, taxes to be shared equally among all the people" he called more loudly as a few cat calls came from the crowd. The Senate has also agreed to your champion" he said these words with a measure of hostility picked up instantly by Marcus as he flicked a glance to Marcus Manlius, his white toga resplendent in the sunshine "to support your wishes as a Senator of Rome" he said with finality as Manlius stepped forwards to a spattering of applause and cheers from some of the crowd, but some of the faces clearly not too sure that Manlius was the right man for the job. Marcus watched Calvus and the two plebeian tribunes as they politely clapped Manlius, whose face showed how much he was enjoying the elevation to the Senatorial ranks. Calvus flicked his eyes to Marcus and smiled a cool smile at him before returning his gaze to Ahala, who was beckoning for silence as he ushered Manlius back into the ranks of Senators, the man clearly enjoying the attention too much for Ahala's liking. "We have asked the favour of the gods and they have agreed" he said, turning to the right as Marcus's uncle the Pontifex Maximus strode forwards, his distinctive robes with the mantle covering his head and the elaborate iron knife of his office in his right hand.

In his deep voice, trained over many years of reading sacrifices and divining the will of the gods the Pontifex Maximus held his iron knife in the air and spoke. "We the people of Rome are beloved of the gods" he said as a silence fell over the crowd, no-one daring to speak over the great priest. "Jupiter Maximus has spoken" he called, his covered head bowed "and the divine readings state that Rome will prevail."

At this Marcus thought of his own augury at the camp of Rufus, the suggestion of war and eventual victory by Rome. He looked back at his uncle as he turned to Ahala and spoke again "Senators the gods favour your actions" he said theatrically as the crowd roared its approval, a great stamping of feet coming from the assembled thousands as the Senators stood and welcomed the cheers.

As Ahala spoke again Narcius nudged Marcus's elbow and nodded his head towards a small slave who was pushing his way through the crowd, the light blue tunic signifying him as a member of the Furii household. Marcus's heart skipped a beat as the man caught his eye and waved, a smile coming to his face as he puffed and panted and pushed his way through the crowd.

"Master, you must return home, your son has arrived" he beamed.

*

*

THE END

If you liked the story, please add feedback to Amazon so that others can enjoy the series.

Thank you for purchasing the book.

Historical notes

This second book of the series brings Marcus to the time when Rome declared war with Veii, its neighbour and possibly the largest of its future enemies within the Latin Delta. The book is mostly crafted around the period 419 – 406 BC and most of the main characters are real people who lived and served Rome during the period. Rome had been steadily extending its influence in the area, with a twenty-year peace with Veii finally coming to an end in approximately 406 BC. However, when writing the book, I had two considerations to make as a backdrop to this story. Firstly, I was interested in the story of Postumius and how he drew his own soldiers to murder him by stoning as very little information exists of the rationale for the actions of the soldiers against their commander. It struck me that it would have taken a lot for men to murder their former general in public and so I decided to make the story central to the initial rise of Marcus Furius Camillus. Little is known of Marcus's role within the Republic at the time but he would certainly have known Postumius and so it made sense to have him pitted against his nemesis from the first book but to ultimately attempt to come to his aide as Marcus was a man driven by the laws and rules of ancient Rome. Secondly, the time lines were too long to keep a sense of order without squeezing the actions of ten or more years into one or two. Hopefully I have crafted the order of action to support a number of the key developments in politics in Rome and in Marcus's life well enough to make the story flow. I needed to shift the timelines to enable Marcus to be qualified enough to be a military tribune by the time he achieves this in the 390's BC, and with his successes at Ferentium and in supporting the return from Bolae I hope to have set his career in motion. Postumius was a real character and did die under a hail of stones by his own soldiers as he presided over the crushing of men who had opposed his withholding of spoils from Bolae and from his denial of the soldier's requests to resettle in the town. Whilst I have fabricated the exact details to fit into the story the thread of the action has a base in history. The main perpetrators of the murder escaped and were tried by Marcus's brother, Lucius, in-absentia before they committed suicide some days after the death of Postumius. It was cleaner for me to have them die on the same day to keep the action flowing and to finish the Postumius link within the story, although Megellus will return in a later book. As an aside the son of Postumius was named Marcus, though with both Marcus Furius and Marcus Manlius I had to change the name to avoid the already overcrowded use of the name.

The attack on Ferentium also occurred, though it is unclear who led the attack at the time. The use of the siege towers is my own creation to continue to show that Marcus Furius Camillus, as with the development of the short sword, was the man to change the fighting style of Rome into that which we know and understand today. Of course, all of this is supposition on my part. Scipio is another real character and is Master of the Horse against Veii, so has a strong part to play in this book and the next. The punishment given to the guards is as accurate as I could make it whilst keeping a level of hostility between Manlius and Marcus for later books. Such punishments in the early Republican army are not as well documented as in the later period so I have used some creative licence to fit what is known from later texts to this period.

The main thrust of part one of the Fall of Veii is to explore the development of political and military thinking in Rome during the period. It is obvious that the plebeian party and patricians continued to have a love-hate relationship and I wanted to show just how deep feelings were running between the two. I also needed to give Marcus Manlius a key role at this time period in support of the plebeians, something he continued to develop later, before and after the sack of Rome by Brennus. Manlius and Marcus will cross swords in a later volume when Rome falls, as the prophecy predicts.

Calvus was to become the first plebeian military tribune and to rule well during his tenure in office, almost too well as many historians have written. Placing Marcus and Calvus together allowed me to build this relationship and fit the changes which Marcus makes during his years as a Tribune and Dictator into context as he almost certainly fought alongside Calvus at some stage of his military career and they would have discussed politics together. The use of Bassano, Tolero and the other plebeian Centurionate fitted the plot-line and allowed me to give a vent for Postumius's anger at the plebeians, almost mirroring the ideals that Calvus and the plebeian council have for a stronger Republic based on shared decision making and control. Sergius and Virginius will also play a part in the next story, their hatred for each other leading to disaster for Rome as they, too, are real historical figures with a part to play in the fall of Veii and the rise of Camillus.

Marcus Furius Camillus is described as the architect of securing pay for the soldiers at Veii by some writers, but this is also dismissed by others. It seems that the true decision maker will never be known, but it certainly started in this period. The year is also disputed, so I simply added this as final action for book one of this two-parter to give Marcus more credibility to strengthen his case for Dictator for the next book as he was clearly a very able politician as well as a military genius. In 403 BC Marcus was made a Censor, along with his friend Regillensis, and went on to introduce some very unpopular (with the Patricians) taxes as well as rebuild the Pons Sublicius which had been destroyed by a particularly bad winter of heavy rain which had followed a period of pestilence in the City. I will skip both of these facts in the next episode of the life of Marcus Furius Camillus as we are now entering the period of history in which facts and (to a degree) dates are known of the man and his actions. To this point the factual details have been sketchy at best and I have filled the gaps with my own creative endeavours. It is now time to return to the military man who won a series of great battles before sacking the town of Veii in circa 396 BC. There are many twists and turns in the story of Camillus to come, and some of the minor characters in this book will continue to play leading parts in the next and beyond into the fall of Rome itself.

The next book will see Camillus sack Veii, but not before he proves himself worthy to become Dictator of Rome in a number of epic battles. Join Marcus as he completes the Fall of Veii, part two, in the next volume and join Marcus on facebook to keep up to date with developments, simply search for Marcus Furius Camillus and send a friend request.

I offer my apologies to any other spirits of the Romans I have used in this text should I have used their names in an unfavourable light.

Please do leave feedback for me on Amazon as it will help me to become a better writer of Camillus's story.

Printed in Great Britain
by Amazon

78921200R00150